"SENSATIONAL, CHILLING, PRO-
FOUNDLY DISTURBING . . . powerfully
narrated . . . enthusiastically
recommended."

—*Milwaukee Journal*

"FASCINATING AND QUICK-PACED . . .
the work of a writer who knows how to
handle suspense without sacrificing the ring
of truth. I was spellbound and convinced."
—Josephine Humphreys,
author of *The Fireman's Fair*

"INGENIOUS, INTRIGUING, ENIGMATIC
. . . a concerned and moving attempt to
understand the interplay of passion and brutality . . . Shreve's prose is clear and com-
passionate, her message moving . . .
powerfully made."

—*Washington Post Book World*

"A POWERFULLY TROUBLING NOVEL
ABOUT THE FINE LINE BETWEEN LOVE
AND VIOLENCE . . . CHILLING."
—*Atlanta Journal-Constitution*

"BRILLIANT . . . ASTONISHING . . . an
immensely complicated, moving book."
—*San Francisco Chronicle*

STRANGE FITS
OF PASSION

ANITA SHREVE

AN ONYX BOOK

ONYX
Published by the Penguin Group
Penguin Books USA Inc., 375 Hudson Street,
New York, New York 10014, U.S.A.
Penguin Books Ltd, 27 Wrights Lane,
London W8 5TZ, England
Penguin Books Australia Ltd, Ringwood,
Victoria, Australia
Penguin Books Canada Ltd, 10 Alcorn Avenue,
Toronto, Ontario, Canada M4V 3B2
Penguin Books (N.Z.) Ltd, 182–190 Wairau Road,
Auckland 10, New Zealand

Penguin Books Ltd, Registered Offices:
Harmondsworth, Middlesex, England

Published by Onyx, an imprint of New American Library, a division of Penguin Books USA Inc. This is an authroized reprint of a hardcover edition published by Harcourt Brace Jovanovich, Publishers.

First Onyx Printing, March, 1992
10 9 8 7 6 5 4 3 2 1

 REGISTERED TRADEMARK—MARCA REGISTRADA

PRINTED IN THE UNITED STATES OF AMERICA

Original hardcover designed by Lydia D'moch

Once Again, for John

Strange fits of passion have I known:
And I will dare to tell . . .
William Wordsworth

On my book tours, I am often asked a number of questions: Did he really do it? Do I think that she was justified? Did they do it for the money or for love?

Then, inevitably, the questions come around to me. Why do I write the kind of books I do? they want to know. Why did I become a journalist?

My books are about crimes—cold-blooded acts of treachery or messy crimes of passion—and perhaps some think it strange for a woman to be as interested in violence as I am. Or they wonder why I chose a profession in which I have to spend most of my time chasing down unpleasant facts or asking people questions they'd rather not have to answer.

Sometimes I say that my job is like being a private detective, but usually I answer (my standard, pat answer) that I think I became a journalist because my father was a journalist.

My father was the editor of a newspaper in a small town in western Massachusetts. The paper was called the *East Whatley Eagle*, and it wasn't much of a paper, even in its heyday in the early

11

1960s. But I thought then, as daughters do, that my father knew a lot about his profession, or his trade, as he preferred to call it.

"The story was there before you ever heard about it," he would say before sending me, his only child and a teenager then, out to cover a theft from a local store, or a fire in a farmer's hayloft. "The reporter's job is simply to find its shape."

My father taught me almost everything about the newspaper business: how to edit copy, set type, sell ads, cover a town meeting. And I know he hoped I would stay in East Whatley and one day take over his press. Instead I disappointed him. I left western Massachusetts and moved to New York City. I went to college there and to graduate school in journalism and then to work for a weekly newsmagazine.

But I did not forget my father or what he had said to me. And in the years after I moved to the city—years in which I wrote articles for the newsmagazine, wrote a book based on one of the articles, which brought me a fair amount of both fame and money, and then made a career for myself as a writer of nonfiction books, almost all of which feature a detailed investigation of a complex crime—I have had to ask myself why it really was that I followed in my father's footsteps. Why, for instance, did I not choose architecture or medicine or college teaching instead?

Because I have learned that it isn't simply a matter of the journalist and the facts, as my father

believed and would have had me believe and
practice, but rather a case of the storyteller and
the story—an ancient dilemma.

Precisely, the difficulty is this.

Once the storyteller has her facts, whether they
be told to her or be a product of her investiga-
tions, what then does she do with her material?

I have thought long and hard about this question. Perhaps I have even been, at times, obsessed
with the problem. So I suppose it wasn't so surprising that I was thinking about just this very
thing as I sat across the room from the young
woman who was perched on the edge of her narrow bed.

I hadn't been in a dormitory room for years—
not since my own graduation from Barnard, in
1965. But though the posters on the walls were of
rock groups I had never heard of, and there was
a telephone and a Sony Walkman on a shelf, the
essential facts of the room were not all that different from my own surroundings in college: a desk,
a single chair, a bookcase, a bed, a quart of orange
juice chilling on a windowsill.

It was February, in the first year of the new
decade, and it was snowing lightly outside the
window, a gray snow shower that wouldn't amount
to much, though the people in this college town
in central Maine had not, I had learned earlier at
the local gas station, seen the grass since early
November.

The young woman sat with her sneakers planted
evenly on the floor and her arms crossed over her

chest. Not defiantly, I thought, but carefully. She was wearing blue jeans (Levi's, not designer jeans) and a gray cotton sweater with a long-sleeved white T-shirt underneath.

I'd met the girl's mother only twice, but one of those times had been an important occasion, and I had needed, for professional reasons, to remember her mother's face. The daughter's hair was the same—a deep red-gold. But the eyes were distinctly her father's eyes—dark and deep-set. They might actually have been black eyes, but the light was bad, and I couldn't tell for sure.

Whatever else the parents had or had not given the daughter—attributes and traits I would never know about—they had given her an extraordinary beauty. It lay, I saw, in the mix of the white skin and the red hair juxtaposed with the dark eyes—a combination, I thought, that must be rare.

She was prettier than I'd ever been, just as her mother had been before her. I have what might be called a handsome face, but it's become plainer in my forties. Years ago, when I was in college, I'd worn my hair long too, but now I keep it short and easy.

Because she was a natural beauty, I was surprised that she wore no makeup and had her hair pulled severely back into a ponytail, as if she meant to minimize whatever attractions she had. She sat warily on the bed. I was pretty sure that she would know who I was even though we had never met.

She'd offered me the only chair in the room.

The package I'd brought was uncomfortable in my lap, and I felt its weight. It was a weight I'd been feeling off and on for years and had driven a very long way to rid myself of.

"Thanks for seeing me," I said, acutely aware of the generation between us. She was nineteen, and I was forty-six. I could have been her mother. I was rather sorry I'd worn my gold jewelry and my expensive wool coat, but I knew that it was more than age or money that separated us.

"I read about your mother," I said, trying to begin again, but she shook her head quickly—a signal, I could see, not to continue.

"I've known who you were for years," she said hesitantly, in a soft voice, "but I didn't think . . ."

I waited for her to finish the sentence, but when she didn't I broke the silence.

"A long time ago," I said, "I wrote an article about your mother. You were just a baby then."

She nodded.

"You know about the article," I said.

"I've known about it," she said noncommittally. "Do you still work for that magazine?"

"No," I said. "It doesn't exist anymore."

Although I didn't, I could have added that the magazine no longer existed because it had been run on a system that had been ridiculously expensive: Writers, based in New York, had traveled widely to report and write their own lengthy features on the most pressing stories of the week. The magazine had not used foreign bureaus, as successful newsweeklies do today, but instead had sent its writers into the field. The expense accounts had been magnificent and legendary and had eventually led to the demise of the magazine, in 1979. But I was gone by then.

Outside her door, in a corridor, I could hear laughter, then a shout. The young woman looked once at the door, then back at me.

"I have a class," she said.

Although her eyes were dark, by then I'd decided that they were not exactly like her father's eyes. His had been impenetrable, and while hers had gravity, more gravity than I'd have thought possible in a girl only nineteen years old, they were clear and yielding.

I wondered if she had a boyfriend, or girl-friends, or if she played sports or was a good student. I wondered if she, too, kept a journal, if she had inherited her mother's talents, or her father's.

"This belongs to you," I said, gesturing to the package.

She looked at the parcel on my lap.

"What is it?" she asked.

"It's the material I used to write the article. Notes, transcripts, that sort of thing."

"Oh," she said, and then, "Why?"

There was a pause.

"Why now? Why me?"

"I know your mother probably told you what happened," I answered quickly, "but in here there is more. . . . In here your mother makes a reference to the story she would one day tell her child, and I thought that if she didn't have a chance to do that, well, here it is."

All week I'd rehearsed those sentences, so often that I'd almost come to believe them myself. But now that the words lay between us, it was all I could do to keep from telling her that this was not the real reason I'd come, not the real reason at all.

"I don't know," she said, looking steadily at the package.

"It belongs to you," I said. "I don't need it anymore."

I stood up and walked across the small space that separated us. My boot heels clicked on the wooden floor. I put the package on her lap. I returned to my chair and sat down.

I was thinking that in a short while I could leave the dorm, walk to my car, and drive back to Manhattan. I had a co-op there on the Upper West Side that was roomy enough and had a good view of the Hudson. I had my work, a new book I was beginning, and my friends. I'd never married, and I didn't have any kids, but I had a lover, an editor with the *Times*, who sometimes stayed with me.

My friends tell me I'm the kind of woman who lives for her work, but I don't think that's entirely true. I'm rather passionate about physical exercise and opera, in equal doses, and I've always liked men for their company. But since I decided early on not to have children, I've found it hard to see the point of marriage.

I'd wrapped the package in brown paper and

sealed it with Scotch tape. I watched as she undid the tape and opened the package. I had let it begin with the memo. I'd included everything.

"I don't have your mother's handwritten notes," I said. "These are my typewritten transcriptions. I've always found it easier to work from typescript than from handwriting, even my own. And as for the rest, it's all here, just as I heard it."

But she wasn't listening to me. I watched her read the first page, then the second. She had shifted her weight slightly, so that she rested on a hand at her side. I shook open my coat. I suppose I'd hoped that she'd glance at a sentence or two, or would flip through the pages, and then would look up at me and thank me for coming or say again that she had a class. But as I sat there, she kept reading, turning pages quietly.

I thought about her class and wondered if I should mention it.

I heard another commotion in the corridor, then silence.

I sat there for about ten minutes, until I realized that she meant to read the entire batch of notes, right there and then.

I looked around the room and out the window. It was still snowing.

I stood up.

"I'll just go for a walk," I said to her bent head. "Find myself a cup of coffee."

I paused.

"Should I . . . ?"

I stopped.

There wasn't any point in asking her if I should come back. I knew now that it would be irresponsible not to, not to be there for her reaction and to answer her questions. And then I had a moment's sudden panic.

Maybe I shouldn't have come, I thought wildly. Maybe I shouldn't have brought the package.

But I had long ago trained myself to deal with panic attacks or doubts. It was simple. All I had to do was force myself to think about something else. Which I did. I thought about how I ought to find a motel room now, and after that a place to eat.

She glanced up at me, her eyes momentarily glazed from her reading. I saw that her hand, turning a page, was shaking.

She looked at me as if I were a stranger who had not yet entered her room. I could only guess at what she was thinking, what she was hearing, and what she feared.

Yet I knew better than anyone else all about this particular story and the storyteller, didn't I?

And all about the storyteller who came after that . . .

The Notes
and
Transcripts

From: Helen Scofield
To: Edward Hargreaves
Re: The Maureen English story
Date: August 2, 1971

I think we can go ahead with the English piece now, and I'd like your OK on this. If you recall, when I last mentioned it a month ago, I thought we were going to have to kill it because I couldn't get to Maureen English, or "Mary Amesbury," as she now calls herself. I had gone up to Maine with the idea of interviewing her for the piece. I visited St. Hilaire and interviewed a number of the townspeople there and got some good background material. Then I drove to South Windham to see Maureen. I'd met her only once before. She had left the magazine just before I had really come on board. I'd seen Harrold around, of course. I knew him to speak to, but not much more than that.

Maureen met with me, but wouldn't agree to talk to me. I tried everything I could think of to persuade her, but I just couldn't get her to open up. I drove home feeling pretty disappointed. I thought I had a great story, but without her there were just too many holes.

* * *

I started work on the Juan Corona story and tried to forget about the English piece. Then, last week, I received a package in the mail. It's a series of notes written by "Mary Amesbury." There are shorter ones, and then some longer ones. It is, I suppose you could say, a kind of journal to herself and for herself, except that in her notes she is sometimes writing to me. Apparently the tape recorder or my presence in the visitors' room had put her off, but back in the privacy of her cell she was able to write her story down. I think that I must have reminded her of her former life, and that had put her off too.

Actually I'm not sure what it is that she's sent me. I do think, however, that the basic facts are here, and I'm pretty sure I can do the piece with this and the interviews from the others I've already got. I know it's unorthodox, but I'd like to give it a try. I've received just the one package, but she says that she'll be sending others.

I'm quite drawn to this story. I'm not sure why, except for the obvious. It's got a lot of strong, raw elements, but I think that if handled discreetly, it could be a fantastic piece. And I'm not sure that the issues involved in this story have really been dealt with before by the media. That alone seems to me a good reason for tackling it. I think that it's particularly interesting that this could happen to them. I know we were all stunned when we found out what had been going on. And then, of course, there's the inside angle—the fact that they both worked here. I'm thinking of in the vicinity of 5,000 words if you can give me the space.

I should tell you right off that I couldn't get to Jack Strout. He positively refused to talk to me. But I think the story can be done without my interviewing him.

Let me know what you think. I'd like to get started on this right away.

December 3–4, 1970

———

Mary Amesbury

I was driving north and east. It was as far east as I could go. I had an image in my mind that sustained me—of driving to the edge and jumping off, though it was just an image, not a plan. Along the road, near the end, there were intermittent houses. They were old and weathered, and on many the paint was peeling. They rose, in a stately way, to peaked roofs and had els at the back that sometimes leaned or sagged. Around these beautiful houses were objects that were useful or might be needed again: a second car, on blocks; a silver roll of insulation; a rusted plow from the front of a pickup truck, set upon a snowy lawn like an inadvertent sculpture. The new houses were not beautiful—pink or aqua gashes on a hillside—but you understood, driving past them, that a younger, more prosperous generation (the snowmobiles and station wagons) lived in them. These houses would have better heat and kitchens. The town that I had picked lay at the end of the road. I came upon it like a signpost in a storm. There was an oval common, a harbor, a white wooden church. There was, too, a grocery store, a post office, a stone library. At the eastern edge of the common, with their backs to the harbor, stood four tall white houses in varying stages of disrepair. In the harbor there were lobster boats, and at the end of a wharf I saw a squat cement building that looked commercial. I thought it promising that the essentials of the town could be taken in at a glance.

I parked across the street from the store. The sign said Shedd's, over a Pepsi logo. In the window there was another sign, a list: Waders, Blueberry Rakes, Maple Syrup, Magazines, Marine Hardware. And to its right there was a third sign—a faded relic from a local election: Vote for Rowley. A boy in a blue pickup truck, parked by the Mobil pump out front, brought a paper coffee cup to his lips, blew on it, and looked at me. I turned away and put my hand on the map, folded neatly on the passenger seat. I put my finger on the dot. I thought I was in a town called St. Hilaire.

The village common to my right was shrouded in snow. The light from a four o'clock December sun turned the white surface to a faint salmon. Behind the steeple of the church at the end of the green, a band of red sliced the sky between the horizon and a thinning blanket of clouds. The crimson light hit the panes of glass in the windows on the east side of the common, giving the houses there a sudden brilliance, a winter radiance. Yet I noticed, above the wooden door of the church, the odd graceless note of an electric cross lit with blue bulbs.

The storm was over, I thought, and was moving east, out to sea. The street in front of Shedd's had been plowed, but not to the pavement. I imagined I could actually see the cold.

I shook open the map and laid it over the seat, with Maine crawling up the backrest. With my finger I traced the route I had driven, from my parking place at Eightieth and West End, up the Henry Hudson and out of New York City, onto the parkways that led to the highways, along the highways and across the states and finally north and east to the coast of Maine. In ten hours, I had put nearly five hundred miles between myself and the city. I thought it might be far enough. And then I thought: *It will have to be.*

I turned to see my baby. She was sleeping in the baby basket in the back seat. I looked at her face—the pale eyelashes, the reddish wisps of hair curling around the woolen hat, the plump cheeks that even then I could not resist reaching back to stroke, causing Caroline to stir slightly in her dreams.

The stuffy warmth from the car heater was fading. I felt the cold at my legs and pulled my woolen coat more tightly to my chest. The horizon appeared now to be on fire. Gray swirls of clouds above the sunset mimicked smoke rising from flames. Along the common, the lights in the houses were turned on, one by one, and as if in

invitation, someone inside Shedd's snapped on a
bulb by the door.

I leaned against the seat back and looked across
at the houses. The windows at the fronts were
floor-to-ceiling rectangles with wavy panes of
glass. The windows that were lit reminded me of
windows I used to look into when I was a girl
walking home after dark in my town. The windows of the houses there—warm, yellow frames
of light—offered glimpses of family rituals hidden
in the daytime. People would be eating or prepar-
ing supper, and I would see them gathered round
a table, or I would watch a woman, in a kitchen,
pass through a frame, and I would stand in the
dark on the sidewalk, looking in, savoring those
scenes. I would imagine myself to be a part of
those tableaux—a child at the dining table, a girl
with her father by a fireplace. And even though
I knew now that families framed by windows are
deceptive, like cropped photographs (for I never
saw during those childhood walks a husband
berating a wife or hitting a child, or a wife crying
in the kitchen), I looked across the common and
I thought: If I were in one of those houses now,
I'd be sitting in a wooden chair in the kitchen. I'd
have a glass of wine beside me, and I'd be half-
listening to the evening news. Caroline would be
in an infant seat on the table. I would hear my
husband at the door and watch as he kicked the
snow off his boots. He would have walked home
from . . . (Where? I looked down the street. The
building on the wharf? The library? The general

store?) He would crouch down to pet a honey-colored cat, would bend to nuzzle the baby on the table, would pour himself a glass of wine, and would slide his hand across my shoulders as he took his first sip. . . .

I stopped. The image, filled as it was with critical falsehoods, was a balloon losing air. I looked at my face in the rearview mirror, quickly turned away. I put on an oversized pair of dark glasses to hide my eyes. I draped my scarf over my hair and wrapped it around the lower part of my face.

I looked up again at the simple white houses that lined the common. There was snow on the porches. I was thinking: *I am a settler in reverse.*

I know you are surprised to hear from me. I think that I was rude to you when you came to visit. Perhaps it was the tape recorder—that intrusive black machine on the table between us. I have never liked a tape recorder. It puts a person off, like a lie detector. When I was working, I used a notebook and a pencil, and sometimes even that would make them nervous. They'd look at what you wrote, not at your face or eyes.

Or perhaps it was your presence in that sterile and formal visitors' room. There was something that you did that reminded me of Harrold. Sometimes he would sit, as you did yesterday, your legs crossed, your face expressionless, your fingers tapping the pencil lead on the table, quietly, like a brush on a snare drum.

But you're not like Harrold, are you? You're just

a reporter, as I was once—your hair pinned back behind your ears; your summer suit wrinkled across your lap—just trying to do your job.

Or possibly it was simply the process itself. You'd think that I'd be used to that by now, wouldn't you? But the problem is that I know too much about how it works. I'd be talking to you, and you would seem to be looking at me, but I would know that you were searching for your lead, listening for the quotes. I would see it on your face. You wouldn't be able to relax until you'd got your story, had seen its center. You'd be hoping for a cover, would be thinking of the length. And I'd know that the story you would write would be different from the one I'd tell. Just as the one I am going to tell you now will be different from the one I told my lawyer or the court. Or the one I will one day tell my child.

My baby, my orphan, my sweet girl. . .

I took the name of Mary, like a nun, though without a nun's grace, but you will know that, just as you will know that I am twenty-six now. You'll have seen the clips; you'll have read the files.

You'll describe me in your piece, and I wish you didn't have to, for I can't help seeing myself as you must have seen me the day you came to visit. You'll say that I look older than my years, that my skin is white, too washed out, like that of someone who hasn't seen the sun in weeks. And then there is my body, shapeless now in this regulation jumpsuit, and only two or three people, reading your article, will ever know how it once was. I don't believe that any man will ever see my body again. But that's hardly important now, is it?

I know that you're probably wondering why it is that I've decided to write to you, why I've agreed to tell my story. I have asked myself the same question. I could say that I am doing this because I don't want a single other woman to endure what I went through. Or I could tell you that having been a reporter, I suffer from a reporter's craving—to tell my own story. But these explanations would be incorrect, or only partially correct. The true answer is simpler than that, but also more complex.

I am writing this for myself. That's all.

When I lived it, I couldn't clearly see my way. I understood it, and yet I didn't. I couldn't tell this story to anyone, just as I couldn't answer your questions when you came to visit. But when you left, I went looking for a piece of paper and a pen. Perhaps you are a good reporter after all.

If you can find the facts in my memories, in these incoherent ramblings, you are welcome to them. And if I tell this story badly, or get the dialogue wrong, or tell things out of sequence, you will hear the one or two things that are essential, won't you?

When I opened the door to Shedd's, a bell tinkled. Everyone in the store—a few men, a woman, the grocer behind the counter—looked up at me. I

was holding Caroline, but the glare of the fluo-
rescent lights and the sudden heat of the store
were confusing to me. The lights began to shim-
mer, then to spin. The woman standing by the
front counter took a step forward, as if she might
be going to speak.

I looked away from her and moved toward the
aisles.

They'd been talking when I walked in, and they
started up again. I heard men's voices and the
woman's. There was something about a sudden
gale and a boat lost, a child sick with the flu and
not complaining. For the first time, I heard the
cadence of the Maine accent, the vowels broad-
ened, the r's dropped, the making of two syllables
out of simple words like *there*. The words and sentences had a lilt and a rhythm that was appealing.
The accent grows on you like an old tune.

The store was claustrophobic—you must know
the kind I mean. Did you see it when you were
in St. Hilaire? A rack of potato chips and pretzels
had been squeezed next to a cooler of fresh produce. There were two long rows of cereal boxes
and canned goods, but at least half the store
appeared to be given over to shelves of objects
associated with fishing. I moved along to the back
wall and picked up a quart of milk. I held the
baby and the milk in one arm and slid a packaged
coffee cake into my free hand from the bread
aisle. Walking to the front of the store, I passed
a cooler filled with beer. I quickly snagged a six-
pack with my finger.

When I returned to the front of the store, a man was at the counter, a man about my age and about my height. He had a handlebar mustache and was wearing a denim jacket and a Red Sox baseball cap. The jacket was tight in the shoulders, and I doubted it would button across his waist. It seemed like a jacket he had worn for years—it had a frayed and soft look—but now he had gained a bit of weight across his middle, and the jacket was too small. He wore a navy-blue sweater, and he moved his feet while he stood there. He seemed jazzed up, nervy, in perpetual motion. He tapped a beat on the counter, where he had placed a package of fish cakes, a can of baked beans, a six-pack of beer, and a carton of cigarettes. I thought he must be cold in such a thin jacket.

Across the counter was the grocer, an older man—in his late fifties? He had discolored teeth, from cigarettes or coffee, and an ocher chamois shirt that had an ink stain, like a Rorschach, on the pocket. He rang up the purchases on the counter with only one eye on the cash register. The other one was glass and seemed to be staring at me. My scarf was slipping from my hair; I had my arms full and couldn't fix it.

The only woman in the store was standing by the coffeemaker and reading *The Boston Globe*. She was wearing a green hand-knit sweater and a taupe parka. She was an impressive woman, not fat, but tall and big-boned, and I thought it was possible, though she was well-proportioned, that had she stepped on a scale, she'd have out-weighed the grocer. Her eyes were watery in color, bluish, and her eyebrows nearly nonexistent in a roughened face of high color. Her teeth were large and very white, and there was a slight gap between the front two—a trait I would see often in the townspeople. Perhaps you saw it too. Her hair was graying, clipped short, in a style I would describe as sensible. I thought she was probably fifty, but I also thought she was a woman who had early on settled into a look that would last her many years. When she turned the pages of her newspaper, she looked up at me.

"That's five hundred and eighty-two dollars," said the grocer.

The man with the handlebar mustache took his wallet out of his back pocket and smiled at the weak joke. He handed the grocer a ten-dollar bill and began to speak to him. I may not have the dialogue quite right, but I remember it like this:

"Everett Shedd, you're goin' to make me a poor man."

"Don't be bellyachin' to me, Willis. You're poor all by yourself."

"That's so. It's a bitch season. Jesus. There in't a man in town makin' a dime this time a year."

"You pull your boat yet?"

"No; I'll do it on the fifteenth, like I do every year. Tryin' to eke out a coupla more miserable weeks, though the pickin's is pitiful."

"Don't get sour on me, Willis. You're too young to get sour."

"I was born sour."

The grocer snorted. "That's the truth."

The man with the handlebar mustache picked his change off the counter and lifted the paper bag of groceries. I moved forward with the milk and coffee cake and beer and set them down. Quickly I tightened the scarf around my head with my free hand. The man with the handlebar mustache hesitated a minute, then said, "How you doin', Red?"

I nodded. I was used to this.

"What can I do you for?" asked the grocer. The glass eye was looking at me. It was blue; the other eye was a grayish green.

"I'll take these," I said, "and I was wondering if you knew of a motel where I could spend the night, with my baby."

This came out fast, as if rehearsed.

"Passin' through?" the grocer asked.

I touched the items on the counter, reached in my purse for my wallet. The strap from my shoulder bag lurched down my arm, causing me to have to shift the baby.

"I don't know. I'm not sure. I might stay," I said. I lowered my eyes to the counter—a scuffed rectangle of gray Formica, bordered on one side by a canister of beef jerky strips, on the other by a display of candy canes. I knew the grocer must be wondering why a woman alone with a baby wanted a motel room on the northern coast of Maine, possibly for more than one night, the first week in December.

"Well, I'm afraid there's nothing in St. Hilaire," he said, as if genuinely reluctant to disappoint me. "You have to go over to Machias for a motel."

"There's the Gateway, halfway to Machias," said the man with the handlebar mustache, who was hovering near the magazine rack. I looked at the magazines—*Yankee, Rod and Gun, Family Circle*, and others. I saw then the familiar title, and my eyes stopped there, as if I'd just caught sight of my own face in a mirror, or the face of someone I didn't want to be reminded of.

"Muriel has about a dozen rooms. She'd be glad of the business."

"That's so," said the grocer. "Save you goin' into Machias proper. Motel's not much to look at, but it's clean."

Caroline began to whimper. I bounced the baby to quiet her.

"That's three thirteen," said the grocer. He said the number like this: "thuh-*teen*," and I always think of that pronunciation when I think of the Maine accent.

I paid the man and opened my coat. I was sweating in the hot store.

"Where you from?" asked the grocer.

I may have hesitated a fraction too long. "New York," I said. The two men exchanged glances.

"How do I get there?" I asked.

The grocer put the food into a paper bag, counted out my change. "You go north on this coast road here till you hit Route One. Take a right and that'll take you toward Machias. The

Gateway is about seven miles up, on the left. You can't miss it—big green sign."

I gathered the paper bag into my left arm, held the baby in my right. The man with the handlebar mustache moved toward the door and opened it for me. When he did, the bell tinkled again. The sound startled me.

The horizon had swallowed the sun. The dry, bitter air slapped my face. My boots squeaked in the snow as I hurried to the car. Behind me, from the top of the steps, in the cold silence of the night, I could hear voices, now familiar, casual and well-meaning in their way.

"She's alone with the baby."

"Left the father."

"Maybe."

"Maybe."

Everett Shedd

You could tell she was in trouble the minute she
walked in the door there. She had a gray scarf
wound all round her face, 'n' those sunglasses,
'n' I know she meant to hide herself, but the fact
is, she looked so unusual, don't you know, with
those dark glasses when it was already sundown
outside, that you had to look at her. You understand what I'm sayin'? It was like she was tryin'
to hide but drawin' attention to herself instead, if
you follow me. 'Specially when she wouldn't take
the glasses off inside; then you knew she had a
problem. And the way she held the baby. Real
close, like she might lose it, or it might be took
away from her. And then later, the scarf fell back
down off of her head, 'n' you could see, 'n' I
thought right away that she'd been in a car accident. It was slick as spit outside—had been all
afternoon. Not all of the roads had been plowed
yet, 'specially the coast road, 'n' so I figured she
was going to tell us she'd been in an accident,
except that the bruises didn't look exactly *fresh*,
don't you know, I mean to say *recently* fresh. And

42

then there was the fact that she'd tried to hide
them. You don't try to hide bruises from a car
accident. At least in my experience you don't.
And I've had a little bit of experience. I expect
you know that I'm the town's only officer of the
law, apart from when I'm authorized to deputize
someone else. Me 'n' my wife, we run the store,
but when there's trouble, I'm supposed to sort it
out. And if I can't sort it out, I call over to Machias, and they send a car. And I'll tell you something: I hardly ever see a face looks that bad. Not
to say we don't have our fair share of altercations.
We got some fellas here get to drinkin' 'n' go off
their heads, 'n' I seen a few black eyes, even a
broken arm here and there, but this was different.
Her lower lip, on the right side, was swollen 'n'
black, 'n' she had a bump, big as a lemon, at the
edge of her cheekbone the color of a raspberry,
'n' I suspect if she'd taken off those glasses we'd
a seen a coupla humdinger shiners, and Muriel,
who saw her in the morning, and Julia, they say
it was bad. This was important, don't you know,
what we saw that day, we had to say so at the
trial. I think Julia might of said, right there when
she walked in, was she all right, and she said,
fine, but you could see she wasn't. Dizzy, she
was. And it seems to me she had a limp. I
thought there was something wrong with her
right leg. So I was standin' there, puttin' in the
groceries, thinkin' to myself. She in't askin' for
help. She says she's from New York. We don't
get many people from New York 'tall up here.

So me and Willis and Julia are all three of us lookin' at each other on the sly like, 'n' then she's gone. Just like that.

I can tell you I've pondered many times if I did the right thing that night. I could of quizzed her, you know. Got her to tell me what was goin' on. But I doubt she'd a told me. Or anyone. She was on the run, if you want to look at it like that. And we knew she was probably goin' to be safe at the Gateway, though I didn't like to send her and the baby out in such cold. It was goin' to be brutal that night, they were sayin' minus sixty with the wind chill, so I called up to Muriel to tell her someone was on their way. And then Muriel put her onto Julia the next day, and I think we all figured Julia, she was keepin' an eye on things, had the situation under control, as if you could control a situation like this. But we talked about it later, after she left. We were interested; I won't say we weren't.

She was skin and bones, like them New York models is, undernourished, 'n' I'll tell you something else. You're goin' to think this is strange, but I had the feeling she was pretty. You wouldn't think I'd say that, now would you. But she was. You could see, even with the dark glasses 'n' that hurt lip, she was meant to be a little bit of a looker. She had red hair; alive it was, I've said it since: not orange, like you sometimes see, but red-gold, real pretty, the color of polished cherrywood. Yup. Cherrywood. And a lot of it, fallin' all around her face, framin' it. (Course, I'm partial to redheads. My wife used to be a redhead once; she had pretty hair too, all pinned up at the back of her head. But that's gone now.) It was like . . . let me try to explain this to you. You see a beautiful ancient statue in a picture book, and the statue has been ruined. An arm is gone, or the side of the face has been chipped away. But you know, lookin' at the statue, that once it was perfect and special. You know what I'm sayin'? That's how you felt when you looked at her, that something special had been damaged or broken. The baby had that hair too. You could see it in the fringe, outside her cap, 'n' later, of course. Have you seen her yet?

Have you met Mary yet? Well, I've seen her a few times since . . . well, you know. And I can tell you right now, she don't look the same as she did last winter when she came to us. But you take my word for it, 'n' you write this down when you do this article of yours. Mary Amesbury was a looker.

Not that it ever did her any good. 'Cept with Jack. And that's another story, in't it.

You have to talk to Jack. You talk to him right, he'll tell you some things. Maybe. He's close, our Jack.

Willis will talk to you. Willis will talk to anyone. I only mean that Willis likes to talk, and he was there. He lives in a pink trailer you might of seen just south of town, with his kids and his wife, Jeannine. And speakin' of Jeannine, I'll tell you something confidential. You don't repeat this now, or put this in your article there, but you're probably goin' to hear this around, so I'll tell you now, about Willis. It's said of Willis—that is to say *in connection* with Willis, the way whenever anybody ever talks about Julia they always say how Billy went from the cold afore he went from the drownin'—that Willis's wife, Jeannine, has three . . . that is to say . . . well, breasts. They say that the third one, a little bit of a thing, is located on the right side, up in the hollow where the shoulder meets the collarbone. I've never seen it, of course, 'n' I don't actually know anyone who has, but I do believe it's true, although I would never bother Willis about it. And Jeannine is as good a mother as they come. Everybody says so, 'n' so I wouldn't want nothin' bad said about Jeannine. It's from inbreeding, tell you the truth, but don't you go repeatin' this in your article there. This is private town business, not for the world. Just an aside, don't you know.

Now, you asked me about the town. You come to the right place. I guess you could say I'm a little bit of the town historian, but I 'spect you know that already, which is why you're here.

I was born here, lived here all my life, like Julia and Jack and Willis. Muriel, she come over from Bangor when she got married. Her husband left her—that's another story—'n' she stayed. We're a fishin' town, you've seen that, lobster mostly, clams and mussels and crabs when the season's on. The main business in town is the co-op on the wharf there. We ship down to Boston. There's some blueberry farms too, just inland; they ship all over the country in August. But the lobsterin' is what we're all about. Me, I inherited the store from my father, never any question about what I was goin' to do. But Willis and Jack, now, they're lobstermen. And Julia's Billy was, afore he died. They're a different breed, you know, not your average Joe. Independent is a nice way to put it. They can be a cussed lot. It's in the blood, lobsterin', handed down from father to son, the way minin' is in a town, because that's the only way to make a livin' here. Don't get me wrong. This is a good place to live, in its way. Can't imagine livin' down where you come from. But it makes you hard, stayin' here. You got to be hard, or you won't survive.

Now, the lobstermen, most of 'em, they'll haul their boats just afore Christmas, 'n' they won't put their pots back in till the end of March or so. Willis, for example, he drives a truck for a haulage company in January and February. Then in March he'll start gettin' his gear in shape. Some of the men, though, they don't pull their boats till January. Jack don't, usually. Well, he's got a difficult home situation, don't he? His wife, Rebecca, had what we call the blues real bad. Some of the women, they get them in the winter. It's a dreary thing—they can't stand the water when it's gray for days on end, and they start to go a bit melancholy on you, cryin' all the time, or they cut off all their hair, till it gets spring, and then they're OK. But Rebecca, she was melancholy summer or winter, a trial to Jack, though if you want to know the truth, maybe he's not the sort of man she ought to have married. Jack keeps to himself, he does, pretty quiet. Maybe a bit disappointed in life too, if you want to know. He had himself two years at the University of Maine, don't you know, more'n twenty years ago that was, on a track scholarship, but his father got both his arms broke on a shrimp boat and the family run out of money, so Jack come home to take care of his father. He took over the lobsterin' and married Rebecca. He did his best with the kids. He's got two, nineteen and fifteen their ages are, I think; decent kids. The boy, he's in Boston at school there now. Northeastern, I think it is. Jack's puttin' him through.

But anyway, Jack, he'll go out in a thaw or when it's not blowin'. Works on his pots the rest of the time at the fish house over to the point. That's where he keeps his boat—the *Rebecca Strout*. They name 'em for their wives. Well, at least on this part of the coast they do. Elsewheres they name 'em for their sons, don't you know. That's where she was, by the way, over to the point. Mary Amesbury, I mean. You've seen the cottage?

You understand that when they do go out, summer or winter, the water's still so cold a man can't last ten minutes in it. That's what happened to Billy Strout—Julia's husband, Jack's cousin, don't you know. Got his foot caught in a tangle of pot warp, and he went over. Not uncommon, sorry to say. It was November, if I remember cor-

rectly. They say he went from the cold afore he
went from the drownin'. The medical people up
to Machias, they can tell when they get the body.
Sometimes we don't ever get the body, but Billy,
he washed up over to Swale's Island. We knew,
of course, the day it happened. It's a disturbin'
sight, I'll tell you, someone findin' the boat,
unmanned, the motor still goin', movin' in slow
circles. That's how you know. Course, Billy was
a drinker, part Indian from his mother, don't you
know, so that may have been the problem right
there.

I can't allow as Julia was all that sorry to lose
him, tell you the truth. Don't write that, either.

Anyway, the town.

About four hundred people, give or take a few.
The young ones in their early twenties, they go
off, some come back, live at home a few months,
go off again, hard to keep track, till they lose heart
and settle down here for good, or go off for good.
We've sent four boys to Vietnam, and we've lost
two. Their names is on the town memorial over
there. Most of the boys, they're already lobstermen and feedin' families by the time they get
the call—and a lot of 'em don't go. We got some
patriots in town, but most folks don't think the
war has much to do with us up here.

The town was first settled in the seventeen hundreds by the French over from Nova Scotia, which
is why we have a French name, like Calais or
Petit Manan further south. During the War for
Independence, the town was mostly British, I'm

sorry to say, so that after the war, they tried to get rid of anything foreign and rename the place Hilary, but it never caught on. There are some families can trace their roots back to the war, others that come from Bangor or over from Calais. We had Indians here too, but now they're on the reservations down to Eastport. I say reservations, but we're talkin' about cinderblock housing projects that'd make you sick to look at. Unemployment and alcohol—it's a sin. What we did to 'em, I mean. Anyway, it's not a problem I can solve.

We got a library, open two days a week. Elementary school. For high school, the kids go over to Machias. The church, the post office, my store. Tom Bonney got sick of lobsterin', tried to start up a marine supply store, don't you know, but it didn't take off—most of the men, they make their own pots, and the gear gets handed down father to son. And Elna Coffin tried to get the co-op to go in with her on a clam shack, but like I say, we're out here at the end of the road—not a road *to* anywhere—and they wouldn't back her.

Those houses over there, they're from the shipbuilding days. A hundred and fifty years ago, this town was big in shipbuilding. We had a hotel too, but it burned down; was at the other end of the common. We had twenty-five hundred people in the town at one time, if you can believe it. You'll see some of the houses on the coast road, abandoned a lot of them. Old Capes, some farmhouses. These houses here now, there's two still in the family, but the people in 'em don't have two sticks to rub together, and they're livin' in only one or two rooms in the winter. Shut the rest off. One of the other houses belongs to the schoolteacher, and the fourth is Julia's. Julia does her best to keep the house standin', but it needs work, you can see that. She come from a bit of money years ago, and she went to college too. Up to Bates. Her mother sent her. Nearly killed her mother when Julia up and married Billy Strout. Anyway, Julia had some money afore Billy run through it, but she kept the house, and she's got the three cottages. We get a coupla dozen summer people. Water's too cold 'n' we're too far north for most people. And the black flies are wicked in June. Still, you wouldn't believe the rents people from the city are willin' to pay in the summer, just to get away from it all. Julia makes a bit of money rentin' out June to September. Uses it to live on the rest of the year.

You read the tourist brochures, the shortest paragraphs are about St. Hilaire. And you won't find a single advertisement for anything in town. There's nothin' here.

So that's about it, as far as the history of the town is concerned. I can't think what else to tell you. 'Cept that we never had a murder as long as I can remember. We've had some violence, what you would call aggravated assault, and I've had to bring in a coupla lobstermen took some whacks at poachers. Dennis Kidder got both his hands broke bad. And Phil Gideon got shot in the knee last year. You take your life in your hands you fiddle with someone else's pots.

And another thing. I know I just said the word *murder*, but you won't find many people in town refer to the events of last winter as murder. They'll call it "that awful business up to Julia's cottage," or "that terrible story about the Amesbury woman," or even "the killing over to the point." But there's not too many willing to say the word *murder*. And to tell you the truth, I guess I feel the same way too.

Mary Amesbury

I drove along the coast road leading out of the village. I was driving only twenty-five, but less than a mile from the store, I felt the rear wheels slip out from under me so that for a moment the car skated sideways to the road. My stomach lurched with that feeling you get when the earth seems to have deserted you, and I whipped my hand around to hold the baby basket in place. I straightened out the car, put it into first, and inched even more slowly than before through a nearly silent landscape. Headlights coming toward me seemed like large ships at sea, and when I passed them I gave them such a wide berth I nearly skidded the car into the deep drifts at the side of the road. I hadn't seen that kind of snow since I was a girl. There must already have been several feet, even before the day's storm, and it surprised me that there could be such an accumulation so near the coastline. Pine trees, with their branches overladen, swept gracefully toward the ground.

I watched for the turn onto Route One that I

had been told to look for. Occasionally I could see a pinprick or a glow of light behind or between the pine trees, the only hint at all that the land was inhabited. I almost missed the warmth of the store then, the bright lights overhead, the reassurance of commonplace objects—a newspaper, a cup of coffee, a can of soup—and I understood why it was that the man with the handlebar mustache had lingered by the magazine rack, why the woman in the taupe parka had wanted to read her paper by the counter. I was looking at the pinpoints of light the way a sailor lost in a fog might strain to find the shore.

At a bend in the road there was the stop sign and the slightly wider road to Machias. I took the right as I had been told to do, and drove for what seemed like too long—perhaps twenty minutes. I was certain that I had made a mistake—that I had missed a turn or had failed to see the motel—and so I reversed direction and retraced my journey. I was impatient; Caroline had begun to cry. I pushed the car back up to twenty-five, then thirty, then thirty-five. I was hunched forward over the steering wheel, as if that posture might help keep the car pinned to the road. But when I reached the village again—the lights surprising me too soon, it seemed—I realized I hadn't made a mistake. I sat for a minute, releasing my hands from the wheel as if they had been sprung, trying to make up my mind whether or not I ought to go back into the store for better directions. I imagined the people in the store looking up at me as

I entered, and decided to turn the car around and try again. I glided along the coast road, took the right onto Route One, and looked more closely at all of the buildings I passed, just in case the motel sign hadn't been lit yet. As it happened, the motel was there, a mile or so beyond the point where I had stopped before, the script of the word *Gateway* outlined in lime neon. By the time I angled into the parking lot—it wasn't plowed, and the car fishtailed as I made the turn—Caroline was almost hysterical. I pulled to a stop near the only lighted window.

The proprietor of the motel was an obese woman who was reading a women's magazine when I walked in. She stubbed out a cigarette and looked up at me. A drop of catsup or tomato sauce had congealed on her pink sweater. Her hair, a brownish gray, was permed into tight curls, with two circles caught at her temples by X's of bobby pins. On the counter in front of her was what was left of a TV dinner. In the distance, I thought I could hear a television set and the sounds of children.

The woman breathed through her open mouth, as if her nose were stuffed by a cold. She also seemed to be out of breath. "I been waitin' on you," she said. "Everett called, said you were comin'. Nearly an hour ago, it was."

I was surprised by this. I started to explain why I hadn't arrived sooner, but she interrupted me.

"All I got is rooms with two single beds," the obese woman said to me. She turned back to her magazine and studied an article as if trying to concentrate all the more intensely because I had interrupted her.

"Fine," I said. "How much?"

"Twelve. In advance."

A key was slapped onto the counter. A ledger with a pen was turned around. The motel owner said the words *name and address* as if from very far away.

The baby began to squirm, crying fretfully. Bouncing her against my shoulder, I picked up the pen, tried not to hesitate, tried not to give myself away. I knew I must identify myself; I must now choose a name. I put the pen to the paper, beginning a slow script, composing as I wrote: *Mary Amesbury, 425 Willard St., Syracuse, New York.* I took the name of Mary; it was my aunt's. But in the forming of that *M*, I thought of other names: Didn't I wish for a name more intriguing than my own? An Alexandra or a Noel? But something sensible—a practical need for anonymity—stopped a possible *A* or an *N*.

The Amesbury had come without thought. It was from my drive that day, the name of a town at the side of a highway. I didn't know if there was a 425 Willard Street. I'd never been to Syracuse.

I put the pen down and studied the black script in the ledger. So be it, I was thinking. This is who I am now.

"What's the baby's name?" asked the obese

woman, turning the ledger around and examining it.

The question startled me. I opened my mouth. I couldn't lie about my baby's name, couldn't call her something she wasn't. "Caroline," I said, burying the word in my baby's neck.

"Pretty name," said the owner of the motel. "I had a sister named her daughter Caroline. Called her Caro."

I tried to smile. I shifted the baby to the other arm. I put twelve dollars on the counter.

"Number Two," said the motel owner. "I've had the heat up in Two for an hour now. Put in extra blankets. But you come get me if you and the baby get too cold. Supposed to be minus sixty with the wind chill tonight." Once inside the room, I locked the door. I sat on one of the beds, opened my coat and my blouse as quickly as I could, and nursed the baby. She drank thirstily, making greedy sucking sounds. I closed my eyes and tilted my head back. No one could get to me now, I thought. The realization filled my chest, expanded.

I opened my eyes and looked at the baby. Caroline was still in her snowsuit and her woolen hat. It was freezing.

The motel room felt crowded and dark, even with the single light on overhead. The cloth of the bedspreads and the curtains was a venomous plaid of black and green. The walls were finished with a thin paneling meant to look like knotty pine. I thought the grocer may have been exaggerating when he said the room would be clean.

When Caroline had finished nursing, I changed her, washed my hands, ate a piece of coffee cake, and drank the milk almost as greedily as she had. Then, leaning against the headboard, I opened one of the beers, drank it quickly down. I thought fleetingly that I ought not to drink while I was nursing, but I couldn't get much beyond the thought. The baby was on her back, content, her arms and legs tickling the air. I removed her hat, stroked her head, enjoyed the feeling of the warm fuzz at the crown. My own hands, I noticed, were still trembling. I opened another beer, drank it more slowly than the first.

I liked watching Caroline, sometimes was content to do only this. But that night the pleasure had an undertow I could not ignore. This thought, unwanted, caused other images to press against the edge of my consciousness. I shook my head to keep them at bay. I put the beer can down, picked up the baby, wiggled her out of the snowsuit, and laid her next to me, in the crook of my arm. I thought if I could hold the baby like that, the images would go away. The baby would be my talisman, my charm.

And is it possible that sometime during that night I left the baby safely on the bed and went into the bathroom and took off all my clothes and looked at my body and at my face in the mirror behind the door? I will not bore you with what I observed, or with the feelings I had when I made these observations in that bare frigid bathroom with only a cold metal stall for a shower, except to say that on my body there were flowers—bright bursts of flowers in rainbow hues.

I woke to see that the baby and I had fallen asleep on the bed with the light on. I rolled Caroline over onto her stomach and made a secure place for her with pillows and my duffel bag. Even if she woke up, she couldn't go very far—she wasn't six months old yet and had not begun to crawl. Though she could wiggle herself to an edge if she wanted to.

I put on my coat, my scarf, and my gloves, made sure I had my keys, and went out into the night, closing the door behind me. The cold was motionless—it hurt just to breathe. The lurid green neon script that had read *Gateway* earlier in the evening had been turned off. I had no idea what time it was. I didn't have a watch with me. I walked to the edge of the parking lot, crossed the road, and went into the woods. Only by starlight and a stingy sliver of moon could I keep my eye on the door to the motel room.

I touched the prickly needles of a nearly invisible pine tree. Already the cold had begun to seep into my boots. I thought I could smell, on the thin air, the ocean, or the scent of salt flats at low tide. Far off I could hear the cry of a gull or an animal, something inhuman.

My insides felt hollow. I was still hungry

despite the coffee cake. When I looked at the motel, the baby seemed far away. The distance caught me by surprise, as if I had just discovered that the boat I was on was moving away from the dock. I saw an angry, rigid face, a woman hitting the wall with her back, her arms outstretched to protect her head. I heard a baby cry and was momentarily confused: Was the cry coming from the motel room or the waking dream?

I remembered then a woman I had been in labor with when Caroline was coming. She had occupied the cubicle next to mine on the labor-and-delivery floor, and I hadn't seen her face, but I had never forgotten the sound that had come from her room. It was an otherworldly sound, heard through the wall, like that of an animal afraid for its life, and if I hadn't known that this cry, this howling, had to come from a woman, I would not have been able to identify the sound as belonging either to a male or to a female. The cries grew deeper and louder, and seemed to rock the woman from side to side. The nurses on the labor floor were quiet. Even the other women, in their own cubicles, who had been moaning with their own pains, became silent out of fear and respect for the sound. The woman's doctor, who sounded frightened himself, tried to bring his patient back to reason by calling her name in sharp, angry bursts, but you could tell his presence was nothing to her, less than nothing. I heard the howling and began to shiver. I wanted to talk about the woman, but no one would discuss her with me, as if the howling were too personal to be shared with strangers.

Yet it was pain, pure pain, and nothing more. And it was, I thought then, a useful measure against all future pain, a standard against which I would always be able to quantify my own, even though I knew I would not be able to howl with the freedom of the woman I heard that night. I never saw the woman, but I knew I would never forget her face as I had imagined it to be.

I stomped my feet in the snow and pulled my coat tightly around me. It is possible I heard, on the edge of the silence, the ceaseless ebb and flow of the ocean against a rocky shoreline. I looked across at the motel and pictured my baby sleeping behind the pine-paneled wall.

I have been wondering—you won't mind my asking you this?—are you the sort of writer who changes the quotes? In the early days, when we used to talk, Harrold and I would debate this question endlessly. I was, I suppose, more literal-minded than he was. I thought one ought to report what a person had said, exactly as the person had said it, even if the words were awkward, or had no rhythm, or didn't fit, or didn't precisely say what you knew the person actually meant. But Harrold, who was more used to entitlement than myself, believed in license. He would find the nuggets in a transcript or a file, and keep these kernels, but would embroider the rest, so that his quotes, and thus his stories, would have insight, wit, momentum, even brilliance. Yes, especially brilliance, like rough-cut stones made into polished gems. And only he, and possibly I, and certainly the person whom he was writing about, would ever know that what was written had not been said.

I used to marvel that he was never caught. Indeed, the reverse was true: The more license he took, the more successful he became. The license gave him a style, a pungency, that other writers envied. I think that perhaps the people he interviewed were at first stunned to see their words misstated in print but, after the initial shock, came to like the charming, more intriguing voices Harrold had created for them.

Ironically, it was myself, precise notetaker that I was, who had more complaints from the people I wrote about. For their quotes, though accurate, would sound prosaic, seldom witty, and, even if important, rarely intriguing. Such people would want to disown their quotes. I would, of course, have my notes. I could tell them, if they asked: This had been put just this way; that word had, indeed, been used. And yet I knew exactly what it was they objected to. What had been written wasn't what they had meant to say at all.

And this was the question Harrold and I would debate: In his writing, did the truth get lost? Or did he, with his license, preserve it better than I did?

*   *   *

You asked, when you were here, about my background. I'm not sure what to tell you, what will be relevant.

My mother was the first in her family to make it to the suburbs and to the middle class simultaneously—though it seems to me now, looking back, that this had more to do with geography than with economic status. My mother was a single parent, a working mother, when all the other mothers were at home. She had never had a husband; my father, barely out of his teens, had abandoned her on the day she told him she was pregnant, and he had joined the army within the week. I don't think she ever heard from him again, and he died, in France, before I was born. My father's parents owned a bar on the south side of Chicago, not far from the tenement in which my mother had grown up, and they gave her money after my father died, so that she would not have to work to support me. Instead she used the money as a down payment on a small white bungalow in a town twenty miles south of the city. She went back to work then, as secretary to the president of a company that distributed office supplies. Until I went to school, I was cared for during the day by a neighbor, at the neighbor's house. My mother was determined that no matter what the cost, her own child would not be raised amid the perils of the city, as she had been.

At five-ten every evening, I would walk down the narrow street on which we lived to the austere wooden train station at its foot and meet my

mother, who would alight, in her hat and her
long woolen coat, from the high top step of the
second car on the train. She would be carrying
her pocketbook and a satchel, in which she took
her lunch to work, and would have come from her
office building in Chicago, a trip that took her
forty-seven minutes. Our suburb, barely a suburb,
was a cluster of prewar bungalows, each like the
other, so that the streets had about them an
ordered and tidy quality noticeably missing in the
city from which my mother had so recently
escaped. Our walk up the street—the pastel
houses lining each side—was my favorite time of
the day, a time out of time, when I had my
mother to myself, and she had me, and there
were no distractions. My mother would be ani-
mated, smiling, and might even have a surprise
for me—a gum ball wrapped in cellophane, a
paper strip of caps—and if she was tired, or her
day had gone badly, she did not share this fact
with me. She kept to herself whatever hardships
she had to endure in the city, or perhaps her train
journey home to her child had erased any discom-
forts of her job.

During this walk up our street—she would walk
slowly to prolong our time together; I would walk
backward or twirl around her or, when she was
speaking to me in a serious way, would put my
hands in my pockets and try to match her stride—
she would ask about my schoolwork or my
friends or tell me stories of her "adventures," as
she referred to them, in which I would be expected

to find the hidden homilies. She was also given to heartfelt lectures on various essential lessons of life, which I listened to as though receiving the word of God. There was a hierarchy in the universe, she told me, and I would be happy only if I found my place. Things happened to a person; one must learn to accept those things. One must not rebel too much against the natural order; the price one had to pay would be too high—a life of guilt or loneliness.

I would savor the twelve or fourteen minutes we had together each evening from the station to our bungalow, for I knew that when my mother crossed the threshold, she would be burdened by her chores. She did not complain, but she would become quieter as the evening wore on, like an old Victrola winding down, until it was time for me to go to bed. Then she would come into my bedroom—a tiny room connected by the bathroom to her own—and brush my hair. It was a characteristic that we shared, the color and texture of our hair, and this practice, the faithful hundred strokes, sometimes spilling into another hundred when she was lost in a story or an anecdote, was a ritual we never failed to observe, even when I had grown older and could certainly brush my hair myself.

When I had been tucked into bed, she sat in the living room, on the sofa, and sewed or watched TV or listened to the radio. Sometimes she read, but often when I got up to get a glass of water or to tell her that I couldn't sleep, I would find her with her book or her sewing in her lap while she stared at a distant point on the wall. I don't know what she dreamed of.

When my mother had removed her long coat and her hat, and had changed from her suit or her work dress into something looser, I thought that she was beautiful—the sadness of which I will not dwell upon, for I did not think this sad in my childhood, only now. Maybe all daughters think their mothers beautiful; I don't know. There was her hair, and the color of her eyes, a light green that I did not inherit, and a complexion that has not betrayed her, even in her older years. She was most beautiful, I always thought, on a muggy evening, resting in the middle of her chores, on an aluminum-and-plastic chair on the small screened-in porch off the back door. She would have on a sundress, and her skin would be faintly damp from the heat. Her hair, an untidy but voluptuous mass, would be falling loose from the pins, and she might be smiling at a juicy bit of gossip about our neighbor that I was telling her while we sipped a lemonade. I knew my mother liked me to gossip about our neighbor; it eased her jealousy, the fear that someone else had been a mother to her child.

I was a trial to our neighbor, deliberately so, I think now, and the woman, whose name was Hazel and who had three rebellious children of her own, didn't like me much. The dislike was mutual, or perhaps it was that I disliked living out my childhood in someone else's house. As soon as I was old enough, I begged my mother to let me stay alone at our bungalow after school, and she allowed this privilege, trusting me not to drink or to smoke or to do the other things she sometimes heard that girls my age were trying then. Of course, in time, with my friends, in my house and out of it, I did participate in the wildness she feared—I smoked, I drank some beer—but she was wrong to think that these essentially innocent pastimes would be the traps that would ensnare me.

Sometimes my mother invited men to the house. I did not think of them as her boyfriends, do not even now. They were men who had befriended my mother in some way—single or unattached men who plowed a driveway for which we had no car, or mended broken windows; or men whom she had met in the city and who would come out to the house on a Sunday afternoon for a meal. But once there was a man whom I think my mother loved. He worked as a supervisor for the company that employed her, and she got to know him well at work, for she would sometimes talk about him, in passing, in the middle of a story, and I would notice the pleasure that referring to him, even in this small way, gave her. His name was Philip, and he had dark hair and a mustache and drove a shiny black Lincoln. For a time, he came regularly on the weekends for a meal, after which he would take my mother and me for a drive in his car. I would sit in back; my mother would sit beside him. He would reach over and squeeze her hand from time to time, a movement I never failed to notice. We would go for ice cream, even in the dead of winter. When we got back from these drives, I would go to my room to play, or outside to find my friends. I was eight then, or nine. Philip and my mother would be alone in the living room. Once I came around a corner; Philip was kissing my mother on the sofa. I thought his hand was on her breast, but she moved so quickly away from him when she heard me that the motion is blurred, and I am not sure now what I saw. She blushed and he stood up, as if I were the parent. I pretended I had seen nothing, asked the question I had blundered into the room with. But I hated the moment, and I cringe even now when I think about it. I did not hate the fact that Philip had kissed her—I was glad that she had someone to love after all those years. I hated myself instead, my burdensome presence.

As it happened, however, Philip also abandoned my mother, after a time. For months, I thought that Philip had left my mother because of me, because he did not want to love a woman who was "saddled" with a child, as the expression went then. When other men came to the house—and there were not too many after Philip—I went to my room and would not leave it.

My mother was Irish and Catholic and had been raised in a crowded apartment, one of seven children. She was devout and attended Mass every Sunday of her life, and I am certain that she viewed my birth out of wedlock as the most serious moral lapse of her life. I could not be persuaded, from a very young age, to accept the Church as wholeheartedly as she did, and I know that this minor rebellion on my part was a source of aggravation to her. If we had fights—and actually I remember very few—it would be over this, my irregular attendance at church. But in later years, when I was working in New York City, and when I was already in trouble, I passed each morning, on my walk to the office, an age-darkened brick Catholic church called St. Augustine's, and I would sometimes be overwhelmed by a desire to go inside it and kneel down. I never did, however. I was plagued by the notion that I did not deserve comfort from a church I had scorned, and in any event, I was almost always late for work.

We had other visitors to our bungalow. My mother had many relatives, most of whom still lived in the city. Our tiny suburban house was far enough away to seem like an excursion on a Sunday afternoon. My grandparents and aunts and uncles and cousins would arrive by train at the bottom of the street, and the entire entourage would noisily make its way up the hill to our bungalow, where my mother would have prepared a meal. She knew they did not approve of her single-parenthood, approved still less of her determination to live outside the city and support herself and her child by working as a secretary— a *private* secretary, she always said, as a point of pride—but she invited them faithfully to the house every other week, even cajoled them when they balked. I would not have any brothers or sisters, she knew; and she wanted me to feel that I belonged to something larger than just the two of us. The noisier and more crowded our house became, the happier she appeared to be.

She urged me, too, to have my friends to the house, and there would be food that she had made in the refrigerator or on the counter to tempt us, or she would ask my friends to dinner or to spend the night. She was vivacious when my friends came to the house, as if she were trying to make it seem as though more people lived there than actually did, as if we were, in fact, just like all the other families on the street. I had girlfriends, later boyfriends, and I remember a kind of frenzied race forward through my teens, my energies channeled into my schoolwork and into trying to be more popular than I was constitutionally meant to be. But my fantasies, nebulous though they were, were focused on a distant point, after high school, when I would live away from home. I loved my mother, and I did not like to think of her alone after I had left, but I understood that neither she nor I would be happy unless I did what I was supposed to do, unless I seized for myself those things that she had been denied.

In the daytime, when my mother was off to Chicago to her job, if I was not in school I would walk the tracks with my friends or by myself. We would walk to other towns (more easily reached by railbed than by road), hopping off the tracks when we heard an oncoming train. We felt ourselves "adventurous." The tracks were peaceful and gave a sense of the lay of the land, but the true attraction of this pastime was the illusion of freedom. There would be an endless stretch of rails and ties with no visible impediment and a sense that one could walk forward forever. Even now, when I hear the rhythmic clacking of a passing train, I think of my mother and of the promise of a journey and of that distant desirable point where the rails seem to converge.

Muriel Noyes

What's this story all about, anyway?

I won't be part of no article that is critical of Mary Amesbury, so you can put that thing away right now if this is some kind of hatchet job. Mary Amesbury is innocent. Trust me, I know. How do I know? Because I've been there before. And any woman who has been there knows the truth about this kind of thing.

I had a husband who beat me. The goddamn son of a bitch ruined my life. Goddamn ruined my life. Took away the best years of my life. You can't ever get them back. You know what I'm sayin'? I had my babies, I couldn't even love them. I mean, I loved them, but I couldn't ever enjoy anything, because I had to be so afraid all the time, scared to death every time he walked in the door, scared for them, scared for me. He hit my son in the high chair once, the baby was only seven months old. Jesus Christ, I ask you. Seven months old. I hadda take the baby to the doctor. I hadda lie. I hadda lie every goddamn day of my life because I was so ashamed and scared.

I'll tell you something. I'm not afraid of anyone or anything now. Ever.

So I know all about this. There isn't anything about this I don't know.

Though I will say I didn't realize about Mary Amesbury until the next morning. You catch me while I'm readin' my magazines, forget it. Anyway, she came in, and when I looked at her, I was really lookin' at the baby, so I didn't see it.

But next morning she came into the office, and she had the scarf around her and the dark glasses, and I knew, right then, and she saw I knew, and she looked at me, and I swear to God, I thought she was goin' to pass out. Then she says to me, when she recovers, do I know of a place where she can stay awhile, a cottage like. I mulled it over in my mind and said how Julia Strout might have something. Julia rents cottages in the summer.

I guess it was 'cause I had a feeling of what she'd been through, and with the baby and all, that made me call Julia myself. Up here, we usually don't bother much with strangers, but this was different, you understand?

I couldn't take my eyes off of her. She was tryin' to keep it hidden, but you could see it. You wouldn't of believed it if you'd seen it. It's a nightmare, a goddamn nightmare. Havin' to go out into the world with your life story all over your face.

You're a reporter, right? Well, no one's goin' to tell you the truth about this kind of thing, so I'll tell you a story. I lost two of my top front teeth.

I been knocked out. I had a broken arm and a shinbone fracture. I've got scars from cigarette burns where they shouldn't be. For five years I never once had what you would call intimate relations and liked it. Even now I can't think about sex without thinking about what he done to me. So that's another thing he took away from me. One time he thought the police were comin', he stole the kids and ran away to Canada. I didn't see my kids for six months. When he came back, I was so scared he'd take them again, I let him do whatever he wanted. Until he started on the kids. I couldn't take that. I called the police in Machias, he ran away. I prayed it would be for good. That was eight years ago. I hope he's dead.

We had a share in a blueberry farm. I sold it and bought the motel. It was abandoned since the early fifties—an unbelievable mess. Some people from the town, they helped me fix it up. I've got three kids. We get by. They're good kids, but raisin' kids on your own, you better believe it's hard.

I love my kids, but when I said he ruined my life, I meant it. I'm still angry. You can tell, right? I'm still angry. I see other families, they come into the motel in the summertime and they look happy, and at first I'm sad for myself, and then I look again—and I don't trust the happiness.

Julia Strout

Yes, I knew Mary Amesbury. She rented a cottage from me at Flat Point Bar from December 4 until January 15.

The rent was minimal. Is that important?

I saw her first on the afternoon of December 3, when she came into Everett Shedd's store.

I would say that, yes, I thought at the time something was wrong. She appeared to me to be in distress. She seemed ill or undernourished. It was extremely cold that day. Extremely cold. It was all anyone talked about that afternoon. On the news, the weatherman had said that the temperature might go as low as minus sixty with the wind chill. In fact, it went to minus twenty, an actual reading. We aren't used to such low temperatures here, even as far north as we are, because we're on the coast.

I may have asked her if she was all right. I can't remember now.

*   *   *

Yes, Everett and I did discuss her after she left the store. We thought perhaps she might be running away from something. I know I thought about that, and possibly Everett and I talked about it. Everett may have suggested to me the idea that she'd been hurt, but I'm not sure about that now.

My husband died in a fishing accident years ago. I'd really rather not talk about myself. I understood your article was about Mary Amesbury, not about the people in the town, isn't that correct?

I don't think I can participate in this article if you're going to write about the town. I'm here only to talk about Mary, to make sure that the truth gets told. That is to say, the truth as I understand it. I can't pretend to know the whole truth. I'm not sure anyone does, apart from Mary herself.

Yes, of course, I am aware that her real name was not Mary Amesbury. But that's how we knew her here, and I suspect that that is how she will be remembered in this town.

Though Mary Amesbury is gone for good now, isn't she.

I saw her again in the morning. Muriel Noyes called me and asked me if any of the cottages were winterized. I have one winterized cottage, over to Flat Point Bar.

I wasn't concerned about making money. I don't normally rent cottages in the winter. The cottage had been winterized by a couple who planned to retire to St. Hilaire, but the husband died, and the widow went back to Boston last summer. I had been renting the cottage to an engineer who was working on a dredging project in Machias, but he left just before Thanksgiving. The timing was fortunate, as it happened, because I hadn't had the water or the heat turned off yet.

She came to my house. She came to the door.

She was wearing a gray tweed wool coat and a gray scarf. Later, when we were at the cottage, and she took her coat off, I saw that she was wearing blue jeans and a sweater and black boots, I believe. She was very thin.

You've met her, I assume.

She reminded me of a thoroughbred. She had what my mother would have called a patrician chin.

I never did any more than any decent person would have done. There are people in the town you have to look out for, give a hand to when you can. I would say it was slightly unusual for

Everett and myself to be concerned about a stranger, except that when you saw her, of course, there was no question of not helping her. And then there was the baby.

What happened next? We got in her car, and I took her to the cottage.

One thing I would like to say now, however. Something important I think you should know.

This is a terrible story, and there are many tragedies to think about. But I will tell you this: I believe in my heart that the six weeks Mary Amesbury spent in St. Hilaire were the most important six weeks of her life.

And quite possibly the happiest.

Mary Amesbury

In the morning I opened the curtains. The daylight was blinding—a blazing glare of light, the sun shearing off the snow in all directions. Caroline lay on the bed looking up at me, two tiny teeth winking from the bottom of her smile. I picked her up and began to walk with her. She was happiest when I did this—she liked the view from the top of my shoulder, or she liked the motion—and I felt good and whole when I held her, as though a piece of me that had been missing had temporarily been restored.

I tried to sort out the immediate future while I walked. I didn't like the room, but I knew I couldn't relinquish it until I had found something more suitable. I thought I should try Machias; the larger town might have more to offer in the way of long-term housekeeping units, or even an apartment. I needed a newspaper and food, and that meant having to go into a store again—a task I dreaded.

I decided that I would ask the motel owner for the room for another night. In that way, Caroline would have a place to nap during the day if I didn't find anything right away.

I dressed the baby and myself, put on my scarf and coat and glasses, and went to the office. The motel owner wasn't there, but I rang a bell and she came. She looked at me as though she had never seen me before. I asked her if I could have the room for another night, and I saw then that she knew.

There was a time when I'd wanted people to know, and I'd been unable to tell them. But now that the truth was apparent on my face, I wanted more than anything else to hide.

I raised my face to the motel owner and asked her if she knew of a place, a rental, where I could stay awhile.

Around the woman, and emanating into the room, there was the stale drift of cigarette smoke. The motel owner peered at my face, at the small bit that was visible, as if trying to confirm her suspicions. She took a long pull at the cigarette, gestured with the cigarette between her fingers.

"There's a woman in St. Hilaire rents cottages in the summer," she said. "I think one or two of them are winterized."

"How do I get in touch with her?" I asked.

The motel owner hesitated, then picked up the phone and began to dial. She kept her eyes on me, spoke to me as she was dialing. "Her name is Julia Strout. She don't rent much in the winter; no one ever comes here. But there's one cottage out to the point, another south of town, I'm pretty sure. The one out to the point that's winterized, there was this older couple from Boston, they was goin' to retire there, and so they winterized it, but then the husband died and she went back to Boston, sold it to Julia Strout, she rents . . . Julia? This is Muriel. . . . I'm fine. Don't know if my car's goin' to start this mornin', though. You survive the cold last night? . . . Good. Good. Listen, Julia. I got a woman here with a baby needs a place to stay, and I was tellin' her about that cottage over to Flat Point Bar that's winterized. . . . Is that right? You think you can get the heat up over there? Be cold out to the point with the wind off the water. . . . There's the baby, don't you know. . . ."

There was a bit more conversation, and then the motel owner hung up the phone, looked at me. "She says she saw you yesterday in the store," she said.

I thought about the tall woman in the taupe parka. I wondered if the motel owner would call the tall woman back again as soon as I'd left the motel parking lot and tell her what she had seen, or what she thought she had seen. I thought then of moving on, to the next town, or to the next.

"Here, let me hold the baby for you while you go try to get your car started, warm her up," said the motel owner. "You can't put a baby in a cold car today. Freeze her tootsies off."

I said thank you and walked out to the parking lot to start the car. The engine didn't catch on the first three tries, but at the fourth coughed anemically. I put my weight on the gas pedal, tried to rev the car into life. I looked up through the windshield, could see nothing. Thick frost coated the glass. While the engine was warming up, I got out and scraped the frost away from all the windows. The sun was brilliant but ineffectual in the deep cold.

When the car felt warm enough for the baby, I packed the duffel bag and threw it into the trunk. I went back to the office. The motel owner was playing a game with Caroline, swinging the baby's arms high into the air. When she did this, Caroline laughed—a deep belly laugh. I felt a pang of guilt. It had been days since I had made my baby laugh, since I had played with her.

The motel owner turned around and reluctantly gave Caroline back to me. "I got three of my own, in grade school now. I miss 'em, the babies. How old is she?"

"Six months," I said.

"You know how to get back to town?"

I nodded.

"All right. When you get to town, you'll see four old colonials across from the store. Julia Strout's is the one with the green shutters. Green front door. She's waitin' on you now."

"Thank you for arranging this for me," I said.

The motel owner began to light another cigarette.

"Don't forget the key," she said.

I took the room key from my coat pocket and put it on the counter.

*   *   *

I circled around the oval common and parked in front of the only house of the four with green shutters. The house was the most prosperous-looking of the group, with a generous wrap-around porch at the front. I climbed the steps of the porch, having left Caroline in the car, and knocked at the door. The woman who answered it was already dressed for the cold in her parka, her hat and gloves, and a thick pair of blue corduroy pants stuffed into her boots. She shook my hand and said, "Julia Strout. I saw you in the store yesterday."

I nodded and said my new name; it caught in my throat. I had never said the name aloud before.

"Your car started," she said, locking the door behind her. "You're lucky. They had to call school off today because they couldn't get the buses started. We'll go in your car, if that's all right with you. I haven't taken mine out of the garage yet."

I said yes, that would be fine. She sat across from me in the front seat. She was a large woman, larger even than I had suspected the previous day in the store, and she took up all the space around me in the car. I looked quickly at the woman, but she didn't return my glance, as if she had already seen what there was to see and was too discreet to stare.

"The cottage is just off the coast road, a bit north of town," she said. "Sorry to make you have to double back, but there was no way to direct you to the cottage on your own. The landmark is a pair of pine trees, and I doubt I'd have been able to describe them."

Julia Strout, too, had the Maine accent, but her speech was more refined than that of the grocer or of the man with the handlebar mustache or of the motel owner.

The road was nearly uninhabited and ran close to a serrated shoreline. The view of the water was unimpeded now—a vast, frigid gulf of blue, strewn with islands, stretching out to the Atlantic. There was a wind up; there were whitecaps.

She said, "Here we are. This right."

We turned onto a rocky road, covered by layers of snow and ice and bordered on each side by tall hedges that she said were raspberry bushes in the summer. We slipped and lurched down this narrow lane until we came, unexpectedly, into the open.

A relentless tide licked at a waterline of dark seaweed. We were looking at a spit of land, with a smooth sand beach on one side and a flat mass of pebbles on the other. In between was a rangy swath of dried grasses, thinly covered with snow. A ruined lobster boat, doubtless tossed by a storm onto the grass, lay on its side, its weathered blue-and-white paint almost too picturesque against the desolation of the beach. Farther along the spit was a shingled shack, no bigger than a single room. And beyond the spit itself, four lobster boats—one a forest green and white—were moored in a channel.

"There's three or four men keep their boats

here, not in town," she said, "but they won't be bothering you. They'll be hauling their boats in a couple of weeks, except for Jack Strout, my cousin, and he'll haul his mid-January. And when they do go out, they go before daybreak and are out all day." The shack, she explained, calling it a "fish house," was for the lobstermen when they did not go out in their boats; they worked on their gear there during the winter months.

A pine-covered island, barren of dwellings, made a dark backdrop for the boats, and beyond that a broken necklace of similar islands, each receding island a paler green than the one before, stretched out to the horizon.

"The cottage is behind you, to the right," she said.

I made a turn on a patch of wet sand and found better ground on a gravel drive that led to the cottage. It was on a promontory, with views out to sea on three sides, and when I saw it I thought: Yes.

It was a modest house of white clapboards, like a Cape but not as well-defined, with a screened-in porch at the side. It had a second story with a wide dormer, no other ornamentation. The clapboards came all the way to the ground and were not shrouded by bushes or shrubs. Looking at it, one had a sense of neatness. A square lawn, surrounding the house, had been cut from a profligate thicket of wild beach roses, now dormant and broken here and there from the weight of the snow. The house looked naked, sun-soaked, freshly washed.

"The key is in the doorframe," she said, unfolding herself from the seat.

I took the baby from the back of the car and followed Julia Strout up the small hill to the cottage. She struggled with the key in the lock.

There weren't many rooms inside the cottage— a living room, the kitchen, a bedroom downstairs, the larger bedroom upstairs, the porch. It was a simple house, sparsely furnished, and I must have noticed the white gauze curtains at the windows, for that is a detail I would have liked, but my memory of those first few minutes is of a glistening wash of corners, windows, shadows. I followed where Julia Strout led; she spoke plainly, defining objects, spaces.

We returned to the kitchen. The table was made of pine, but it had a worn green-and-white-checked oilcloth cover on it, and around it were four chairs, mismatched, one painted a dark red. Julia was concerned about the heat—the cottage had been frigid when we entered—and was busy for a few minutes turning up the thermostat and descending into the basement to look at the furnace. She showed me where the hot-water heater was and turned it on. We talked about the lane down to the cottage: She said she would have one of the men plow it later in the day.

I wanted to sit down and did. I kept the baby bundled in her snowsuit and her hat. She began to fuss; I opened my coat and nursed her. I sat sideways in a kitchen chair, one arm resting on the table. Through the window in front of me, I could see a gull rise nearly thirty feet straight up in the air with a clam in its mouth, then drop the shell to break it open on the rocks.

Julia tried the plumbing in the bathroom and switched on all the lights to see if they worked. She was examining a light fixture over the stove when I asked if her husband was a fisherman. It was meant to be a pleasantry. I was looking at a gold wedding band on her finger. I looked at the indentation on my finger where my own wedding band should have been.

"He's passed on," she said, turning to me. Unlike most large women, she stood up straight and was graceful.

She explained: "It was a squall, and he caught his foot in a coil of pot warp when he was throwing his pots over, and he went in too. It was Veterans Day. The water was so cold he had a heart attack before he drowned. Usually they go from the cold before they go from drowning," she said plainly.

I said that I was sorry.

"It was years ago," she said with a movement of her hand. She paused.

I thought that she would go on, but she moved toward the counter and looked for a light bulb in a drawer instead.

I turned back to my view. The gulls, several of them now, swooped high into the air with their booty, like feathers in an updraft. In the silence of the kitchen I could hear what I'd been too distracted to hear earlier—the business of the day outside the cottage: the gulls cawing and calling; the swell of the waves over the pebbles, the settling of these stones in the ebb; the drone of a motor on the water; the rattling of a windowpane from a gust. The cadence in those natural sounds brought on a sudden sleepiness.

Julia Strout finished her inspection of the cottage and came over to the table where I was sitting. She had her hands in the pockets of her parka.

I was still wearing my scarf and sunglasses. By tacit agreement, I had not removed them, nor had she referred to them. But the scarf and glasses were cumbersome, unnecessary now. With my free hand, I unwound the scarf, removed the glasses.

"I was in a car accident," I said.

"I can see that," she said. "It must have been a bad one.

"It was."

"Shouldn't that lip be bandaged? Or have stitches?"

"No," I said. "The doctor says it will be fine." The lie came easily, but I found I could not look at her when I said it.

She sat in the chair opposite. She seemed to be studying me, making, I thought, a judgment of some kind.

"Where are you from?" she asked.

"Syracuse," I said.

"I used to be at school with a girl from Syracuse," she said slowly. "I don't suppose you would know the family."

"Probably not," I said, avoiding her glance.

"You've come a long distance."

"Yes. It feels like it."

"There's a clinic in Machias—" she said.

I looked up sharply at her.

"For the baby," she added quickly. "And of course yourself, if you should need it. It's a good idea to know where to go in case of emergency."

"Thank you," I said. I reached for my pocketbook on the table. "I'd like to pay you now. What is the rent?"

She hesitated, as if thinking to herself, then said, "Seventy-five dollars a month."

I thought: Even in St. Hilaire in the winter, she could get twice that. I had three hundred dollars in cash in my wallet. I calculated that if I was very careful I might be able to last at least two months before I had to find a job or figure out how to get into my bank account without anyone discovering where I was.

Julia accepted the money, folded it into the pocket of her parka. "You don't have a phone here," she said. "I don't like to think of you here alone with the baby without a telephone. You have a problem, you'd better go up to the LeBlanc place—that's the blue Cape just before we turned in. I'm pretty sure they're on the phone. For other calls, you can come use my phone, but I'm afraid we don't have a public phone in St. Hilaire. You have to go to the A&P in Machias. There's one inside the door."

She shifted her body in the chair and looked at Caroline. "I think you'll find St. Hilaire a very quiet place," she said.

I nodded.

"You'll need a crib," she said.

"I have the basket."

She studied the baby again. She was thinking. "I'll get you a crib," she said.

I noticed that her glance tended to slide off my face and rest on my baby's instead.

She stood up. "I'll be on my way, then," she said. "That is, if you don't mind running me back to town."

"No, that's fine," I said, gathering up the baby and my keys.

"It feels warmer in here, don't you think?"

I did think it was warmer and said so.

Julia moved toward the door. She looked out at the ocean. I was behind her with the baby.

A sharp gust rapped at the glass. I glanced beyond Julia to the seascape outside. I saw the snow-covered grass, the gray-black rocks, the deep navy of the frigid gulf. The sun glinted painfully off the water now. I thought the view was brilliant in its way, but inhospitable.

I had the impression that she was thinking about the ocean or the view, perhaps thinking of her husband, who had been lost in the gulf, for she stood at the door longer than was natural.

I was about to speak, to ask her if she had forgotten something, when the tall woman turned, looked down at my face, then at the baby.

"This may be none of my business," she said, and I felt my heart begin to lurch. "But whoever did this to you, I hope he's in jail."

I am tired. It is late, but you would never know. The lights are on in the corridors, and it is noisy here, very noisy.

I will write tomorrow and the next day, and then I will send this off to you. You will be surprised.

I have traveled so far—farther than you will ever know. Sometimes I remember my life as it was just a year ago, and I think to myself: That can't have been me.

We drove to town in silence, the droning of the motor or the vibrations of the car causing Caroline to drift off to sleep just seconds after we had emerged from the lane onto the coast road. When we reached the village of St. Hilaire, Julia told me to park in front of the store. She would watch the baby in the car, she said, so that I would not have to wake Caroline in order to buy supplies. It was a sensible solution to a logistical dilemma, and I accepted it as that. I put the car in neutral, left the motor running and the heater on.

I shopped quickly, perfunctorily, trying to think of staples, composing lists in my mind as I wheeled the small shopping cart up and down the aisles. The grocer was there behind the counter, making notations in a ledger. He nodded, squinted at me with his good eye, asked if I had liked the Gateway. I told him it had been fine, that Julia Strout was renting me a cottage.

"The cottage," he said. "The one over to Flat Point Bar?"

"I think so," I said. "It's north of town on a small peninsula."

"Yup," he said, satisfied. "That's the one. Tight little place. You'll be all right there. Well, well. Good for Julia."

The groceries cost me twenty dollars. I felt my own motor revving with the car and wanted to leave the store. But the grocer seemed reluctant to let me go, as if he had questions he wanted to ask, but had to make small talk before he could reasonably get to them. I didn't want him to get to the questions, and was impatient as he slowly put the groceries into the paper bags. I suspected that he functioned as a central source of information, and that he would be expected to report on the new woman who had come to town, the new woman who wore large dark glasses at night and covered her face with her scarf. Or possibly he already knew some of the answers to the questions. Would Muriel have called Julia, and Julia, in turn, have called Everett Shedd? I thought not. I didn't know why, but I trusted Julia Strout, could not imagine her as a gossip or as a woman who would give away much of anything very easily.

The grocer appeared not to like the arrangement of the groceries in the bags; he began to take some of the items out and then to replace them. I inhaled two long breaths to keep myself from sighing out loud. He counted my change with elaborate care. I thought of Julia with Caroline in the car. I did not want to be indebted to anyone. Before the grocer had finished with his repacking job, I whisked one of the bags off the counter and said quickly, "I'll start taking these out to the car."

I put the groceries into the trunk, drove around to the other side of the common, and let Julia off in front of her house. There were people about now—a group of school-age children throwing snowballs near a war memorial, using the large stone monument as a fort; an elderly woman shoveling snow in the driveway of the house next to Julia's. The old woman, lost amid the woolen layers of her clothing, was bent nearly double over the shovel, her progress snail-like across her driveway. Down by the co-op on the wharf, there were capped pickup trucks in soiled rusty colors.

Julia stepped out of the car without ceremony and repeated that someone would be by to plow the lane. I didn't like to think about how Julia had seen my face and had not believed my lie, and so spun off from the curb perhaps a little faster than was necessary. It was only near the end of the drive back to the cottage, alone in the car with Caroline, still sleeping in the back seat, that I could begin to release the crabbed muscles in my back.

At the cottage, I lifted Caroline, basket and all, into my arms and walked with this bundle into the house. Gently, so as not to wake her, I placed the basket on the rug in the living room. As long as the baby stayed asleep, I would have time to bring in the groceries and put them away.

This task pleased me, made sense to me in the same way that caring for Caroline often did. I placed the perishables in the refrigerator, the packages and cans in the cupboards. I looked at the dishes and the silverware. The dishes were white plastic with blue cornflowers, the kind supermarkets offer as promotions. In a cupboard under the counter, I found a cache of pots and pans and serving bowls.

When I had finished with the groceries, I turned to examine the interior of the cottage, as if for the first time. I was thinking that it was mine now, mine and Caroline's, and that no one could tell me how to live here, could tell me what to do. I walked around the corner into the living room. The furniture was spare, even homely: a lumpy sofa covered in a frayed and faded chintz; a wooden rocker with its caned seat coming loose; a maple end table I associated with my mother's house; a braided rug, worn smooth over the years. The walls were plain, painted several times, the last coat a pale blue, but the windows were appealing—large multipaned windows with white gauze curtains at the sides. There were pictures on the walls, trivial paintings of mountain scenes, painted by amateurs for tourists, I suspected. I began to take them down, to stack them behind the sofa. I found a hammer in a kitchen drawer to remove the nails. The walls should be bare, I thought; nothing could compete with that view.

I opened a door and walked into the downstairs bedroom. There was a single bed with a cream chenille coverlet, a tall maple dresser in the corner. The crib might fit in there, I thought, but I wondered if I shouldn't have the baby with me, in the upstairs bedroom.

I climbed the stairs to see if there was space for the crib there. In the center of the room was a large double bed with a carved mahogany headboard. The bed was exceptionally high—I could almost sit on it from a standing position without bending my knees—and on it was a heavy white quilt, intricately pieced together with hundreds of patches in rose and green. I ran my hand over the cloth, admiring the stitches with my fingers. I tried to imagine who it was who had made this quilt and when: Julia as a younger woman, Julia's mother? The widow who had gone back to Boston? To the right of the headboard was a bedside table with a lamp. And to the left was the view— a view farther out to sea than could be seen from the lawn. I sat on the bed and gazed at the seascape through the bank of multipaned windows. In summer the gauze curtains would billow out over the bed.

I could see the boats moored in the channel from a different perspective here—the painted floorboards, the traps stowed in the stern, the yellow slickers hanging just inside the wheelhouses. I could also see the tip of the point, with the gravel beach and the sand beach meeting at a place where the slope cut sharply into the water. To my right, south along the coast, I could make out the map of the shoreline, with a large rock jutting up through the surface of the ocean. Far out to sea, there seemed to be a momentary pin-prick of light, a lighthouse, though I thought it might have been a hallucination.

I relaxed my gaze on the horizon and let my eyes drift from the area where I had seen the light, to allow the signal, if it was really there, to come into my vision. It was then that I heard it: it was a small sound, an intrusion. I clutched the fabric of the bedspread, stopped breathing altogether so that I might hear more keenly. It was the click of a key in the lock, the sharp tread of footsteps in the hallway. He was home sooner than I had thought he would be, I was thinking. I must pretend to be asleep. I must turn out the light.

But it was not the sound of a man in a hallway. It was merely a car, an engine straining, in the lane. I released the fabric and looked at my hands.

I listened to the car in the lane, heard it backing up, then the sound of something hard scraping gravel or ice. It must be the man with the plow, I realized. I stood up to peer out the window, but I could not see him from there.

In the living room, Caroline was stirring. I was distracted and busy then—changing the baby, feeding her, putting clothes in drawers. In the background was the whomp and scraping of the plow.

I heard the truck pull into the gravel driveway. I walked with the baby to the living room window, glanced down. The truck was a rusty red pickup with a cap, much like the ones I had seen that morning at the co-op. Below the driver's-side window there was a pattern of scrollwork in flaked gold. The driver alighted from the cab. He was wearing a Red Sox baseball cap and a denim jacket that was too tight across the waist.

He rapped at the glass. I walked with the baby to the door and opened it. He stood on the steps with a crib, staring at me, seemingly unable to move.

Then I remembered.

"I had a car accident," I said.

"Wow. You all right? Where did it happen?"

"New York," I said. "Come in. I don't want the baby to catch cold."

He maneuvered the crib through the door. He asked me where I wanted it. I said I'd like it upstairs, in the bedroom, if he could manage it.

"No problem," he said.

I laid the baby in the basket and meant to help him with the crib, but he was halfway up the stairs by the time I turned the corner. I could hear the crib being opened, the sound of the casters as he shifted it into position. Then he was back on the stairs, pulling a pack of Marlboros from his jacket pocket. He was short and stocky, but he seemed strong. He made his way down the steps as though moving to an inner jittery beat.

"Mind?" he asked as he reached the bottom step.

I shook my head. I walked into the living room. He followed me.

"My name is Willis, by the way," he said. "Willis Beale. I saw you in the store yesterday."

I nodded, but we did not shake hands. "I'm Mary," I said. "Mary Amesbury."

"When did it happen?"

I looked at him. Instinctively, my hand rose to my face, but I lowered it.

"A couple of days ago," I said, picking up the baby.

"Oh," he said. "I thought it mighta been on account of the storm."

His hands were rough, the fingernails cracked and broken. I could see, too, that his jeans were worn, frayed, with grease marks, like finger paint, along his right thigh. He walked to the large window overlooking the point and studied the view. He had a day's growth of beard and used his cupped hand for an ashtray. Despite the sense that he was in constant motion, he seemed in no hurry to leave.

"That's my boat out there," he said. "The red one."

I looked at the boat he was pointing to. I could see the name *Jeannine* on the stern.

"Me and a couple of other guys, we use the point. The channel's deep, and that island there gives good shelter. It's faster out to the grounds from here. You can get yourself a good head start. My father, he used to keep his boat here too. So when it came my turn, I started comin' here."

"Thank you for plowing the lane," I said, "and for bringing the crib."

"No problem," he said, turning, looking almost startled as he again saw my face. He shivered slightly. "Cold out there," he said.

"You should have a warmer jacket."

"I got one; I should wear it. But I dunno, I always wear this jacket. It's a habit. My wife, Jeannine, she's always naggin' at me, 'Put on your parka.' I know, I should. She says I'll get pneumonia."

"You might."

"How old is the baby?" he asked.

"Six months."

"Cute."

"Thank you."

"I got two kids, four and two. Boys. My wife, Jeannine, she'd die for a girl. But we're on hold now. For a while, anyway. They dropped the price of lobster on us last summer; times is tight. You alone here or what? Your old man comin'?"

"No," I said. "I'm on my own now."

The *now* had slipped out without my wanting it to. He heard it, caught it.

"So you left him or what?"

"Something like that."

"Jesus. Winter, too. You goin' to be alone through the winter?"

"Oh, I don't know," I said vaguely.

He reached over and tickled Caroline under her chin. He looked for a place to stub out his cigarette, could find nothing, walked over to the sink, turned on the water. He opened the cupboard under the sink and threw the butt into the trash basket. He leaned against the counter, his arms crossed over his chest. I thought he must be expecting a cup of coffee, as payment for plowing the lane. Perhaps it was the custom here.

"Can I get you a cup of coffee?" I asked.

"Oh, no, thanks, but I'll take something stronger if you got it."

I remembered that he had seen me buy the six-pack at the store.

"I do," I said. "I've got some beer. In the fridge there. Help yourself."

He opened the fridge, took out a can of beer, and looked at the label. He popped open the top, swallowed long and hard. Then he leaned against the counter again, holding the can with one hand, the other in the pocket of his jeans. He seemed somewhat more relaxed, physically calmer.

"So are you from New York City or what?"

"No," I said. "I'm from Syracuse."

"Syracuse," he said, pondering the city name. "That's north?"

"Yes."

He looked down at his feet, at the heavy work boots soiled with dirt and grease.

"So what brought you to St. Hilaire?" he asked.

"I don't know," I said. "I just kept driving, and it was getting dark, and so I stopped."

That wasn't true. I had picked St. Hilaire deliberately, picked the town because its dot on the map had been small and far away.

He opened his mouth, as if about to ask another question, but I said, quickly, "What is pot warp?" to deflect him.

He laughed. "Yeah, you really aren't from around here. It's rope. Warp is rope, the pot is . . . well, you know, the lobster pot."

"Oh," I said.

"Give you a ride out on my boat if the weather warms up some," he said.

"Oh, well, thanks, maybe," I said.

"Course, I'll be pullin' it the fifteenth, so you want to go, it'll have to be afore then."

There was silence in the kitchen.

"Well, I guess I better be goin'," he said after a time.

He walked to the door. He paused a minute, his hand on the knob. "So, OK, Red, I'll be goin'. You need anything, just give old Willis a call. Watch out for the honeypots, now."

"Honeypots?"

He laughed. "Come here; I'll show you." He gestured for me to come to the door. I walked over to where he was standing. He put his hand on my shoulder, pointed with his other hand.

"You see out there—that salt muck? Low tide in a couple of hours. We get extreme tides here; the bay will be almost drained by suppertime—

apart from the channel, that is. Anyway, you look carefully you can see gray patches in the brown, right?"

I looked closely, thought I could see small circles of gray, about three or four feet in diameter, in the wide expanse of brown.

I nodded.

"Those gray patches," he said, "are called honeypots. They're like quicksand. You walk into one of those, you'll be up to your waist in muck in a matter of minutes. Not too easy to get you out, either. And if you're still stuck when the tide comes in, well . . ."

He released his hand from my shoulder. He opened the door wide, turned on the top step, faced me, his shoulder holding the door open.

He braced against the stiff wind at his back. He nodded, as if to himself.

"You'll be all right," he said.

Willis Beale

That's W-i-l-l-i-s B-e-a-l-e. I'm twenty-seven. I been a lobsterman since I was seventeen. Ten years. Phew. Jesus.

My boat, she's a winner. I don't want to brag or nothin', but she's pretty fast. Every year they have the lobster boat races over to Jonesport on the Fourth of July; I always place in the top three. I come in second this year. She was my dad's afore he retired, but I trimmed her down some. I fish the grounds nor'east of Swale's. My dad fished there, and his father afore him. It's my grounds now, you understand that. No one in town, they'd dare go near 'em. That's the way it goes—handed down father to son, it's your territory. I catch a poacher out there, I put a half hitch on his buoy spindle. I don't give no second chance. The next time I catch the son of a bitch, I cut his pots. My grounds is my livin'. You put your pots out to my grounds, it's just like walkin' into my house and stealin' the food off of my table. You follow me?

When is your article comin' out, anyway? You goin' to put my name in it?

Oh yeah, I knew her. I was around here and there. I keep my boat over to the point, and I had to help her out some. Plowed the lane. Like that.

I thought she was real pretty. Real nice. She was always nice to me. I coulda gone for her, you know what I mean, if the circumstances was right. But of course, I'm married and I love my wife, so anythin' like that was out of the question.

But you see, this whole mess, I have my own ideas about it. It's a complicated problem.

Well, we only ever had her say-so, didn't we? I'm not sayin' she was lyin' or anythin' like that, but you take Jeannine and me. I love my wife, but I won't say that we haven't had our moments. And maybe once or twice we kinda got into a little pushin' and shovin', you follow me. Nothin' heavy. Just a little somethin'. It takes two to tango, right? I'm just sayin' how are we ever goin' to know? And she took the kid, right? Well, I'll tell you the truth: If my wife ever did a thing like that, I'd knock her block off. What guy wouldn't, if you're goin' to get truthful. You steal a guy's kid and run off where he can't find you, that's goin' to make a fellow pretty wild, I don't care whose fault it was. I mean, there's ways to deal with problems in a marriage. You don't have to run away. You got to talk it out or get divorced or whatever, right?

And then there's other things to think about.

Well, I been thinkin' about it. Afore Mary Amesbury come here, this was a peaceful little town, right? Not much to write home about, but the people here is decent, law-abidin', and so forth, you know what I mean. Then she comes, and it's like some hurricane blew through town. Don't get me wrong. I liked her and all. And I'm not sayin' she was tryin' to cause trouble. It's just that she did, didn't she?

I mean, look at it this way. By the time she left us, we got one murder, we got one alleged rape and assault, we got one suicide, and three kids don't have mothers anymore.

I mean, she's got somethin' to answer for, don't she?

Mary Amesbury

I watched Willis Beale make his way down the hill to his truck. He stepped up into the cab and started the motor. I saw him turn the corner, and then he was gone. I moved back from the window, still holding the baby. The tide was going out now. Fast. Already I could see almost fifty feet of salt flats below the waterline. Just a couple of hours earlier, the tide had been high, licking the seaweed.

I didn't know what time it was, but thought it must be the middle of the afternoon. I made a mental note to buy a clock, perhaps a radio. The sun was weaker than it had been; on the horizon there was a darkening, like a gathering of dust. It would be night by four-thirty, I thought. The sun would set behind me.

I stood by the kitchen table, watching the waning sun turn the navy of the water to a teal, the boats in the channel catching the light at anchor. I saw the afternoon and evening stretching ahead of me. Empty time, empty spaces. I was glad the day would end soon, that darkness would come early. The night had a rhythm of its own, with a meal, with putting Caroline to bed. I could cope with that. Then I remembered that I had no book with me, I had nothing to read.

I heard a car engine in the lane and thought briefly that Willis had come back, that he had forgotten something. But it was a different color truck, a black pickup with a cap. I watched the truck drive along the hard wet sand almost to the end of the point. A man got out, and the wind blew his hair and filled his short yellow slicker like a sail. He wore long black boots, and his hair was the color of the sand. Turning his back to me, he withdrew one oar and several coils of rope from the back of the truck. He walked to one of the rowboats, beached by the low tide, and untied a rope, pulling the boat down to the water. He pushed the boat out, hopped into the stern, and began to scull with the oar, standing up in the boat as if it were a punt. When he was far enough away from shore, he sat down, sculled expertly with the oar in the direction of the green-and-white lobster boat. I watched him tie the rowboat to the mooring and leap onto the bow of the larger boat with his coils of rope. He walked along the narrow deck to the cockpit, jumped down inside. I saw him disappear into the little cabin at the front and then reappear without the rope. He reversed his journey then, from the larger boat to the dinghy to the shore, pulling the rowboat high up onto the beach to the iron ring at the waterline. The small boat tilted onto its side. He carried the oar to his truck. He looked up, saw my car in the driveway, swept the cottage with his glance, but I didn't think that he could see me. Then he got into the cab of his truck, turned it around, and drove back up the spit, into the lane.

The landscape was suddenly quiet, seemingly motionless. The water lay flat, like a pond. The wind had stopped; there were no gulls. Inside, it was as still as death, except for dust motes that were slowly moving in a beam of sunlight. The baby had fallen asleep in my arms. A wave of something like fear started then, even as I held the baby.

I decided I would clean the cottage. It would keep me busy for hours, keep the fear at bay.

I found the tools that I would need—a broom, a dust mop, rags for dusting—in a broom closet next to the hot-water heater. I had bought a can of Ajax and a plastic bottle of dishwashing liquid. These would have to do, I thought.

I worked on the house. I swept all the floors, wiped down the walls with the dust mop. I ran the rags over all the furniture, scrubbed the tub and toilet in the bathroom. In the kitchen, I cleaned the sink and cupboards and washed the linoleum floor with hot water. I sponged down the refrigerator, scrubbed the shelves.

When I could, I left the baby in the basket to sleep or, when she woke, on the rug to play. Sometimes I stopped to nurse her. Once, when I was mopping the kitchen floor, I looked up to see that she was on all fours, trying to propel herself forward. I watched her make a tentative move. My heart swelled. I looked around as if there might be someone in the cottage I could tell about this feat, this milestone. But I was alone. There was no one there to see my daughter. I went to her and picked her up and kissed her. I held her then a long time.

After the sun had gone down, and I thought it must be close to seven o'clock, I dressed Caroline in her pajamas and put her to bed upstairs in the crib.

Hungry now, I made my first real meal in the cottage—a bowl of canned soup and a salad. I drank a beer while I was cooking, another while I ate at the table with the green-and-white-checked tablecloth that I had scrubbed nearly raw with a sponge and the dishwashing liquid. The soup tasted good to me. I liked looking at the cottage from the table, felt a sense of accomplishment in the cleaning.

When I had finished my dinner and washed the dishes, I decided to reward myself with a bath. I walked into the bathroom. The tub looked inviting, sparkling. I filled it with water as hot as I thought I could bear. I took off my clothes and lowered myself into the tub. The steaming water stung at first, then was soothing. I lay back against the rounded lip of the tub, let the water close over me. I picked up a washcloth and a cake of soap and gently massaged my skin, wanting to make myself as clean as I had made the cottage.

My skin was pink when I emerged from the

tub. I dried myself gingerly with an orange towel hanging from the rack. I slipped on my night-gown and put over that a large white cardigan sweater that I had decided would do for a bath-robe. When I sat at the table, to dry my hair with a towel, I could hear that the wind had started up again outside. I heard the press of waves against the rocks, a loose rattling of the window-panes. I thought that I would indeed like a radio, just to have a bit of music in the background. I had never experienced quite so much silence and wondered if it was good for the baby.

The chores or the beer or, more likely, the long soak in the tub had made me finally drowsy. I did not know whether it was nine o'clock or ten o'clock or even later, but I thought that time didn't matter much, anyway.

When my hair was almost dry, I hung the tow-els on the rack in the bathroom, turned off the lights there and in the kitchen. I felt my way around to the stairs, climbed them to the landing. Inside the bedroom at the top of the stairs, I could hear the soft rhythm of Caroline's breathing. I waited for my eyes to adjust to the small bit of moonlight coming through the bank of windows, then peered over the crib. I could just make out the dark shape of Caroline's head on the sheet, the bundled body under the blankets.

I drew back the covers of my own bed, took off my socks and the cardigan. The sheets were cool cotton, and I shivered slightly as I slipped between them. I thought I would just drift off to sleep: I was tired now, very tired. The baby would wake early, I knew, and would need to be nursed.

But I didn't drift off to sleep. I didn't sleep at all. Lying on my back in the bed, I had instead a clear and distinct vision of exactly where I was— a luminous vision of myself perched on a high bed at the top of a cottage on a hill overlooking the Atlantic. I had driven to the edge of the continent; there was nowhere else now to go. The slight shiver I'd felt earlier deepened along my spine.

I had been foolish to imagine I was safe. It had been silly to mop floors, wash tables, as if I could scrub away the past. He would not let me get away with this. He would not let me take his child. He would not let me outwit him. He would find me; I was sure of this. Even now, he might be in his car, driving toward me.

In the darkness I covered my face with my pillow—for there was something else that I knew.

This time, when he found me, he would kill me.

June 8, 1967–December 3, 1970

Mary Amesbury

We met my first day of work. I came around a corner—he was in an office. I saw him only, though it was another man, my editor, I had come to speak to. Harrold had been standing, hovering over a desk, looking at a layout. He straightened up, watched me walk toward the desk. I had on a blouse. It was new, ivory-colored, and I had worn a necklace—a string of beads? I brought my hand up, touched the beads. I had forgotten already why I had come, and I cast about for a question I could ask: It was, after all, my first day on the job, and I had an array of questions to pick from. My editor said our names. We didn't speak, and he felt compelled, I think, to fill in the gaps: She is from Chicago, just out of college; he is off to Israel in the morning. Maybe I asked a question then: What would he do in Israel in the morning? and perhaps he answered, Find a decent cup of coffee.

He was large, I think massive; I have always said massive in my mind, though you could see he'd never had an extra ounce of fat. His hair was

large too—that's how I think of it: large and loose
and dark, and it curled slightly below his collar.
But it was his eyes I remember most clearly. They
were black and deep-set, almost lost beneath a
wide expanse of brow. They were dark eyes and
impenetrable, and when he looked at me I felt
lost. I believe he saw this immediately, and it
pleased him, possibly even thrilled him. He put
his hands on his hips, brushing back his sport
coat. His tie was red, loosened at his collar. His
shirt was light blue. The sport coat was a navy
blazer, and he wore khaki pants. It was a uniform
of sorts. He smiled at me. It was a smile that
started at one corner and stayed there. You would
say, if you saw it, it was a crooked smile, and
that would suggest he had charm, and he did.
But that day I understood the smile differently.
He had plans, and time was short, and he was
off to Israel in the morning.

I left the editor's room, and I am absolutely sure
I knew it even then. I knew it the way when
you're told you have a certain illness you understand you will not get better; or the way when
you see a particular house on a particular landscape you think: Yes, that is for me, I am going
to live there.

I was given a cubicle in a maze of cubicles. I had a
telephone, a typewriter, a small rectangle of desk
space, a few drawers, a bookshelf. I remember
most of all the noise, a cacophonous crush of tele-
phones and typewriters, punctuated by staccato

bursts from the wire services. Even so, everything I said in the cubicle could be heard by those adjacent to me, just as I could hear what they were saying. There was an intimacy in that large room, even as you were insulated by the noise.

I was assigned that day to a section called Farewell and told to write a one-paragraph obituary of Dorothy Parker, who'd died the day before. I had only six sentences to write, and though I put more thought into it than I would ever have time for again, I finished it before lunch. I had the rest of the day to kill. I read past issues of the magazine. I observed the faces in the office—the camaraderie, the hostility, the jealousy. You could see it all, in one afternoon: those who had power, those who didn't, those who thought a lot of themselves, those who had longings elsewhere. I wondered where it was that I would fit. People spoke to me, made jokes, asked questions. They smiled with their mouths but not with their eyes. Even the friendliest were cautious. There were pressures there, and for some the stakes were high. Or seemed so then. It was remarkable, the air of importance created in that office—extraordinary to remember now how much it all seemed to matter.

I saw him too, moving through the office—to his own office, adjacent to the editor's; to a coffee machine across the maze of cubicles; out to lunch; back from lunch; to another writer's desk. In each of these journeys, there was the fleeting look, the sidelong glance, the eyes locking quickly in a

turn, and I felt—actually I knew—that I was sealing a bargain with those brief glances. So that
when he came to my desk at five o'clock and said
some words about a drink at six, I was not surprised, merely nodded.

We went to a bar around a corner. It was filled
with men in sport coats and loosened ties. He
knew the place well, moved through it like a regu-
lar, took a table in a corner—I had the feeling the
table had been left for him. He ordered a gin martini and I said I'd have a beer. He laughed at that;
he said I didn't look the type to drink a beer. I
asked, recklessly, what type was I? and then he
had his opening: an easy shot straight to the
center.

He said that I made lists and that I never would
be late. He said I would be steady, though I'd
rather drift. He said I'd do the job, though my
heart would not be in it—that routine was more
important to me than the work. He said I would
be fast and dexterous but that I would not enjoy
reporting: I was the type to listen but not to pry.
He said it was his guess I'd rather edit: It was
quiet work, and I'd be left alone.

A waitress came and brought me a frosted
glass. I put my hand around it—my hand was
burning. Was I so transparent after all? He loved
this game; he would always win. It was a dance,
and he was leading. I wonder now, was he not high,
too, with the knowledge that we had found each
other, the perfect team, the perfect symbiosis?

I changed the subject and asked a question about the Middle East. I knew that there was heavy fighting in the Sinai. He leaned back, let his jacket fall open across his belt. His answers were full of understatement, but in the understatement you could hear his skill, his own dexterity. He had a byline I had seen before: Harrold English. Already when you saw the name you had images of the man. I was looking at his wrist, at his wristbone exposed beyond the cuff of his jacket. It was tanned, and I was thinking while he talked—fatal, lethal, self-destructive thought— if only I could touch him there.

You understand that it was physical. Before the night was over, I was in a room alone with him. We hadn't even had a meal. There were silk ropes, or possibly that came later. This was a movie I had never seen before, might never have seen if I had not said yes to his questions. I was frightened, but I was ravenous, complicitous. I thought, believed, that this was love, and before the night was out, I had said the word, or he had. We said the word together, and christened what we did.

He went to Israel in the morning, and I went back to work. I think the others must have seen it: I was like a toy top someone had spun and walked away from. I did not know for how long he would be away. He hadn't told me, and I couldn't ask the editor—it was too obvious. I did my work, took on more and more, stayed late into the night at the office, as the others did. The longer I stayed in that building, the more chance I had of catching some brief word of Harrold, overhearing his name in a bit of gossip from the field. There was nothing else I wanted to do. At night I did not go out. It was enough just to sit in my room and think of him, replaying the same images over and over again in my mind.

I was moved from Farewell to Trends. This was thought to be a step up.

I think it was then that the pattern began—his leaving and his coming back, my never knowing when he would come back, so that always I seemed to be living life on the edge, keen and waiting. I was sitting in my cubicle, on the phone doing an interview, when he walked into the room and looked at me. He'd been gone for seven weeks; I had not had a word from him. He'd been to Israel and Nigeria, Paris and Saigon. I didn't even know for certain if he had another woman; I had imagined, from time to time, that it was someone else he wrote to. I didn't know then that he wouldn't ever write or call when he was away; it was part of his plan, to keep me always waiting.

He came to my desk. I put my hand over the mouthpiece of the phone. He said that he had work to do—two, three days at the most. He asked me how I'd been. I had the sense that we were being looked at, watched by others. I said that I'd been fine. He said that on the third night we would go to dinner. It wasn't a question.

So that's how it began. Do you need other details? He had a large apartment on the Upper West Side, large and mostly empty. I had a tiny room in the Village, and so we lived at his place. He had been to Yale, and his father was a wealthy man. They were from Rhode Island, on the water. Harrold was twenty-eight when I met him, established at the magazine. It was understood that he was meant to be a star. His mother had died when he was a boy, and there was me without a father, and somehow that seemed fitting: Our backgrounds were symmetrical.

What else can I tell you about him?

He had a habit of running his fingers through his hair, and he would seldom comb it. He didn't eat breakfast, he was hard to rouse when asleep, and he almost always ordered eggs for lunch. He typed with two fingers, very fast—a dazzling display, I always thought, of compensation.

He was addicted to the news. He read four papers a day and never missed a TV news program if he was at home. When he read, he always had the radio on, to music or to the news. He said it was a consequence of having lived alone so long. He couldn't bear the silence.

His taste in music was contemporary. He liked Dylan and the Stones and a guitarist named John Fahey. He played them loud and often. But though he liked the music of the moment, he didn't take to drugs: They made him lose control, he said, and made him queasy. Instead he liked to drink in bars—as if he were a character from another era. He liked bars in foreign cities best, he said. The women there intrigued him.

He was often out of town, and later sometimes I was too. When he was home, we'd go to a bar, then to bed, then I'd cook a meal. We'd be up until two or three in the morning. We never had people to the apartment, and we never went to parties. This was essential, that we be alone: My dependence on him must be absolute.

I think now about that isolation, how complete it was. The world around us, as you know, was jagged and screaming. There were the riots, and there was the war. We knew about these things, often wrote about them for the magazine. Harrold was a witness, and sometimes so was I. But strangely the reporting and the writing isolated us even more. What we wrote were words, like the ones we read in newspapers. There would be an event, and we would be above it or beside it. If you were there to tell the facts, you didn't have to feel. Indeed, we thought detachment from the world essential. And if, in the office, we could talk about a protest or a killing because we had the facts, these were not the stories that mattered in the empty rooms at night.

We weren't like other couples. How can I make you understand? In the office there would be the heat between us, and possibly others felt it, but in public he went his way and I went mine. I was seen to be friendlier with other people than I was with him. We did not have lunch together or touch in the office or display the kind of public possessiveness that new couples sometimes revel in. What we were and did was secret, and even when we married, the sense of secrets kept us separate from the world, like women veiled in harems.

Later, as a consequence, I would think: There is no one, no one in the world, that I can tell this to.

Sometimes—often, in fact—I would wonder: Why had Harrold chosen me? For I had sometimes found among his things pale-blue air letters from women in Madrid or Berlin.

It was my hair, he'd say, teasing me; it was a flame that had drawn him to me like a moth. But no, really, he'd add later, coming toward me, backing me up against a wall, it was my feet. He liked small feet, and mine were white and neat, and had I ever noticed that before? Or later still, and in a more serious mood, he'd say it was the way we worked together: We had minds that thought alike when it came to putting words on paper.

But once, when we were in a taxi late at night, speeding uptown from the office on a rain-soaked street, the lights swimming on the wet pavement, I asked him why, and he said lightly—his hand was resting on my thigh, his smile had started at the corner of his mouth—*You let me have you.*

*   *   *

I wrote my mother. I wrote that I had met a man and that I loved him. I said that he was smart and well respected at the magazine. I said that he loved me too. I told her that he was tall and dark and handsome, and that when she met him she would find him charming.

I knew that she would like this letter.

The things I wrote were all the truth, but they didn't tell her anything like the truth, did they?

The truth was that we drank. There would be the drinking in the bars, with all the world around us. And then there'd be the wine, the open bottle and the glasses beside the bed. Or champagne in a bucket; we often had champagne. The drinking then was festive: Every night was a celebration. The empty rooms in his apartment would be lit with candles, and I would find, in the morning, clothes in a hallway, delicate glasses beside the tub. I cooked in a robe he gave me. It was navy cotton terry cloth, too big for me, and I felt small and lost inside it. There was a round table in the kitchen—a wrought-iron table with a smooth glass top. Around it there were dark-green metal chairs such as you'd see in France. And there would be the red wine on the table for the meal, and it seemed to me that we would drink until the fevers, both erotic and mundane, had burned their way out of us, and we could go to sleep then.

I had had a lover in college, but he was just a child by comparison. He had no dark secrets that he let me see. Of course, I was a child then too, and though we drank sweetened drinks on weekends, it was an innocent pastime, meaningless.

With Harrold, the drinking was different: We were drowning.

I have memories. I remember this: We were in the bedroom after work. It was late, a hot night, and I was in my slip. He lit a cigarette and leaned across the darkness to give it to me. I did not smoke often, but I sometimes smoked with him. His cigarettes were foreign, and I liked them. He bought them on his trips, and they had a dark and fruity scent, like flowers in a damp woods.

He was still dressed in his clothes from work. I remember particularly the cloth of his shirt, a stiff blue oxford weave. He had his tie on, but he had loosened it. We smoked together and we didn't speak, but I had the sense that soon something would happen.

I was sitting on the edge of the bed, my legs crossed, my feet bare. He was sitting not far from me, slouched a bit in his chair, his legs crossed too, one ankle resting on a knee. He was watching me, studying my face, examining my gestures as I smoked, and I felt self-conscious under his scrutiny and wanted to laugh to deflect him.

But then he stood and took my cigarette from me and put it out. He lifted me under the arms and laid me down on the bed. I remember that he was hovering over me, hovering in that way he had, and that he hadn't taken his clothes off. He raised my wrists to the brass bars of the head-board. He undid the knot of his tie. I felt the small stab of his belt buckle against my rib cage, the cloth of his shirt against my face, the silk of his tie against my wrist. I inhaled the cloth of his shirt—I loved the smell of him through the weave. And later, when he was saying that he loved me and was calling out my name, I thought: When he had been watching me, had he read this scene on my face?

It was morning. I was standing by a closet and a mirror, getting dressed for work. I had on a dress I liked—it was cotton, muslin, a long smock from India, and had intricate hand embroidery on the bodice. He was in front of his bureau, lifting socks from a drawer. He had on his pants but not his shirt. He turned to me and examined me—a long, cold stare of examination. He said, You should wear your skirts shorter; you have nice legs. And then: Don't put your hair up. It looks better long.

I took the pins out of my mouth, put them on a table. I unwound my hair, let it fall.

He said, You could look sexy if you wanted to. You've got the raw material.

I had known him three months then, or maybe four.

That day, on my lunch hour, I walked to a department store and bought two skirts that were shorter than those I normally wore. But even as I handed the money to the woman behind the counter, I was thinking: He is changing me. Or rather: He wants me to be different than I am.

The presents started then. Harrold had money and would bring me things from Europe or from California. Or from Thailand or Saigon. At first the gifts were jewelry and sometimes clothes. Then mostly clothes—beautiful, expensive fabrics I could not afford and would not have bought for myself. The clothes were unlike those I'd ever worn before—sensuous and exotic. I put them on to please him and seemed to change as I wore them, to become the person he'd imagined.

And then there was the lingerie. He bought me risqué bits from Paris or the East. He said I had to wear them to the office, and only he would know, and I thought, talking to myself, trying to still just the smallest voice of worry: This is harmless and fun, isn't it?

He said I should stand up straighter; I should unclasp my hands; I should stop a nervous gesture I had of fingering my hair.

He said to me, I tell you these things for your own benefit. Because I love you. Because I care about you.

He was my mentor at the office. I had a modest talent only, but he took me in hand. This was exciting, you understand, being tutored by him. He had power, and I sometimes found that irresistible. In the bar, after work, he would look at a story I had done, suggest improvements. I'd be stumped in my reporting, and he'd have a name to call, a golden source. He told me, too, how to talk to the people above me—what to show them, what to withhold. When I was sick once, he did my story for me; he even wrote it in my style.

He told me I should refuse to write only about trends, and I said no, I'd lose my job. But he goaded me and pushed me, and one day I did as he had said to do, and I didn't lose my job: I was moved to the national desk; I was given a bigger cubicle.

I took everything he offered me, acquiesced to his design. This was the bargain we had made, wasn't it?

We had been together a year, maybe longer. I had gotten home before him. I was in the kitchen, at the table, reading a newspaper. I didn't want a drink. I hadn't gone to the bar to meet him. I had a headache. Actually I had the flu but didn't know it yet. I heard him in the hallway, and I stopped reading. There was his key in the lock, his footsteps in the hallway. I realized with some surprise that I didn't want to see him, I wanted to be alone. Do I need a reason? I was tired. I didn't want to have to give anything—or to have to take from him, either. It was the first time since we'd met I'd felt this way.

He came into the kitchen, and he must have seen it. Perhaps it was in the way I wouldn't look at him and kept my eyes on the newspaper: Something in me resisted this intrusion.

He took his jacket off, hung it on a chair. He pulled his tie loose, unbuttoned his collar. He put his hands on his hips, looked at me. He said, Don't you want a drink? and I said, No, I have a headache. He said, Have a drink; it'll help the headache, and I said, No, but thanks.

He came up behind me, put his hands on my shoulders. He began to massage the muscles at the base of my neck. I should have relaxed for him, but I couldn't. I understood this gesture. He would touch me even when I didn't want it, especially when I didn't want it.

I tried to sit there, pliant, thinking: This will be over soon. But his fingers kneaded the knots in my shoulders too vigorously. I wrenched away suddenly, stood up. I was going to say, I'm not feeling well, I'm better off alone tonight, but he grabbed my wrist, held it.

I don't remember everything that happened— the room seemed to spin around me very fast. He had me up against the refrigerator; the handle was in my back. His strength was absolute: I'd had only hints of this before. He raised my skirt to my waist. I tried to push him away from me, but he slammed my wrist up against the metal. I felt a sharp stab of pain; I thought that he had broken it. I was frightened then. I knew that he could hurt me, was hurting me. He was a large man—have I said that before?—and though I fought, my fighting him was useless.

And then I stopped resisting and became a part of it, a passive player. And it seemed, when it was over, and he was holding me, and I didn't want to think about the implications of those few moments, that possibly love or sex or violence was simply a matter of degree. Seen in a certain light, was what had happened against the refrigerator so very different from all that had gone before?

He carried me to the bed and wrapped me in a blanket. He put ice cubes on my wrist—it was bruised but not broken. He put his mouth on my wrist and said that he was sorry, but curiously, I understood that he meant he was sorry the wrist was hurt, not that he was sorry for the act.

He made a meal for us, and we ate it on the bed. He seemed grateful to me, and I was aware of a strange sense of our having grown closer to each other, more intimate, as though the more risks we took, the more secrets we shared, the further we pushed the boundaries of what was done, the more entwined we would become.

In the night I got the fever, and it is possible I am confusing the sequence of what was said or felt, but that was when he wrote my story for me. And that was when he asked me to marry him.

In the months and years that followed, it was often like that: He'd take something from me, or hurt me, and then offer me something larger in return. And if I took the something larger—a promise or a commitment or a dream—it was understood that I forgave him.

He never said, then or ever, the word *rape*, and I could not say the word aloud myself.

I said that I would marry him. He went off to Prague to do a story. I had his apartment to myself. I was sick with the flu. I was sometimes feverish. I didn't go to work.

Already I felt addicted, or obsessed. I would drink alone, just as we had done together, because it was a thread, it connected us. I would walk to windows, bare windows looking out at traffic and at buildings, and sit for hours, thinking just of him and of us. I would wander rooms and touch his things, go through pockets to find bits of paper that would tell me more about him. I read his notebooks on his desk, tried to think the way he thought.

Yet even as I did, I knew that we were not like other people. Or if we were like other people, this was a side of love I had not heard anything about. Harrold had had a vision of who I might be, had seen this vision even on the first day we met, was relentless in his pursuit of it. Who I actually was or might have been was merely clay to play with. He saw me as a star, like himself, his protégé, his possession. Perhaps I am oversimplifying this, but I don't think so. I was in trouble only if I resisted the vision he had—only if I spoke or acted or felt in a manner that was incompatible with his design.

Was this my failing, then? My failure to embrace wholeheartedly this new self that was being offered to me, even as I wore the expensive lingerie to the office, shortened my skirts, listened avidly to his advice?

For always there was something in me, as yet unidentified, unrecognizable, that resisted the shaping and the molding. In the beginning it seemed that this resistance was maverick, merely confusing to me, there almost despite my best interests or my wishes.

And later, when I did resist at last, his repertoire was extensive, magisterial: subtle scorn, veiled ridicule, icy silence, absence, presence, absence. He was skilled, a virtuoso, a concert pianist.

But I am getting ahead of myself.

There were good times, have I told you that? At the table in the kitchen, he would tell me stories of his travels, wonderful stories of misadventures and comedies, peopled with characters I could clearly see as he described them. He was a gifted raconteur, and he saved for me all the bits he could not put into his articles, so that when he came home from a long trip, I'd be entertained for days.

Or maybe we would lie side by side on the living room floor, with only our arms touching, our heads propped up on sofa pillows, and listen together to music he had chosen. We might smoke together or drink the wine we had brought from the bedroom, and between us for those moments there would seem to be a deceptive feeling of perfect ease.

And sometimes, before the others knew about us, we would be at a large oval conference table in a meeting room at the office, and everyone would be arguing about a cover, or story ideas, and someone would say something that wasn't meant to be amusing but was, and I would seem to turn my head to look at the clock or out the window, and I would catch his glance in that moment and see just the most imperceptibly raised eyebrow or upturned corner of his mouth, and in that split second between us there would be an invisible smile big enough to last a morning.

When he returned from Prague, he said that we would go to Rhode Island, tell his father that we were getting married. He had not said much about his father, although I knew his name was Harrold, with the same double *r*. It was, too, the father's father's name and so on. Perhaps once, years and years ago, it had been an affectation or possibly a mistake, but now it was so deeply a part of the passing down of the name that Harrold, my Harrold, could not bring himself to drop the extra *r*—even though he himself did not know its origins.

The house was on the water, cavernous, filled with empty rooms, the prototype of the apartment with the empty rooms in Manhattan. It was Victorian, or turn-of-the-century; I never knew for sure. It had gray shingles and a porch and many windows of different sizes. The furniture inside was heavy, dark, and masculine. We drove up the driveway, and already I could feel a sea change in the man beside me. He grew quiet, taciturn. He turned off the radio. There were lines on his forehead, a tightening around his mouth. He said before we had even parked the car that this was a bad idea, but I said nonsense, I was dying to meet his father.

There had been, in the city, a sense of manic joy as we'd set out, like opening the shutters and letting daylight flood into darkened rooms. Perhaps we would join the world, after all, we thought but didn't say, by getting married. There had been, after that night in the kitchen, a sense of striving for something like normalcy: We had, just the day before, on his first day back from Prague, told the people in the office that we were getting married. And we had both enjoyed, even more than the announcement, the surprise on the faces there.

His father was a wizened man, a man who had once been large, like Harrold, but now was shrunken, caved in. His face was gray, like his hair. His hair was combed back straight from the brow in a style that seemed to be a holdover from an earlier era. You could see at once that he wasn't well, hadn't been for some time. He had Harrold's eyes, black and impenetrable, catching you suddenly in what might have passed for an indifferent glance. He held a cigarette, and there was a tremor in his hand. There were nicotine stains on his fingers. He was sitting in an oversized captain's chair of darkened wood that seemed to mold itself around him. He was wearing a suit, a formal gray suit that doubtless once had fit him well but now hung poorly over the wasted body.

I remember a housekeeper standing by a window. Harrold walked to the center of the room but didn't go to his father. I had the feeling they hadn't touched in years, so couldn't now. Harrold turned around to look at me—I was behind him— as if he would have me leave the room, as if his father were something I shouldn't see, or the other way around. Harrold seemed lost. I had never seen him like this—smaller, diminished. His father, in the polished chair, was now the larger man. I walked to where Harrold was standing. Harrold said my name, said his father's name. I walked to the father, shook his hand. His hand was dry, like yellow dust in my own.

Get us a drink, Harry, will you, his father said. It was not a question. I heard the diminutive. Harrold was never Harry, though sometimes he was known as English. Once in a while a colleague or the editor would call him that: Hey, English, they would say. I watched Harrold's hand reach for a glass on a sideboard. He made a large Scotch for his father, one for me. I had not been invited to sit down, but I did so, on a leather sofa. The room was not a living room, not a room that people lived in, though his father lived in here. It was a study, leather and wood and masculine, but there was a chaise by a window, with a throw. Beyond the window, you could see the water. The house was quiet, still, with dust motes drifting in the air.

You make your living scribbling for that rag too, his father said to me. There was a scratch of metal in his voice; it turned questions into pronouncements.

By the sideboard, Harrold had downed his drink already, had quickly poured himself another. I was sure his father had seen him do this. You had the sense the eyes saw everything, even though the body was immobile. I said yes, I worked with Harrold, and then because I was nervous and Harrold had not yet spoken, I said inanely, to fill the silence, that I had heard a lot about him, which was not true, and that I'd heard about the textile mills and how he'd made them out of nothing, which was true and which Harrold had mentioned to me, in passing.

The business was his if he'd wanted it, but now it's gone to strangers, said the father, as if the son were not in the room. The bitterness in his voice was unmistakable.

We're getting married, Harrold said in a rush, like a schoolboy in his father's presence who wanted only to change the subject, and I winced that what we had come to tell had been used by him like that.

There was a silence in the room. I thought that possibly Harrold had shocked his father too much, had not prepared him for this eventuality, and that his father, understandably, was at a loss for words.

But then his father spoke.

You can stay to supper if you want, he said, but I won't be joining you. I take my meals alone now.

I glanced at Harrold, but he turned away from me, looked out at the water instead. Perhaps his father was deaf, I thought. The deafness would explain his rudeness. If he had not heard what his son had said, I would repeat it for him, I would tell him that I hoped he would come to the wedding. I would say this loudly, and he would understand then. I opened my mouth to speak, but his father cut me off.

What's your family do? his father said. His voiced rasped, and he coughed.

I knew then that he had heard but had chosen not to give his son anything like his blessing or even an acknowledgment.

Harrold left the room, walked out of the room onto a porch. I heard his footsteps on the stairs, saw him, through the window, walk toward the beach.

I answered his father's question about my family, about my mother. I could see that he was disappointed. He had hoped, despite his air of indifference, that his son would marry well, do that right at least. He gestured to the housekeeper to fill up his glass. I wondered if he sat like this all day, drinking Scotch, not moving much in this tomblike house.

I excused myself. I said I would be back. I went out to find Harrold on the beach, saw him walking in the sand with his shoes on, his good shoes filling up with sand. He had his hands in his pants pockets, with his suit coat and his tie blowing in the wind behind him. We had dressed to meet his father. I took off my shoes and ran down to the beach to talk to him, but he didn't want me there, said he'd rather be alone. I chose not to believe this, ran in the sand to keep up with him. His hair was buffeted by the wind; his eyes squinted against the sun.

We shouldn't have come, he said. It was always like this. His father was an alcoholic.

As if that excused everything—the ice, the scorn, the ridicule. But it didn't, not entirely.

What happened to your mother? I asked.

He didn't answer me at first. He turned and walked toward a dune and sat down. He looked almost comical in his good suit sitting in the sand, and I felt sorry for him. His father was an ugly man, but I couldn't say that.

I sat down beside Harrold.

He was ten, he said suddenly, after a time. His mother was dying of cancer. Breast cancer. He didn't know that she was dying. He'd known about the operations and the hospital stays, but his mother had said to him that she was getting better, and he'd believed her. Had to believe her. He was only ten.

And on this one particular day he was remembering, he had walked into the kitchen for a glass of water. It was a hot afternoon, and there was a swinging door into the kitchen. He'd swung the door open thoughtlessly, as boys do, he said, and he'd hit his father in the back. His father and then his mother's sister, who'd come to help with the care. They'd been embracing—not an embrace of consolation, either, Harrold said. He thought now that probably it was just a grope, a pass on his father's part, meaningless in the long run, but the boy did not see it that way. He was at an awkward age, old enough to understand yet not understand fully. He'd run out of the kitchen and gone outside, had gone into the dunes where we were then. He'd cried, he said. He'd cried for his mother and his father and for the shame of it— the hot earnest tears of a ten-year-old boy.

And then, he said, he'd done the one truly terrible thing of his childhood.

Later that night, thinking somehow that his mother would make it right, he'd half told her, or had begun to tell her, and then had realized he couldn't, ought not to, but she had seen it on his face, had heard too much before he could recover and take it back.

And after that day, his mother had not spoken to his father again. She'd died weeks later, not speaking to her husband, and the father had never forgiven the son.

Mine was the worse offense, Harrold said, looking at me. Telling her like that, hurting her.

He'd understood that almost immediately and had tried to tell this to his father. But his father was a hard man. He'd always been hard, Harrold said—it was how he'd made his family, made his business.

I hate the bastard, let's get out of here, he said.

We drove back to the city in silence. The three quick drinks in the middle of the day had not made Harrold drunk, merely made him silent, almost sullen. I was disappointed for myself too, you must understand. It wasn't how I had imagined it might be; I had hoped we would be happy, like other people seemed to be. I didn't see how we could have a wedding in a church: That wouldn't suit us now, though we would be married. That felt inevitable.

I said that I would go to Chicago to tell my mother. I didn't ask him to come. I knew he wouldn't now.

Was this the reason, then? The reason why the man I loved was so twisted, angry, brutal? And if so, do we forgive him his brutality?

Or if so, what then was the reason for his father's brutality and ice? A father's father's sin? A legacy that I have now dismantled?

I am trying to tell you the truth. I am doing this so that you will understand how it was—how it was that I stayed, wanted Harrold, believed in us. Later, yes, I was afraid to leave, that was simple; but in the beginning, when I could have left, could have stopped it from happening, I didn't want to.

You see, I loved Harrold. I loved him. Even on

the day I left, even when I was most afraid of him.

And I wonder now, was this a sickness on my part? Or was it my best self?

I got your letter this morning. I knew that you would be surprised to hear from me, to receive the notes and writings I had sent you. I see you getting the package at your desk, your puzzlement as you look at the first page, wondering what this is, then your face as the wheels begin to turn, realizing you have your story after all, will not have to abandon all the work you've done in Maine, have a story that is viable.

I see you in your white blouse and skirt, your shoes kicked off in the heat. Your suit jacket is behind you, over your chair. You are bent over your desk, reading what I have written. Your hand is at your forehead; you are concentrating deeply. I see your blond hair pinned back with tortoiseshell barrettes, falling behind your ears. Maybe you unsnap a barrette and run your hand through your hair, thinking; it's an excited gesture.

And then you'll have a drink at lunch, maybe a glass of wine. You'll be humming with ideas, your own ideas of how to write the story. You'll think you've got the cover now; it cannot fail to make the cover. You'll have to time it right. The peg will be the verdict. It must come out before the verdict, or the story quickly will grow old. You are thinking—possibly, just possibly—that this story will be the one that will truly make your career. That will let you rise above the others, that will allow the world to see just how good you really are. It's got juice and meat, and you are thinking you can do it justice.

Yet even so, I don't believe it is possible for you ever to know the truth or to write it. For at the end you will have an article, your own ideas, which you will have edited, by necessity, in the process of writing it, and that story will, in turn, be edited by those above you, and *that* final printed story will be read and perceived differently by every reader, man or woman, depending on the circumstances of his or her life, so that by the time all of the magazines are put out with the rubbish, and you are off interviewing someone else, no one will have any idea of my story as it really was at all, will they?

We were married in the winter. My mother came and was radiant, even though we did not get married in the Church. I filled the apartment with flowers, made it seem like a happy place. We were married there and had a party: We invited people from the office.

It was a curious match at the magazine—the subject of much gossip and of speculation: Why had Harrold chosen Maureen? I wore an ivory-colored dress and a wreath of flowers in my hair. I let my mother brush my hair in the morning, and she put it up with combs. I was buoyant with belief in the ritual, drifting lightly with the illusion. If we seemed happy, and had my mother with us, and there was sunlight in the rooms, and there were people there who wished us well, wasn't that enough?

Not long after the wedding, I had to go to Los Angeles to do a story. There was an oil spill off the coast of California, and I was part of a team— two reporters and a photographer.

My colleagues both were men. They had a motel room together; I had the adjacent room to myself. But the three of us moved easily from room to room, sharing takeout, talking of our story, watching television, until it was time to go to bed.

One night Harrold called me on the telephone. Robert, the photographer, was in the room, writing down what I wanted from the Chinese restaurant around the corner. He called out to me as he was leaving, said not to bother with the money, it was his turn to pay. Harrold heard his voice, said, Is that Robert? I said, Yes. He said, What's he doing in your room? I laughed. Possibly that was my mistake. I shouldn't have laughed. I heard the ice in his voice. I said, What's the matter, Harrold? He said, Nothing. I knew that *nothing*. It's what he always said when he was angry and wouldn't talk. I made it worse then; I tried to explain. I said, Robert and Mike are always here. We eat our supper here. It's nothing. Don't be silly.

Don't be silly.

—He said, Fine.

I got in late at La Guardia, took a taxi to the apartment. He was waiting up for me, sitting in a chair in the bedroom. There was a bottle on the table. He'd been drinking, quite a lot by the look of him. He got up, hesitated, started walking toward me. I said, Harrold.

Which one did you sleep with? he asked me, moving closer.

I put my hands up. I remember that, I put my hands up. I said, Don't be ridiculous. A tremor in my voice suggested I was trying to wriggle out of it. He made me feel guilty, even though I was not. Harrold, I said, backing up to the wall. For heaven's sake.

He put his hands on my shoulders, shook me once. He said, I know what these trips are like, what goes on.

What does that mean? I asked.

It means I know what goes on, he said.

I brought my arms up, pushed his hands away. I said, You're crazy; you've been drinking. I turned around, as if I would walk away. I wanted to get out of the room, shut a door.

I don't know if it was my saying he was crazy, or my accusing him of drinking, but I'd said the magic word, ignited him. He grabbed my hair from behind, jerked my head back. I could somehow not believe that this was happening. Revolving as if in slow motion, I saw his hand, his free hand; it made an arc, hit the side of my head. I spun back into the wall, covered my face with my arm. I slid down onto the floor.

I was motionless. I didn't move a muscle. I was afraid even to breathe.

I heard a voice above me. *God*, he said. He hit the wall, put his fist through the plasterboard.

I heard him grab his coat, his keys. I heard the door shutting.

He didn't come back to the apartment or to the office for three days. I covered for him, said that he was sick. I said that a taxi driver at the airport had opened the door when I was bending down and that the door had hit me on the side of the face.

Once you tell your first lie, the first time you lie for him, you are in it with him, and then you are lost.

I want to tell you about something I witnessed when I was in St. Hilaire. Actually it was in Machias, when I was shopping at the A&P. I had Caroline in the baby basket in the front of the cart and was in the fruit-and-vegetable aisle, counting out oranges, when I heard a small commotion behind me. I turned to look and saw a woman walking fast, and with her there was a boy, about six years old or seven. He was crying, trying to catch up to her, trying to hold her hand. She was short and somewhat overweight. She had on a car coat, plaid, and a flower-printed kerchief. She snapped as she was walking, You're the one that lost the money; don't come cryin' to me. There won't be no treats this week. I give you a dollar bill to hold on to, and you lose it.

She was furious, wouldn't look at him.

He ran a little faster then and caught her hand. She whirled around and shook his hand out of hers as if it were a viper, a snake that she had found there. Don't touch my hand! she screamed, and walked away from him.

He followed her; he had nowhere else to go. I knew what he was thinking. He had to get her back. He had to make her like him again, or his entire world would fall apart.

He had on an old woolen winter jacket, a faded navy: a hand-me-down from an older brother? His hair was cut severely short, and his nose was running. He turned the corner after her, and I lost sight of him.

I bought my groceries and paid for them, and went out to the parking lot to put them in the car. Beside my car there was a dented station wagon, rusted here and there from the salt. The man inside was chewing on a cigarette. He had thinning hair that was greasy and dark sideburns that came almost to his jawline. He'd waited in the car while the woman and the boy I'd noticed were shopping. He was sitting in the driver's seat, listening to a story that his wife was telling him in fits and starts, with many hand gestures, some directed angrily to the boy in back. The boy sat sideways in the cargo area, his hood pulled up over his head. He was crying, sniveling, his face bent toward his knees.

The father screamed, Jesus fuckin' Christ! What's the matter with you, givin' the money to the boy. What are you, some kind of moron? Serves you right he lost it.

And then he gave a kind of hiss of disgust and put the key in the ignition.

The wife turned her head away, inadvertently in my direction. She didn't look at me; she was looking at the brick wall. But I saw it all on her face: that mix of anger and of resignation; a desire there to lash out and a desire to be left alone. She was exhausted, drained. She hated the man beside her, but she would never be able to tell him that. Instead she'd shower anger on the boy in back.

I used to think that, like that woman, I never would be free—that freedom was like that distant point on the tracks. You could never get there.

Harrold went to work on the fourth day, came home that night. I did not know where he had stayed, and he didn't tell me. Already I was learning to be careful, not to ask certain questions, not to use a particular vocabulary. He said that it would never happen again, and I believed him. He was contrite, and he explained it—to me or to himself. He said that just the idea of my being with another man drove him crazy. And he'd been drinking. He would cut down on his drinking, but he denied he was an alcoholic: *not like his father*, he said. He wasn't like his father.

And I must not tell anyone. I must promise not to tell a soul.

I did not go out on stories again. I made excuses at the office. I said that I got motion sick, could not travel well in automobiles or airplanes. I could do a job of sorts if I did not go out, but it would hold me back: I'd have to rewrite files, not report them. I wouldn't get the bylines.

He did not hit me again for several months, but there are levels of abuse, and some of it is not physical. The other violence was sometimes worse than being hit. It was more insidious, and he was very clever. I didn't understand it quite, and I don't think he did, either. It was something he could not stop himself from doing.

When you have been hit, it is almost a release. You have power then, because he cannot deny what he has done. He can only threaten you more, and he will, but he has lost a little bit of power. Because even though you never do, it is understood that you could now go to the police, or tell someone and say, Look at what he has done to me. But when the violence is invisible, no one knows. It is the violence that is more intimate than sex, that no one ever talks about. It is the darkest secret, the thing that binds you together.

There was a pattern to our married life. We would be close for a day or two or even a week, and I would have hope, and I would think the worst was over now and that we would be happy and have a family. And then, one day, because he had a story that was difficult, or because I had bristled or raised my voice, or because the ions in the air were crazed—I don't know—we would grow distant, and in the distance I would become afraid and tentative, and he would see that and would find that unattractive. Everything about me would suddenly be cause for criticism. I was growing shrill, he'd say. Or others thought me strident. Or I should learn to laugh a little more, loosen up. It didn't matter what it was—there were a thousand faults I had. My faults were legion, dizzying. It was because he loved me, he would again say when I asked him why. Because he cared so much.

And in the distances my anger would develop, so that what he said about me became a self-fulfilling prophecy. I *was* strident; I seldom laughed. The anger eroded joy, dissipated a life. It is a fallacy that anger makes you stronger. It is like a tide running out, leaving you depleted.

And that would be the ebb and flow of our days: the bait, the anger, his saying with derision, *Look at you*. The tears, my silence.

I told myself then that I would leave him. I tried to think of where to go and how to do it.

I tell myself now that I would have left him if I had not become pregnant.

I had the test in the morning but saved the news for the night. I had hope that the pregnancy would end the distances forever.

I had bought a bottle of champagne; we hadn't had champagne in ages. I made a dinner that I knew he'd like, put candles on the table. He knew at once, when he saw the table, that this was special, and he asked. He said, What's the story? And I said, We're going to have a baby.

He kissed me then and put his hand on my stomach. It seemed that he was happy. I felt a rush of giddiness myself: It would go well; I would call my mother after dinner. He opened the champagne, and we toasted babies.

I didn't want to drink much, so he had the bottle to himself. He said once, during the dinner, What about your job? and I said that I would quit when the time was right. He said, What about us? and I said, We'll be better now—babies bring you closer. I saw a darkening on his brow, but I thought that this was normal: It was only natural for a man to worry some when he had a family coming.

I was drying dishes in the kitchen, thinking of how I would tell my mother, when I saw him standing in the doorway. He had changed into a T-shirt. He was drinking something else now; he had finished the champagne at supper. He said, Come to bed.

I didn't want to go to bed; I had other things to do. I was full of news and plans and wanted to tell more people. But I thought: He needs attention now; I can call my mother later.

I sat on the edge of the bed and began to unbutton my blouse. I felt tender toward myself. You will laugh at this, but I was thinking of myself as a fragile vessel, thinking I should take care now.

It was a delicious feeling, that I was something special, and I was savoring it, unbuttoning my blouse slowly, in a dreamy way, thinking then not of Harrold but of babies, of having them inside you.

And then I looked up, and he was standing over me. He had his clothes on still, but he was furious. His eyes were black and glassy. I put my hands behind me on the bed, moved away from him, but he grabbed my blouse, stopped me.

I won't tell you what he did to me; you don't need all the details. Except to say that he pushed my face to the side with his hand, as if he would erase my face, and that what he did he did ferociously, as if he would shake the baby out of me. When he was finished, I curled up on my side of the bed and waited all night to lose the baby. But (strong girl) she didn't leave me.

In the morning, he wrapped me up with blankets and his arms, and brought me tea and toast and said we'd call my mother now, and what grand way could we break the news at the office?

There were other times, four or five, when I was pregnant. I didn't know then, and I don't know now, why it was that the pregnancy angered him so—angered him even as he was denying it, saying that he had never been happier. Perhaps it was that he felt replaced or that he was losing control over me for good; I don't know.

He would come after me only if he'd been

drinking. He'd come home late from the bar, and I would be afraid of him. I'd be careful to stay away, but sometimes that would backfire. Somehow, sometime during the evening, I would say a word or a sentence that angered him, and he would hurt me when he took me to the bedroom. Later he would always be contrite, solicitous for my well-being. He would bring me things, make me promises.

I believe he couldn't stop himself. I had opened a door for him that he was unable to close. I think that sometimes he wanted desperately to close it, but he couldn't. In wanting control over me, he lost control over himself. He denied it, or he tried to. He was like an alcoholic hiding bottles in a closet; he suppressed the evidence. If you couldn't see the bruises on my face or arms or legs, he hadn't done it. It was how we lived. Once, when he saw me stepping from the shower in the morning, he asked me if I'd fallen.

I started taking sick days when I couldn't go into the office. Then I used my pregnancy as an excuse and did not go back at all.

In February I was five months pregnant. When I went to the doctor, he said, What is this? It was black, a swath of blue-black paint, on my thigh. There was another on my buttocks, under me, but he couldn't see that one. I said I'd fallen on the ice, on the steps of my building, and he looked at me. He said that if I fell, I should call him straightaway. To check the baby. After that visit,

I did not go back for a while. I didn't see how I could tell him that I had slipped again.

Toward the end, Harrold didn't touch me. I grew big, I put on lots of weight, and I think he found me frightening. It was the only time I was ever safe from him, for those two months. I wasn't working then; I stayed inside. Or I walked in the park and talked to the baby. Mostly what I said was that I didn't want the pregnancy to end. Stay inside me, I would whisper. Stay inside me.

Harrold was distant, busy. He was gone for days, and then for weeks. He would say he shouldn't go, that he should be around for when the baby came. I knew I was safer without him, and so I said, I'll be OK, I have friends to help me.

I went to a psychiatrist. I told her what was happening. But I was veiled, cautious. She said, You have longings.

I looked at her.

That was it?

She didn't speak. She waited for me to say something.

I asked a question: Are longings wrong?

I started labor in the night, in June. It was a sultry night, soft and sweet-smelling, and I had all the windows open to the air. Harrold was far away, in London for a story. I got my watch and counted pains, and waited until morning so that

I could call the neighbor who lived in the apartment next to ours. She came at once and summoned a taxi for me and went with me to the hospital. I knew her only slightly, just in passing, but I'd been saving her for just this day. In the taxi, she held my hand, this woman I hardly knew, and shouted at the driver to take it easy. She said to me, Are you all right? I thought she meant the baby, so I nodded.

And then she said, I have sometimes thought— I looked at her.

She stopped and shook her head.

At the hospital, my neighbor said goodbye. I told her I would call her. She said, What about your husband? I said, He's on his way.

There was a woman in the next cubicle, but I have told you that already.

My labor was not too long. Twelve hours or thirteen. They say that that is average. When my baby came, they laid her on my chest, and she looked up at me.

When I came back from the hospital, Harrold seemed at first a changed man, and I had hope. He was calmer; he didn't drink. He came home early from the office. He held the baby and fed her from a bottle, and sometimes sat just watching her. When she woke up in the night, he would walk the floors with her until she'd fallen back asleep. I think he felt that she was his— another possession? He would sometimes say that—*my daughter*—but I understood it differently then, that he was filled with love and pride.

My mother came to visit and said how lucky I was to have both Caroline and Harrold, and I thought when she said it: Yes, that is how I feel, I have my family now, and we will be all right. The past is over, and I don't have to think about that now.

Caroline was six weeks old or seven. It was August, very hot and humid. Harrold had been home for three days. It was his vacation, but we hadn't gone away; we'd said it would be too soon to travel with the baby. There was a fan in the window, revolving slowly, I remember, and he'd had a drink, a tall sparkling one with lots of ice, and then another, in the middle of the afternoon. I thought: It's his vacation after all; if we had a cottage, we might be having summer cocktails.

But the drinking put him in a mood. We hadn't been together for several months. He said, It's all right now? and I nodded. I thought that I was ready and that I needed him. He inclined his head in the direction of the bedroom, and I went in there. We had the baby in a bassinet in the hallway, and she was sleeping.

We began slowly, and he was careful not to hurt me, and I was dreamy, languid, thinking: Babies let you start again; this will be a new beginning.

And then she cried.

I sighed and said that I would have to go to

her. I started to sit up, but he held my arm and
told me no.

Let her cry, he said, ignore her.

I can't, I told him. It isn't right. He held my
arm tightly and wouldn't let me go.

She was wailing now, and I said, Harrold.

He was suddenly angry, furious with me. The
baby, baby, baby, he said. It's all you ever think
about.

He wouldn't let me go.

It was worse than all the other times, worse by
far. Because all the other times, there was only
me, and I could stand it if I had to. But this time
there was the baby, crying in the hallway, crying,
crying, crying, and I couldn't go to her. There is
no way, ever in my life, that I can explain to you
what that felt like.

We disintegrated after that. My voice grew shrill,
everything I said was shrill. I remember standing
in a doorway, shouting out, *I hate you*, not caring
about the consequences. I had the baby in my
arms, and I was thinking: She is hearing this.

He became immensely jealous; he thought that I
was seeing men while he went to work. He drank
heavily every day; the drinks would start at lunch
with martinis, and he would go to bars after
work. He couldn't bear to be wakened in the
night, and if the baby cried, I had to silence her
at once—I was afraid that he might hit her too. I
began to hope that he would travel more, that he

would go away for weeks, so that I could think, could clear my head, but he traveled less than ever. He was convinced that if he left, I would run away with another man. I began to hope that he'd die in an air crash. Are you shocked? Yes, it's true; I prayed for a crash. It was the only way I knew of to get free of him then.

Perhaps because of the drinking, or because he was in more trouble than even I knew about, his work began to suffer. A story he was working on was killed, and then he lost a cover. There was a new fellow in the office, who seemed to be the favorite now. His name was Mark; perhaps you know him. Sometimes Harrold would talk about him with derision, and I knew that Harrold was threatened by this man.

All his life, writing had been effortless for Harrold, but now it seemed that he had lost his way. He blamed me for this; he said that my constant nagging was destroying his concentration. He said that the broken nights were exhausting him, ruining his career.

Oddly, despite myself, I felt sorry for my husband then. It was coming apart too quickly, and he was powerless to stop it.

In October, there was unrest in Quebec, and Harrold had to go to Montreal. He had whittled the necessary traveling down to two nights, but he had to go. I saw this as my chance. I was nice to him all the week before. I had to make him go, I had to make him believe that I'd be faithful, that I wouldn't run away. I was girlish that week, girlish and sweet and pliant, and as sexy as I could muster. You'd think that might have roused suspicions on his part, but he believed that one day I would come around, turn the corner, and he was always watching for that moment. Perhaps he thought I'd given in after all, that I'd seen the error of my ways. I kissed him when he left, and said to him, Hurry back.

When he had gone, and I felt certain he was on a plane to Montreal, I packed a suitcase and got a taxi for myself. I bought a ticket at the airport, and I held the baby on the plane all the way to Chicago. There I boarded the train for the journey to the town where I'd grown up. I carried Caroline and my suitcase up the narrow street to my mother's bungalow.

When my mother came home from work, I said to her, Surprise! I said I'd had a whim, had come home for the fun of it. I said that Harrold was on a story and I was tired of staying alone. She believed me; she had no reason to doubt me. I couldn't bear to have my mother think that all her dreams had turned to dust.

What was I thinking then?

Perhaps I believed that in a day or two a plan would come to me. Or that in a day or two I would be able to tell my mother that my husband and I were having difficulties and that I needed time to think. I don't remember now. In retrospect, it seems naive to have chosen my mother's house to run to. Where else would I logically go?

And he knew that. Knew it at once, knew it when he opened the door to the empty rooms.

He called. My mother answered the telephone. I could not tell my mother not to answer her own phone. Her voice was full of happiness and light, and she said to me, It's Harrold!

I took the phone from her.

I think I had hoped that he would go to the apartment and see me gone, and take some time himself to think. That he might somehow welcome this reprieve. I had acted, extricated myself, released him from our terrible bond. Perhaps he would be grateful.

His voice was ice, full of clarity and intent. He said, If you don't return at once, I will come and get you. If you run away, I will find you. If you ever take my child away from me again, I will not only find you, but I will kill you.

He said these words, and I was looking at my mother, and she was smiling at me, holding Caroline's arm, teaching her to wave to me. My mother was saying to my daughter: Dada! Dada! It's Dada on the phone!

I can see you shaking your head. You're bewildered; you're confused. You think me unwell, as crazy as he was. Why did I go back? Why didn't I call the police?

Why indeed.

I believed that he would kill me if I did not go back. Or I couldn't tell my mother the truth. Or I thought that I had no right to take his child away from him. Or in my own dark way, I loved him still.

These reasons are all true.

When I returned to the apartment, I was seen to have capitulated utterly. I was punished for having run away, punished for having deceived him with charm the week before, punished for having stolen his child. He would hurt me physically, or he would be cold to me, or he would be derisive.

Look at you, he would say to me.

I went outside infrequently. I talked on the phone only to my mother, and everything I said to her was false.

I haven't told you anything about where I am. I think I should, although there isn't that much to tell.

When I came here, they searched my body. They took my fingerprints and my picture.

I have a cellmate, but she is quiet. She has been convicted of having stabbed her uncle, who functioned as her pimp. She exchanges sexual favors with women now for large quantities of tranquilizers and is sleeping out the rest of her sentence. The guards know this but don't mind. A sleeping prisoner is an easy prisoner to take care of.

Although I have a kind of solitude in my cell, the noise level in this block is deafening. I think I mind that the most, the noise. Even at night, there is talking, calling, laughing, screaming. They make you sleep with the lights on. I haven't yet discovered how to ward off all the noise or the light, but I am learning that the writing helps. I am creating a wall with the writing that is a kind of buffer.

I am in here with women who are thieves and drug addicts, but I'm not afraid of the women. I'm afraid of the staff. The staff have power over me; they determine everything I do.

The women who are awaiting trial or sentencing live in a suspended state, like purgatory or limbo. We say at meals or in the yard, Do you have any news? Or, Do you have a date yet?

In June, on her birthday, they brought me Caroline. She was walking. I hadn't been there to see her take her first steps, and though I was proud that she was walking, watched her walk to the table and fall into my arms, I was heartsick too. I could see that she didn't really know me.

They brought a cake, and I had a present for her I had made, a doll of yarn and bits of cloth. We sang to her, and I fed her broken pieces of the cake. All around her, they were saying, Give a kiss to your Mummy. This is your Mummy, Caroline. I wanted everyone to leave us, but I knew they wouldn't, couldn't.

You will ask me, Was it worth it? And I will answer, How can it be worth it to be in hell and set yourself free, and then lose your daughter into the bargain?

And then I will answer, I didn't have a choice.

*   *   *

It was the first week of December, and the magazine was having a party for the editor, who was leaving. It had been almost a year since I'd visited the office. I said to Harrold, Do you think I should go?

He thought awhile and said, Why not? Let's show off the baby.

I bought a dress for the party, a black dress with a high neck and a long skirt, and I put Caroline into a red velvet dress my mother had sent her for the holidays. I wore my hair up, pinned it up with rhinestone combs, and when I held Caroline, and we looked at ourselves in the mirror, I thought: You would never know.

Harrold had said that I should bring Caroline to the office at five, when the party would begin. At a quarter to, I put her in the baby basket and drove to midtown where the office was. When I got to the nineteenth floor, Harrold was finishing up some business, but he came out of his office and smiled at me. Smiled at me. He put a proprietary arm around my shoulder, then took the baby from my arms. People came out of cubicles and offices to greet me. Harrold and Caroline and I walked around the office in a kind of luminous cocoon, and I knew how we must have appeared—a proud husband with his radiant wife and daughter. We were smiling, laughing, making easy jokes about my having traded deadlines for diapers, and Caroline was smiling with us. I thought—I remember thinking—Well, this is partially true. We *might* have been this couple.

It seemed there were a lot of people in the office, mostly familiar faces, some I didn't know. Then we all meandered into the dining room or near it, where there was a bar, and you came up to us. Harrold introduced you, and you shook my hand. I was struck first by your height—you must be five ten or eleven?—and then by your dress. It was khaki, I remember, a shirtwaist, belted, and I recall thinking that it was the sort of dress a woman ought to wear on a safari, in a Land-Rover, in the bush of Africa. It suited you. You held the baby, and Harrold went off to get us drinks.

I wonder now: Did you see anything? Did you know?

Did we chat? Briefly, possibly, about the baby, but then you moved away, and a man I'd never seen before came over to me to say hello. He said his name was Mark. He was tall and thin, with light-blue eyes and blond hair. He wore gold-rimmed glasses. I thought he was attractive. We began to talk. He said he knew Harrold, admired my husband's work, and knew that I had once worked for the magazine as well. I was still high from the illusion Harrold and I had created, and perhaps I was laughing—I think I might have touched Mark on the sleeve in the middle of a joke or a story—when Harrold came around the corner with the drinks. He'd been moving through the crowd, smiling easily, accepting compliments on his daughter, but when he saw me standing there with Mark, he stopped. I wasn't looking at him, but I could feel him staring at me. I turned, against my better judgment, to see him, to call him over.

He was standing motionless, with a drink in each hand. He had on a blue blazer that day; his tie was dark stripes, I remember, loosened at the collar. His eyes were deep circles, fixed on me. He came forward, ignored Mark. He handed me my drink. He said, Get the baby. I want you to hold the baby.

Mark seemed to take the hint and drifted off, or perhaps he saw someone else to talk to, and when he was gone, Harrold said to me, I leave you for a minute, and already you're after some guy.

I didn't say anything. I knew better than to speak. I knew exactly what to do: to hold the baby and to talk only to women until Harrold took me home, and perhaps, if I was lucky, he might forget about what he'd seen or thought he had seen.

I was not lucky. Men came up to me and talked to me and sometimes kissed me; it was only natural. I hadn't seen them in almost a year. They were friends—not even friends, just acquaintances—but Harrold chose not to see that. Each man who came to me, I wanted to say to him, You are sealing my fate, but of course, I couldn't. I waited for half an hour, then I said to Harrold, I'd better go. He said, Do that.

I excused myself, said to anyone who asked

that the baby had to go to bed. I drove home, took the baby up to the apartment, changed my clothes. I nursed Caroline, put her to bed for the night in her crib in her room. I made myself a drink; I was frightened. I knew that Harrold was angry, would drink too much, and would come home in a mood as black as his eyes had been. I had another drink, and I thought: Where the hell can I go now?

It was after midnight when he came. He was drunk, stumbling. His features were blurry, and I thought he might have been sick. His tie was missing, and his shirt was rumpled. I knew then that he'd been with another woman. I turned away. I was frightened, but I was filled with rage. I walked down the hallway to the bedroom and shut the door.

I waited.

He burst through the door like a large figure in a childhood nightmare. He said, Don't you ever shut a door in my face again!

It was the only thing I remember him saying.

He threw me against the wall. I put my hands out to protect my face. Perhaps I screamed; I heard Caroline begin to cry in her crib. I prayed that she would be silent, because I was afraid that he might harm her. I didn't cry out again. I put my hands out to protect my face, but he swatted them away like mosquitoes.

He was a machine, a machine of rage and fury. He had never been so frenzied. He didn't seem to care anymore where he hit me, that the bruises would be visible. Instinctively, I let my body go limp. I could not fight him, but I knew it was important to stay conscious if I could. His hands came down upon me, then he stumbled, missed, jammed his hand into the wall. He cursed, held his fingers, and I scooted out from under him. I ran to Caroline's room, swiftly scooped her from her crib, then locked us both in the bathroom.

He came to the bathroom door, shook the knob once as if he would tear it from the door. I didn't move. I waited. I sat on the tile floor and tried to get my blouse open so that I could nurse Caroline. I wanted to keep her quiet. She fell back asleep while I held her there.

I don't know how long I was in the bathroom, but I didn't hear him again. I didn't know if he had gone away or had fallen asleep or had passed out in the hallway. Or if he was sitting in a chair, waiting for me to open the door.

I sat cross-legged for what seemed like hours. When I moved finally, I felt a bolt of pain in my knee, but I knew I had to stand up. I opened the door, could not see him. Tentatively, I limped out into the hallway. He wasn't there. I walked into Caroline's room and put her in her crib. I inched down to my own bedroom, looked in on the bed. He was lying there, half undressed, his shirt still on, his pants and blazer on the floor. He had passed out, was lying on his stomach; he was snoring.

I have never been so quiet or so cautious or so quick. I picked up my duffel bag from the bottom of the closet, put a few things in it, went to the baby's room, packed the bag with her clothes. I walked back into the bedroom, removed Harrold's wallet from his pants pocket, took the cash there. I didn't even count it. I put on my coat and scarf and gloves, slung the duffel bag and my purse over my shoulder, wrapped Caroline in a blanket, and was out the door like a fox with her prey. I couldn't chance waking Caroline to put her in her snowsuit. I would do that in the car.

I took the elevator to the street, ran with my bundles to the car. The baby basket was in the back seat. I'd forgotten to bring it in. I put Caroline in her snowsuit. She woke up and began to cry, but when I started the engine, she was soothed.

The car was nearly out of gas, so I drove uptown to a gas station. I said to the attendant there, Do you have a map?

He said, A map of what?

I said, Anywhere.

He said, Let me look.

I sat in the car and waited. The city was still, unmoving. He came back and said to me, All I got is New England.

I said, Fine; I'll take it.

I turned on the overhead light, shook open the map, and spread it over the dashboard. I let my eye drift until I found a dot that I thought would be safe. I folded the map, switched off the light. I turned the key in the ignition.

I rolled down the window. I took my wedding

band from my finger and threw it into the night. I didn't hear it land.

It was four o'clock in the morning, and I was headed north and east.

So how's old Ed Hargreaves? Keeping the magazine together, is he?

Exactly. Exactly.

And Mark Stein. What's he up to now? Taken over Harrold's territory, no doubt.

God, this is an awful business, isn't it? Terrible story, terrible. I was flabbergasted when I heard. I had no idea, none. Absolutely nothing.

I was at the magazine until the first of December, as you know. Maureen English had left the previous year. I knew them pretty well. Well, I *thought* I knew them well. Just goes to show, doesn't it?

She was quiet. But awfully good, awfully good. I thought she would really go places, make a name for herself, until she got that motion sickness. Shame, really. She said the doctors had tried everything with her, she couldn't shake it, something to do with the structure of her inner ear. So I put her on rewrites. God, she was fast. Give Maureen English a file, she'd have the story back to you before the day was out.

She was very attractive. You've met her. You could see right away someone was going to snap her up. I don't think I realized for quite a while that it was Harrold, though. They were cool in the office, very cool. I thought she had a bit of class, actually. You could see that. I don't mean from her background. I didn't really know much about her background, although she was obviously Irish. She was Maureen Cowan, by the way, when she first came. No, I mean the way she carried herself, kept to herself, wouldn't toot her own horn kind of thing. They met in my office, by the way.

Yes, they did. Let me think now. I was in the office. He'd come in. He had a beef with me about a headline, I think. I can't remember now. Something. And it was her first day of work. That's right. And she came in to ask a question. She was very nervous that day, very nervous. I remember she kept fingering these beads she was wearing. Looking down at her feet. I could see Harrold looking at her, smiling, but I didn't think much about it at the time. She'd have caught anyone's eye; it didn't strike me at the time as particularly meaningful. Though as I understand it now, they started seeing each other pretty soon after that.

Now Harrold. He did some great pieces for us then. Those were great days at the magazine. We had Joe Ward, and Alex Weisinger, and Barbara Spindell. Great days. I miss them sometimes. Publishing is a different business. I got out of magazines because the late nights were driving my wife crazy, but the pace is different here. You don't get that adrenaline high; you know what I mean. Books have a different evolution: You see the writers a lot less, hardly at all sometimes. And you've got to love a story. You're working on it for months, for years in some cases. Anyway, enough of this; you want to know about Harrold.

Let's see. He came to the magazine in '64, I think. He'd been working for *The Boston Globe* out of school, then wanted to get into magazines, into New York. He came at a good time. There was a bit of a vacuum—a lot of old blood leaving, retiring. I'd been there a year or two myself; I'd come over from the *Times*. So when he signed on, he was able to move up rather quickly. I had him out reporting almost at once. He was a great reporter. Very aggressive in the field. Wouldn't quit till he got the story. He'd hound them to death, or charm them. I think his size helped, actually. He was very impressive physically. You must have met him. About six four, I think; two hundred pounds, anyway, but not fat, just well-muscled. Played for Yale, I'm pretty sure. But he wasn't a blowhard like some guys from the Ivy League you meet. Kept to himself most of the time. And those eyes. Black as coal. They could pin you to the wall, make you squirm. I saw him do it a couple of times. Pretty impressive.

Harrold English was a real pro. We weren't what you would call friends, but we had some lunches. You know the kind of thing; you get to really talking after the second martini. He said once that he'd had a bit of an unhappy childhood, despite the money. His mother died when he was a kid, and he never got along with his father. Bit of a son of a bitch, from what I gather. They weren't close. I never heard about any other family.

I liked his writing style. It was clean, straightforward, not too much of the "I," and I liked that. You could feel his intelligence in the piece, but he didn't let it get in the way. He wasn't one of those let-me-show-you-my-dazzling-virtuosity kind of writers. Just straight. Always got his facts right. The fact checkers loved his pieces.

Maureen, she had a different style. I'd say more feminine, except that would probably get me in trouble. Her rhythms were different, more fluid. I liked her writing, but you had to push her a bit to dig a little deeper for the story. She had a hard time asking the really tough questions. One time she came in to see me and said she didn't want to write only about trends anymore; I'd had her on Trends. I was a little bit taken aback, but I could see her point, so I moved her over to National. She was very good there, detached in a way, but good. Until she couldn't travel anymore.

I think it was a good six months before I knew they were seeing each other. When I heard about it, I have to tell you, I wasn't too happy about it. I've seen these office romances, and they always lead to trouble. You have a fight at home, what are you supposed to do at the office? But Maureen and Harrold, like I said, they were cool. If you didn't know, you'd never have known, if you know what I mean.

That's why it's so—Jesus—unbelievable. I have trouble believing it even now. I just can't see it. I mean, you hear about these kinds of stories once in a while, but it's always some poor woman with six kids in Arkansas or Harlem, and her husband is an alcoholic kind of thing. Rarely do you hear about this kind of thing with people like Harrold and Maureen.

You would think there'd be a hint of something somewhere. And Harrold was no alcoholic. I mean, he drank like the rest of us drank. A martini at lunch maybe, maybe two if the occasion called for it. Cocktails at dinner, that kind of thing.

Although I will say, the last couple of months I was at the magazine, he did seem to be in a bit of a slump. We all get them; I really didn't think too much about it. Was he drinking more then? I really can't remember. I do remember thinking that maybe he was bent out of joint a bit by Stein. Stein was straight out of Columbia, a whiz kid. Very sharp. Very. He was at the magazine a couple of months, and already he was stepping on Harrold's toes. Flavor of the month, that kind of thing. It coincided with Harrold's slump, put the edge on the slump, but I knew Harrold would pull out of it. He'd just had a baby. I could remember what that was like—up all night, out of it all day. I figured he was cutting some slack for a few months, then would pick up speed. And then I left, and really never gave it another thought.

Until I heard. Absolutely stunning. Really.

But it's a hell of a story. In fact, I don't know if you've given this much thought, but you might have a book there. You know, maybe an *In Cold Blood* kind of thing. It depends on what you get, how it shapes up. There are some interesting themes here: the secretiveness of it all, the fact that it was them. Like Scott and Zelda run amok kind of thing.

Yeah, it's a possibility. Tell you what. You put the piece together, send it over to me when you've finished it, before it comes out. I'll take a look, let you know.

She had a lover up in Maine, didn't she?

For the book, we'd want to know about that. These complexities. Makes a better story. It might have some bearing on her motives, don't you think?

December 5, 1970–January 15, 1971

———————

Mary Amesbury

I heard a sound. A muffled sound of tires crunching over gravel. A car or a truck was moving slowly down the lane, as quietly as it could, a sleepy vehicle at daybreak. I tossed back the covers and went to the window. I found my cardigan on a chair and put it on. The floorboards were cold underneath my feet. Outside, there was a field of gray, that half hour of lightening before the sun would rise. I watched the black truck roll along the sand to the dinghy. A man got out. It was the same man as yesterday, although I could see only the yellow slicker clearly through the field of gray; his features were indistinct. The water was still and flat, and when he sculled out to his boat, there was a perfect rippled wake behind his oar.

The rumble of the motor was a complaint, a boat disturbed too early and grumbling under her skipper. I saw flashes of the yellow slicker on the bow, in the wheelhouse, then moving in the boat in its graceful arc out to where the sun would rise.

I sat on the edge of the bed and watched the boat disappear. I wondered where he was headed, how he knew where to go, what it would be like when he got there—another expanse of gray, with colored buoys bobbing in the water? I didn't know what time it was for certain, but I knew that it had to be early: no later than six-thirty, I imagined. To be on the water by six-thirty, I thought, required rising at five-thirty. In the dark with his wife at his side, his children sleeping in another room. And this was in December, with the longest nights of the year. What must a lobsterman's life be like in June, when daybreak came at four or earlier? Do lobstermen eat their supper in the late afternoon, I wondered, go to bed before their children?

I touched a finger to my lip; it was swollen still, and tender. I was aware, too, of other places that I didn't want to touch. There was something wrong with my knee. I wasn't sure what, exactly, but it burned under the kneecap, as if I'd wrenched it in a fall. I thought that perhaps the cleaning yesterday hadn't helped it much, the crouching and the bending.

I heard the baby stir and went to her and lifted her out of the crib. I carried her to bed and pulled the covers up high over us so that we were a warm package together underneath. I nursed her this way and she drifted back to sleep, and perhaps I did too, but I remember listening to the sounds of my new surroundings, trying to orient myself to where I lived. There were the gulls, roused now and cawing over the point, and there was a breeze that was coming with the sunrise.

I slipped out of bed, humped up a secure niche for Caroline, and went downstairs to make myself a cup of coffee and a bowl of cereal. The sun had risen; the day would be clear. The water went from gray to pink to violet even as I watched from the table. I heard another vehicle in the lane, saw a blue-and-white pickup truck emerge from the brush and stop in front of the gray fish house. A man in a pea jacket and watch cap got out, carrying a cardboard box of rope and bits of hardware. He went inside the shack, and in a few minutes I saw smoke rising from a chimney. When he opened the door again, I heard the jarring patter of a disc jockey from a radio inside. The man walked to the back of his truck and removed several lobster traps and carried them into the shack. He didn't come out again.

After a time Caroline began to cry. I brought her down, bathed her in the sink, dressed her, and set her on the braided rug. She seemed intent on mastering the art of crawling, or at least the art of balancing on all fours, despite a few comical false starts and a tendency to propel herself backward. But I was tickled by the look of concentration on her face, the tongue tucked into the corner of her mouth, the goofy expression of surprise when her coordination betrayed her and she collapsed on her tummy.

I had another cup of coffee and made a list. I needed a clock and a radio and a laundromat. The soiled diapers were piling up, and Caroline was running out of clothes. I wanted to see if I could find a baby sling too. I thought if I had one I could walk on the beach with her if it warmed up some. Carrying her in my arms wasn't practical. Even though she wasn't all that heavy—only seventeen pounds—it was an awkward position for long distances, and my arms would grow tired.

In lists there was a kind of order: creating purpose out of aimlessness; rescuing a day from a vast expanse of time. It didn't matter so much that I didn't actually have the clock; it was enough just to have written it on the list. That was progress. I thought that I would dress myself, find my pocketbook, put Caroline into her snowsuit, and make my way into Machias, but for the moment I was content just to sit and look out the window, drink a cup of coffee and watch my baby daughter on a rug, or the water change its color out the window. I had forgotten the fear of the night before, or I had put the taste of it aside. This was a new sensation, drifting with the moment, *enjoying* the moment, with no urgency for the next, and I savored it, or rather, I simply let it happen.

Machias is, I think, considered a small city by the people who live around it, but I was reminded of a suburb. It had more shops and buildings than St. Hilaire, but it, too, was quiet, an only somewhat larger fishing town, on the banks of the Machias River. I saw a lumber mill, a furniture factory, a restaurant, a fish store, a five-and-ten, a gift shop, a church, a hardware store, an A&P, and one historical house that was open for tours in the summer. There *was* a laundromat. There were strollers for sale in the five-and-ten, and I would have liked one, but I was concerned about the money I had left, how long I could make it last. I bought a clock radio, however, thus crossing off two items on my list with one purchase. Along one wall, there was a small shelf of books— a paperback shelf of doomed love. I selected three: *Anna Karenina, Ethan Frome, The French Lieutenant's Woman*. In another aisle, I bought a sling and two presents for my daughter: a string of toys to hang across a crib that she could bat at, and a fuzzy yellow duck I could not resist. As I put the duck on the checkout counter, I was suddenly struck by the idea that just as Harrold had had his legacies, so also did I have mine: I was alone now with a daughter. I was alone now with a daughter for good, just as my mother had been. The woman behind the counter, a woman who looked as if she might be related to the woman who owned the Gateway Motel, had to ask me twice for my money.

I wondered then, as I was walking to my car with the baby and my purchases, what Harrold was doing. He would not, at first, go to the police; he'd be afraid that I might tell them what had happened. He'd try other ways of obtaining information: He would call women I'd known at the office; he would quiz my neighbor; he would keep a careful watch on our bank account. I didn't think he would call my mother. He would know I hadn't gone there again. And then, when I did not return, he might call a private detective whom he had gone to school with and whom he had sometimes used on a story. Harrold would have to be careful; he'd have thought the dialogue through in advance. He would say, in a voice rich with male camaraderie, that he had a ticklish situation, could the fellow help him out? He would explain that I had gone away on a trip and hadn't returned, and he was worried that something had happened to me. He'd tell the man he didn't want a fuss, we'd had a little row, and that all he needed to know was where I was. He'd ask his friend not to tip me off, and he'd say that he himself would drive to where I was, sweet-talk me into coming back—you know how women can be, he'd say—and then they'd laugh together, and one of them would say, Let's have a drink when you're in the neighborhood.

He wouldn't say I'd kidnapped his child. Not yet. That would be his trump card, his ace in the hole. He'd save that for later, in case I did speak up, went to the police before he got to me. What was hitting a wife, he would reasonably argue, compared to stealing a baby?

There were three trucks in front of the fish house when I returned from Machias; one of them I recognized, a red pickup with gold-leaf scrollwork under the driver's-side window. Indeed, no sooner had I entered the cottage and put the baby down than I heard a knock on the door. Willis had a package in his hands, and he spoke to me. This is how I remember it:

"Brought you some fish," he said, walking into the kitchen. "Haddock. Caught this morning. Not me. André LeBlanc brought it in."

I took the package from him. He put his hands into the pockets of his jeans and hunched his shoulders up underneath his denim jacket. He looked as if he were freezing. I said that I had to get some packages from the car.

"Don't you move," he said. "I'll get them for you." And before I could respond, he was out the door.

He brought in all the packages from the five-and-ten and the bundle of laundry from the laundromat. I saw that he was wearing the same pair of jeans as yesterday, the same navy sweater.

"I have to put the baby in for a nap," I said.

I thought that he would leave then, but he said instead, "No problem," and walked over to the window, looking out at the point.

I took off my coat and scarf and carried the baby upstairs. I sat on the bed and nursed her, and when she was finished, I laid her down in the crib and pulled her blanket over her. Below me, I could hear footsteps on the floorboards, the refrigerator opening, a chair scraping the linoleum.

When I came downstairs he was sitting at the kitchen table. He had an open can of beer in front of him.

"You don't mind," he said, lifting the can in my direction.

I shook my head, stood uncertainly in the middle of the kitchen floor.

"Get one yourself," he said genially, as if it were his kitchen, as if we were old friends.

I quickly shook my head again. I turned the heat on under the coffeepot, stood by the stove while I waited for the coffee to warm up.

"Let me pay you for the fish," I said.

He waved his hand. "Wouldn't hear of it. Think of it as a housewarming present." He laughed. "No, seriously," he said. "I didn't even pay for it. LeBlanc gave me a coupla pounds of fish; I just skimmed off a pound for you. I been waitin' for you over at the fish house. I got pots do to myself, but it's too fuckin' cold out there. Anyway, I feel like takin' a coupla days off."

He looked around the cottage. He snapped a beat with his splayed fingers on the table. He bobbed up and down in his chair for a measure or two. I wondered what music he was listening to. "You like the Dead?" he asked.

I nodded noncommittally.

"I gotta get a tree," he said. "Jeannine likes it early. Says it gives her somethin' to look forward to. She puts it in a corner of the trailer. I worry about fire, that's the only thing."

"Fire?"

"You have a fire in a trailer and you're dead. Just like that." He snapped his fingers. "It's like fryin' in an aluminum box. It's the biggest problem with a trailer, fire. So I only allow the kids to have the lights on when I'm in the trailer with them—the lights on the tree, I mean. And I'm a son of a bitch about keepin' it watered. The minute the needles start fallin' off, I get rid of it. But any tree I get won't shed until Valentine's Day." He laughed again. "I'll cut it myself, in the woods across from the Coffin place. Sit down, take a load off your feet."

I poured the heated coffee into a mug, took the mug to the table. He kicked out a chair with his boot, an invitation. I sat down, took a sip of coffee. I'd let it boil, and it burned my tongue. Willis looked at me, seemed to be studying my face. He looked away toward the living room.

"Baby asleep?" he asked. He looked back at me. I nodded.

He stood up, walked to the refrigerator, took out another can of beer. He opened the can and drank it almost entirely down. He returned to the table, stood just to the side of me. He was looking out at the point, with the can in his hand.

"So what's the story?" he said. "You and your old man are definitely split, right?"

"Something like that," I said carefully.

"You're on your own now," he said, more to himself than to me.

"For now," I said vaguely.

There was an awkward silence. I felt his presence beside me. He was standing close to me, calmer, not moving now.

The back of his finger brushed the bruise at the

side of my cheekbone. I flinched, more because of the shock of his touching me than from any pain.

"Oh, did that hurt?" he asked, as if surprised. "Sorry. Didn't mean to hurt you. It must still be pretty raw."

I stood up. The chair was between us. I put my hand on the chairback. "I'm tired," I said. "I didn't sleep well. I think you'd better go now. I'd like to take a nap."

He put his hand on my hand. His fingers were dry and cold. He looked at the place where our hands were touching.

He said, "You wouldn't like to—you know— like fool around, or anything, while the baby is asleep?"

I slowly pulled my hand from his, crossed my arms over my chest. My chest was tight, and for a moment it was hard to breathe.

"No," I said. And then again: "No." I shook my head.

He quickly withdrew his hand, put it into his pocket. "Yeah, well, I didn't think so."

He nodded, as if to himself. He took a last swallow from the can. He sighed.

"Sometimes," he said, "a women gets left by a guy, she needs a little lovin', you know what I'm talkin' about. Nothin' heavy, just a little comfort. I thought maybe . . ." He shrugged.

I didn't say anything.

"So no hard feelings, right?"

I looked down at my feet.

"Come on, Red, let me off the hook."

I looked up at him. On his face was an expression of genuine, if mild, anxiety. Perhaps he had been opportunistic, but there had been no malice behind his request, I thought. He had tried and failed, and that was all right with him; he would think that it had been worth trying.

"No hard feelings," I said.

He made a show of relief, letting his breath out, wiping imaginary sweat off his brow. "Well, good," he said. "That's settled." He began again to move his shoulders from side to side.

I was thinking how long it had been since I had been able to say no to a man and not be fearful of the consequences, since I had been able to say no to a man at all. I was almost glad that Willis had asked, despite the minute of awkwardness between us.

"There's Jack," Willis said, turning away and walking to the window.

I followed him and looked out at the water with him. The green-and-white lobster boat had entered the channel and was closing in on the mooring. We stood together and watched as the man in the yellow slicker snagged the mooring, hitched the boat to the buoy, and jumped back into the cockpit to turn off the motor—a fluid motion, a graceful maneuver.

"He's crazy," said Willis. "You wouldn't catch me out there on a day this cold, but Jack, he don't give a shit, excuse me, about the weather."

We watched as the tall man with the sand-colored hair unloaded buckets of lobster into the dinghy that he had pulled alongside the larger boat. He returned to the cabin then, appeared to be fastening a door.

"Course if I had his home life, I might be out on the water year round too. His wife has got the blues real bad. She don't clean the house or nothin'. Jack does it all. Him and his daughter. I used to feel sorry for his kids. They're good kids, but it's a sad house. My wife, Jeannine, she tried to go over there once, sort some things out; Rebecca was in her room, wouldn't come out. Jeannine swore she heard her cryin' through the door. They got a Cape down the road here. Cries herself to sleep most nights, so I'm told. Jack, he don't say much about it, but you can see it on his face. I'll hand it to him, though, he's stuck by her all these years. She waited for him when he went away, and he came back and married her."

He peered closer out the window, as if something interested him there.

We watched the man in the slicker scull toward shore. The water was a deep, crisp winter blue.

"Rebecca didn't start gettin' sad till after she got married and her babies come. They say that happens to women sometimes. But it's the sea and the weather what does it. The gray and the long winters—that really does 'em in."

The man in the slicker beached his boat, made it fast on the iron ring.

"He's stuck with her for the kids, of course. Although sometimes I think he mighta done better by the kids if he'd got out of there, married someone else. Well, you can't ever know why a person does what they do, can you. Maybe he still loves her; you never know."

Willis turned away from the window.

"I gotta go," he said. "The guys at the fish house, they're goin' to want to know what happened to me. They'll start makin' jokes. And if I drink any more of these, I'll fall asleep; then they'll really be ribbin' me."

He put the two cans in the trash, walked to the door.

"So," he said, "you're all set, right?"

I nodded. I thanked him again for the fish.

He waved his hand as if to toss my gratitude away. He looked at me.

"I gotta go fix some pots," he said.

As it grew toward evening, Caroline began to fret, then to cry. Nursing didn't help; she refused me, twisting angrily away and scrunching up her features in a grimace of discomfort. I thought: If she won't feed, how can I help her? She wasn't content to lie or rock in my arms, and seemed to be trying to jam her fist into her mouth. This convinced me again that she must be hungry, but each attempt to feed her ended in tears and frustration. I put her then up against my shoulder and began to walk with her. She was quiet as long as I was actually walking. If I sat and tried to duplicate the sensation of bouncing up and down from the walking, she quickly saw the ruse and cried almost at once. What was it about the walking? I wondered. It was mysterious and exhausting. I walked in a circle through the kitchen, the living room, the downstairs bedroom, around and around until I thought I would drop, or go mad from the tedium. I was sure she would fall asleep against my shoulder, but as long as I walked, she remained contented and alert. If I stopped, even for a minute, she would begin to cry again. I thought: If whatever hurts her doesn't hurt when I am walking, how can it hurt when I sit down?

I walked for at least an hour, maybe two. Toward evening I remembered the baby sling, endured her wrath as I dressed her and myself for the cold, and struggled to get her into the new contraption. A change of scene might save my sanity, I thought, and the fresh air might let her drift off to sleep.

The air stung: I shielded her face in my coat. The sling allowed her weight to rest on my hip rather than in my arms, and it was such a relief to be out of the cottage, I didn't mind the cold. The sharp air was bracing, but not as bitter as it had been the day before—or perhaps the damp by the sea had taken the edge off; I don't know. I walked down the slope to the pebbled side of the spit, made my way along its expanse. My boots, even with their modest leather heel, were inappropriate for the rough surface, and the walking was slow going. I thought immediately that I would have to be careful, that I could not afford

sand to the dinghy again. He
down. He didn't move.
ned and walked back to the cot-
avel beach. He'd have heard me,
en walking away from him by
'd have been no need to call out
ak. I could have done that. But I

he edge of the point, cradling the
er in her mouth. I was watching the
inghy—only a suggestion of yellow
lack of the sand and the water. The
, what little remained, was playing
my eyes. Already it was impossible to
he water met the shore, and I was no
e I knew where the truck was parked.
lit a cigarette. I could see the sudden
e match, the red ember.
and he sat for perhaps five minutes. I
ow what I was thinking then; I was just
g, trying not to think. I did not con-
decide, yes, I will speak to him; I did not
reason to speak to him beyond a vague
ty or wonder about what his life was like,
is wife and his children and his boat. Possi-
felt that I wanted to dispel the image of tres-
ng, that I didn't like the image of myself
king away. I crossed over the hillock to the
hern side of the point, walking toward him,
ing as casually as I could—as if it were noon-
e, summer, and I were having a stroll on the
ach with my daughter—*hello*, as I walked.

to stumble or to twist an ankle. Apart from the
damage to Caroline from a possible fall, there was
the total isolation of the point. Would anyone
hear my shouts if I was in trouble? I looked
around and thought not. The nearest cottage, a
blue Cape up on the main road, was too far away
to call to: I would not be heard against the white
noise of the surf and wind, particularly if all the
windows and doors in that cottage were tightly
shut, as they must be on a cold night.

Dusk was gathering quickly, seeming to rise in
a mist from the gray gulf itself. Already I could
no longer make out the horizon—only the blip of
the lighthouse at rhythmic intervals. There was
seaweed on the stones, some old weathered
boards—driftwood—empty crab shells, bits of blue-
violet mussel shells. As I passed the fish house, I
could smell the lingering scent of a dampened
fire. I was intrigued by the fish house. I walked
over to it and peered into the windows, but I
could not see much in the gloaming: two or three
aluminum-and-plastic lawn chairs; a stack of slat-
ted traps in a corner; a low wooden bench along
one wall; a small, untidy fireplace. I thought
about the men who gathered there during the
day, imagined their voices as they sat in the stuffy
warmth, mending their gear. I wondered what
they said to each other, what they chatted about.

I crossed the ridge of grasses to the beach side
of the spit, enjoying the comfort of the hard sand
underfoot in place of the uneven stones. I thought
briefly of the honeypots that Willis had warned

against, but I wasn't sure I believed in them; anyway, I reasoned, if I kept close to the high-water mark, I wouldn't step in one.

When I reached the point, the green-and-white lobster boat had lost its color. There was a faint outline of its shape, a sense of rocking from side to side. Only a set of yellow foul-weather gear, hanging on a hook by the pilothouse, caught what was left of the light. The gear looked like a man moving with the boat—so much so, in fact, that I felt as if someone were watching me.

I was thinking about the man Willis had referred to as Jack, and about his wife, Rebecca, who had become melancholy, when I idly stuck my little finger into Caroline's mouth for her to suck on. I sometimes did this if I thought of it, because it seemed to soothe her, but when I put my finger in this time, she immediately bit down on it, and I felt the tiny sharp surprise. That was it, then, the source of her discomfort and irritation: My daughter had another tooth, one on top this time. I could feel only a sliver of a rippled ridge in her gum; I couldn't see the tooth in the darkness. She looked up at me and smiled. She seemed almost as relieved as I was that I had solved her mystery. I remembered then that I didn't have any baby aspirin with me. I wondered what the women of St. Hilaire used when their babies teethed—a sluice of brandy along the gums, a frozen crust of bread to gnaw on, or the prosaic baby aspirin I'd have used if only I had thought to buy it at the store?

I ...
back ...
darkne ...
see the ...
vehicle ...
beach. I t ...
pany—per ...
that it was ...
entire day al ...
the headlights ...
beach, I was in ...
were trespassing ...
I was standing ju ...
was moving along ...
I was sure the hea ...
out, but the truck sto ...
would have found me ...
lights on and got out o ...
his yellow slicker; you co ...
I stood motionless behind ...
I put my finger in Caroline ...
from crying, but it wasn't ...
finally fallen asleep.

I watched as the man called ...
the sand to his dinghy. He ben ...
retrieve a metal box, like a too ...
straightened up, he seemed to h ...
the box on the edge of the dinghy ...
head, as if thinking for a moment. ...
the box in the boat, walked back to th ...
turned off the headlights. I was puzzl ...
barely see him now—just a hint of a yell ...

moving across the ...
got inside and sa ...
I could have tu ...
tage along the gr ...
but I'd have be ...
then, and there ...
to me or to sp ...
didn't.

I stood at t ...
baby, my fing ...
man in the ...
against the ...
natural ligh ...
tricks with ...
tell where ...
longer sur ...
The man ...
flare of t ...
I stood ...
don't kr ...
watchin ...
sciousl ...
have a ...
curios ...
with ...
bly I ...
pass ...
snea ...
nor ...
say ...
ti ...
b ...

I startled him, I could see that. He'd been far away, or he was surprised to see another human being. Probably, I thought, he was used to having the point to himself, had forgotten there was a car at the cottage.

He stood up, stepped out of the dinghy, faced me. I said hello again, and I think he must have answered me or nodded.

I walked close to him. Now that I had intruded upon him, I had to let him see me—though I must have appeared to him as only a gray shape in my coat and scarf.

My first impression of him is distinct and clear. I am not overlaying this with later images, seen in the sunlight, or by firelight or at daybreak. His face was angular, and I was aware that he was taller than I'd thought. There were deep lines running from his nose to the bottom of his chin at either side of his mouth, but I didn't think these were from age, even though he looked as if he was in his forties. They were from weathering; his face was weathered. You could see this even in the darkness: the roughened skin, the wrinkling at the eyes. His hair was average length and curly. You could not see the true color in the darkness, but I knew already it was the shade of dry sand. He wore an off-white Irish knit sweater underneath his slicker; there was a hole unknitting itself where his collarbone would be. He threw his cigarette onto the sand.

"You've got a baby there," he said. His voice was deep and slow, hesitant, but he didn't sound surprised. He had a bit of the Maine accent; it was in the lilt of the words and in his vowels. But he spoke more like Julia Strout, his cousin, than Willis Beale.

I looked down at Caroline.

"She was teething—I just discovered that—and I was trying to get her to stop crying, so I brought her out for a walk in the sling."

"Looks like it worked," he said.

"Yes," I said. I smiled. "I've taken the cottage there."

That seemed to register. He looked in the direction of the cottage.

"I heard someone was there, and I've seen your car."

We didn't tell each other our names, and we didn't shake hands. Why? I thought at the time it was merely economical, as if we imagined we would not know each other long, or at all.

"I've seen you," I said. "And your boat."

"I bring it into town if we get some weather. Otherwise, I leave it till mid-January. We sometimes get a thaw in early January."

"Oh."

"Cold tonight, though."

"But you went out today."

"I did. Didn't get much for my trouble."

"Willis Beale was delivering some fish when we saw you come in. He said he thought you were crazy to go out today."

He made a sound, a sort of laugh. "Willis," he

said, as if I shouldn't pay much attention to Willis. But I already knew that.

He was glancing out to where he'd have seen his boat if there were any light left, and I was looking at the side of his face. Ravaged, I remember saying to myself, by the elements or by something else. What was it about the face? The eyes—they were old eyes, or were merely tired. Yet I was drawn to his face, its shape, the sense of calm around the mouth, or what I took to be calm in the dim light. His body was lean, but you felt its weight, as if it were anchored to the sand. Or its stillness. I had a feeling of stillness when I watched him, when he moved.

A breeze came up, blew a strand of hair across his brow.

"I have to put her to bed," I said, shielding Caroline's head with my arms.

"Getting late," he said.

He bent down to retrieve the toolbox from the dinghy. I walked away.

We didn't say, "So long now," or, "Nice meeting you."

I was halfway down the beach when I heard the motor of the truck start up. For a minute I was walking in its headlights, conscious of my back in the headlights, and then they were gone, veering up the lane. I stopped to watch the progress of the truck, the jostling of the light on the rough dirt, the left turn onto the coast road, the swath of light moving south toward town.

*   *   *

There was a rhythm to my days. It established itself before I had even become aware of it, an insistent pattern pushing at the edge of my consciousness.

Each day I woke with the low rumbling of a motor on the lane. There would be just a hint of gray beyond the window, the first sign of daybreak. I would listen as one or several trucks made their way down the sand, and after a time I began to be able to recognize the sounds of routine: a truck door shutting, the dragging of an object along a truck's metal bed, the small splash as a dinghy was put into the water, the creak of wood under a man's weight, the slap of a wake against a larger boat. And then the other motor would start up, grumble a bit as if it wanted to quit, and there would be the quiet whine out to silence as a boat moved away from the mooring.

Each day I made the high double bed. I smoothed the sheet, drew up the quilt. There was about these gestures a monastic purity, a return to the single self. If the baby was not awake yet, I would go down to the kitchen and make myself a cup of coffee and sit in my nightgown and sweater at the table and watch the water change its colors as the day began.

At first I was unable even to read. I had the books, but for days they lay unopened on the table. I wanted just to look.

It was winter, the dead of winter, when everything was dormant, and yet I was continually surprised by the constant mutability of the landscape.

Sometimes the tide would go out so far that what sea was left was only puddles. At other times, when the tide was high, the spit in front of me would seem to have shrunk to a spindle.

I knew so little. For the first few days, I couldn't predict the tides at all; they were a constant surprise. I somehow always had it wrong. I could spot the gulls, but there were other birds I had never seen before. Sometimes I thought I saw seals, I was sure of this, and yet when I'd look again, the dark hump I'd thought was a seal was only a rock with the water lapping against it.

I had my chores, of course. I took to washing the clothes by hand, boiling the diapers and putting the wash out on a line behind the house. I liked the way our wash looked—the tiny undershirts and my jeans whipping in the breeze.

There was industry all around me, and perhaps I took my cue from that. How could I be idle when every morning men came to the point to mend their broken pots and traps or go out onto the water? First there would be the trucks, then the sound of a boat's engine or a curl of smoke from the fish house. There might be three trucks on the point, or four. From time to time, I'd hear a voice or a bit of music, sometimes a shout and then a laugh. And in the early afternoon, I'd see the green-and-white lobster boat come from behind a pine-darkened island. This would be a milestone in my day, a mark of punctuation, and I never failed to watch the man in the yellow slicker perform his returning ritual.

But when the black truck had gone back up the lane, the day would seem to lose its momentum. The rhythms I had heard and understood and counted on disappeared, and those hours until darkness were somewhat harder for me to negotiate. I tried to fill them with a drive or a walk or a nap. But I understood that these were gestures of defiance, skirmishes against empty time.

Eventually, in the second week, I established a routine that suited me, that didn't feel at odds with the world around me. I bought a few skeins of yarn and began to knit, a sweater for myself and one for Caroline. In the mornings, when the baby napped, I would knit. My mother had taught me how when I was a child, but I hadn't taken it up again since I had moved to New York. I felt it as a link to her, to something she had given me, translated now into something I could give my daughter. I liked also the sense of working with my hands—a kind of counterpoint to the men working around me.

I called my mother once a week on Saturdays, from the A&P in Machias. It was a habit we'd established, and I knew she'd be alarmed if she didn't hear from me. I didn't tell her where I was or what had happened. I pretended everything was fine.

Willis came by almost every day, on one pretext or another. He might have fish for me or want to warm up in the kitchen. Once he had whittled a small wooden figure for Caroline. Each day he took a seat at the kitchen table. He would look at my face. The bruises were healing, I knew, and didn't appear as raw as they had when I had first come to the cottage. But when he examined me, I would look away.

I almost always let him in, from politeness if nothing else, and he seldom stayed long. I think he felt proprietary toward me. He never asked again if we could "fool around," as he had put it that day, but the question always seemed to be in the air: If he was persistent enough, would I not change my mind?

You will perhaps wonder why I permitted these visits and I sometimes ask myself that too. I believe I didn't want to alienate Willis—or anyone else from the town, for that matter. Nor did I want to draw attention to myself any more than I had to. I think I hoped that Willis would grow tired of my lack of response and stop coming.

After Willis had left, I would feed the baby and then make a lunch for myself. Usually I'd done my chores by noontime. Then I'd go out with the baby. If the day was reasonable, I'd put Caroline into the sling, and we would walk to the end of the point and back, or south along the rocks. I had bought for myself, on one of my forays into Machias, a pair of sneakers so that I could make my way better along the stones. Sometimes I'd look for things: smooth mauve pebbles one day, pure white shells the next. There were jars and cups of stones and shells collecting on the sills in the cottage.

After a walk, I'd put Caroline into the car, and we would drive into St. Hilaire. I shopped every day at the store there, selecting in the early afternoon what I would have for supper. I learned to weather the baleful glass eye, the small talk, and the questions—even, after a time, to look forward to them, a tenuous thread of connection to the town.

Two days a week, when it was open, I'd go to the library. I'd begun finally to read, and once I'd begun, I became hungry for more books. I read in the evenings and long into the nights, sometimes devouring a book a day. I hadn't ever had this kind of time, it seemed to me, and the books were a luxury I'd rediscovered.

The library was a poor one, I suppose, as libraries go—there wasn't much new in it—but it had the classics, plenty to keep me occupied. I read Hardy, I remember, and Jack London, and Dickens and Virginia Woolf and Willa Cather.

I looked forward to walking into that small stone building. There was a woman there, a Mrs. Jewett, who balked at first when I requested a library card, since I was only renting, but finally, after much wheedling from me, she gave in. An extraordinary reticence on her part, now that I think of it, since I was almost always the only visitor she had, and I know that she looked forward to these visits.

Eventually I took to going around to Julia Strout's for a cup of tea. Yes, I was sometimes lonely—even if I savored my solitude: an odd paradox—and it was this loneliness, after a long spell of gray days in the second week, that prompted my first visit to the tall woman with the gapped teeth. I'd come out of Everett's store and seen Julia Strout's house across the common. I thought: I could just stop by on a pretext—the kitchen faucet leaked? I needed extra blankets?—but when I climbed her porch steps with the baby in my arms and knocked on her door, pretext left me, and I said, when she answered, her eyes momentarily startled but her face not giving away much of her surprise, that I'd just come by to say hello.

I had not been inside her house before and had the idea that it would look fussy, if homely, with knickknacks and knitted tea cozies. Did I think this only because she was of a different generation than myself? But her rooms were not fussy, were rather surprisingly spare and inviting. I remember most of all her floors, burnished dark hardwood floors that she later confessed to me she polished on her hands and knees. She had a ritual, she said, of rising at six every morning and spending her first two hours cleaning and polishing, so that she did not have to think about chores the rest of the day. Her kitchen was quite large, with white vertical boards on its walls and a gray-green slate floor. She invited me into her kitchen and said she'd make us a cup of tea. There was a fireplace and a large round oak table. She was wearing that afternoon, as she always wore, a pair of thick corduroy pants and a sweater. I don't think I ever saw her in a skirt the entire time I knew her. She had strong, muscular hands and forearms, which I noticed particularly when she brought the kettle to the stove. I remember, too, that there were a great many books in her kitchen—not cookbooks but novels, biographies, and histories—and I had the sense that she lived in this room, at least in wintertime.

I put Caroline on the floor and let her creep around, always keeping my eye on her and the fireplace. Julia put the screen across, and she, too, kept watch, once getting up and bringing Caroline, who had wandered too close to the hearth, back to the other side of the room.

"You settling in?" Julia Strout asked as she fetched two mugs from her cupboard.

"Yes," I said. "The cottage is wonderful. Very peaceful."

"You have any idea how long you're going to stay?"

It was an idle question—I'm not sure she really cared—but it took me by surprise, and I must have hesitated, or she must have seen the alarm on my face, for she quickly added, "It's yours for as long as you need it or want it. There's no one else signed up for it."

"Oh," I said.

"Milk or brandy?" she asked.

"What?"

"I prefer brandy on a cold afternoon," she said, "but suit yourself."

"Brandy," I said.

I watched her pour large dollops of the amber

liquid into the mugs. Perhaps she wasn't as sensible as I'd imagined.

She brought the steaming mugs to the table. I took a sip from my own. The liquor was strong, and I could feel it hit my stomach, the warmth spreading.

She sat across from me, took a swallow of her tea.

"Are you going to be looking for work?" she asked.

I wasn't sure of the answer to this question. I looked at Caroline.

"I don't know," I said. "I suppose I'll have to eventually. But there doesn't seem to be much work available. I'm not sure what I'd do."

"You have a certain amount of money," she said carefully.

"Yes."

"And when that's gone . . . ?"

"Yes."

"I see." She turned in her chair.

"I like living alone myself," she said, "though this house is ridiculously big for just one person. The cottage is nice, though."

"Very nice," I said.

"I've shut off most of the rooms here. Can't imagine living with anyone else now. Comes from too many years on my own."

I heard the hidden message—that I did not have to be afraid of living alone. I took another swallow of tea. Caroline was making cooing sounds in a corner, entranced by the carved and spindly legs of a tall wooden chair she'd found there.

"You're on the run, aren't you?" Julia Strout said suddenly and plainly. "You've run away."

At first I didn't speak.

"You don't have to tell me," she said. "It's none of my business."

"I had to," I said finally.

She stared for a time at her knee, which was crossed over her other leg. She wore work boots, laced up over the ankle.

"Not a good idea to be alone with a baby all the time," she said. "I can always take her for a couple of hours if you want a break."

"Thank you," I said, "but I couldn't . . ."

"Well, you think about it."

"I will."

A silence descended upon the kitchen. In the corner, up on all fours, Caroline lost her balance and bumped her head on the chair leg. I went to her and picked her up. I had nearly finished my tea, anyway, and said I ought to be going. Julia seemed at first reluctant to let me go, and I thought that possibly she was sometimes lonely too.

She walked me to the door.

"You come again for tea," she said to me.

I thanked her and said that I would. She watched as I put Caroline into her snowsuit, wound the scarf around my head.

"He won't find you in this town," she said.

*   *   *

That day I did not go back to the cottage but instead drove into Machias. There was something at the five-and-ten that I wanted to get. I went into the store and bought a nightgown for myself—a long flannel nightgown in a pattern of small blue cornflowers, a long prosaic nightgown to keep me warm in my solitary bed, the sort of nightgown that might grow soft and threadbare from use.

A nightgown that Harrold would not have approved of.

In the middle of December, about ten days before Christmas, there was a flurry of activity on the point, as three of the four boats in the channel were hauled onto cradles for the winter. There were boat trailers and winches and heavy pulleys and more men on the point than I had ever seen before. One of the boats that was being pulled that day was *Jeannine*, Willis's boat, and he made a show of coming to my cottage twice, once for coffee, and once for a drink when the boat was safely hauled, as if to suggest to the men on the point that we were old friends and the cottage nearly a second home to him. I wondered if the other men ever asked Willis about me, and if they did, what he told them. Would he confine himself to the little that he knew, or would he feel compelled to embellish these few facts so that I might appear more mysterious or intriguing in his stories? The green-and-white lobster boat did not get hauled that day, was not even in the channel. It had gone out at daybreak, as was its custom, and did not return until nearly dusk, when all the other boats had been hauled and the men had gone home to their suppers.

On the day after the boats had been hauled, I dressed Caroline and myself for an excursion. I was short of coffee and dishwashing liquid and a baby cereal I had begun to give Caroline, and thought I would just run into town and pick up a few things at Everett Shedd's. It was a gray day, cold and overcast, with a hint of snow in the air, and I was thinking that I had better do the errand before dusk and possible bad weather. I put Caroline into the basket in the back seat and started the car. I was halfway down the gravel drive, however, when I realized something was wrong. The steering wheel kept pulling to the right. I stopped the car and got out. I had a flat, the right front.

You will probably be amused by this—I see you as someone who prides herself on being competent—but I had not actually ever changed a tire before. I had been shown how to do it by a male friend of my mother's, who had taught me how to drive, but I had never done the deed myself. Out of habit, I looked around me, as if someone might materialize—where was Willis when I really needed him?—but the landscape was particularly cheerless that day and empty. Now that the boats had been hauled, the men seemed to have taken a day off. And the green-and-white lobster boat had not returned yet. I thought to myself that I could wait until the next day, when someone might appear, but I did not like to think of myself and the baby stranded without a car, in case of an emergency. I carried Caroline back into the house, so that she would not freeze in the back seat, and laid her in the baby basket on the braided rug. All the coming and going had thoroughly woken her up, and she was crying.

I mumbled something to her about being right back, which was, in the circumstances, wildly optimistic, and went out to forage through the trunk of the car. I found the jack and the spare and a lug wrench. I understood the theory of changing a tire. I got the jack to work, but I could not get the nuts off. I stood on the wrench, but even my weight wouldn't budge them. Inside the cottage, I could hear Caroline wailing.

I was thinking that I might have to wait until she was asleep, but by then it would be dark outside and the task even more difficult. I thought that if I jumped up and down on the wrench, that would loosen the nuts, and so it was that I was standing on the wrench, jumping up and down for all I was worth, holding on to my car so that I would not lose my balance, perhaps even cursing my bad luck into the bargain, when I heard a voice behind me.

I hadn't seen the boat come in. From the gravel drive, the channel was not as visible as it was from the cottage. And I hadn't heard the familiar sound because I'd been too distracted by Caroline's cries.

"The way they put them on, it's a wonder anyone can get them off," he said. "Here, let me give it a try."

He bent down and gave the wrench a hard push. I could only see the back of his head. His ears were red from the cold. I had never seen him wear a hat. He loosened the nuts and tossed them into the hubcap. Caroline sounded hysterical in the cottage.

"I have to see to the baby," I said.

He nodded once, took the flat off the axle. I went in to Caroline, lifted her into my arms, and returned to watch the man in the yellow slicker fix my tire. He worked with dispatch, methodically changing the tire as if he'd done it a hundred times before. He turned the damaged tire carefully in his hands, examining it. Then he put it into my trunk.

"Can't see offhand what the trouble is. You take it into Everett's, he'll fix it for you if he can." He was wiping his fingers on a rag in my trunk.

"I'm glad you came by," I said. "I don't know what I'd have done on my own."

"Someone would have come along," he said. "Is she still cutting teeth?"

I looked at Caroline. "Not any more since that night," I said. "She's been pretty good, actually."

I glanced up. He was staring at me, at my face. I hadn't given a thought to the scarf while I'd been trying to change the tire. He looked hard at me for four or five seconds, not speaking, and I didn't look away. I was thinking how unusual his eyes were, how they didn't seem to belong to the rest of his face. He seemed about to speak, then stopped.

He threw the rag into the trunk, shut it.

"Thank you," I said.

"It's nothing," he answered, and turned.

Just then a red pickup truck came around the corner of the lane at a fairly fast clip, pulling to a stop beside my car, spewing gravel so that it hit my car like bullets. The man in the yellow slicker, on his way back to his own truck, gave a wave to Willis but kept walking.

Willis jumped down from the cab, looked toward Jack Strout, then at me.

"What's the story?" he said, sounding out of breath.

"What story?" I said.

"With Jack. What's he doing here?"

I thought, all in all, it was an odd question.

"I had a flat," I said. "He saw me trying to fix it and came by to help."

"That so."

He shook a cigarette from a pack in his jacket pocket, put the cigarette to his lips. He seemed particularly jumpy.

"I've got to go," I said. "I have to get the tire fixed at Everett's."

"Let me take it for you," he said quickly. "I'll bring it right back, put it on for you."

"No," I said, "but thanks, anyway. I have to get some things." I moved toward my car.

"I come by to tell you about the bonfire," he said.

"The bonfire?"

"Yeah; it's a town tradition. Every Christmas Eve, we get together on the common, the whole town, and we have a bonfire and sing Christmas carols. Everybody goes. The women from the church, they make hot cider and sweets for the kids. You should come; wrap the baby up. You'd be amazed, the heat from the bonfire, it keeps you warm, even on the coldest nights." He looked up at the threatening sky. "Think we're going to have another storm tonight," he said.

I thought he must be running out of excuses to come to the cottage. Christmas Eve was more than a week away.

"Well, I'll see," I said.

He took a long drag on his cigarette.

"Want me to follow you into town? Make sure you're all right, with no spare now and all?"

"No," I said. "I'll be fine."

"You're sure about that now, Red."

"Yes," I said, moving toward my car. "I'm sure."

"OK, then," he said, looking down at the figure in the yellow slicker moving toward the end of the point.

"Think I'll go see how old Jack is doin'," he said. "Too bad I didn't get here sooner. I could of changed the tire for you; you wouldn't have had to bother old Jack."

"I didn't bother old Jack," I said. "He just—"

"Yeah, whatever," Willis said, cutting me off. "Watch yourself now, in the storm, if it starts snowin'."

"I'll be fine," I said, with more firmness than was perhaps necessary. I got into the car, put Caroline in the back, shut the door. Willis was walking down the point, his shoulders hunched up inside his jacket. I put the key in the ignition, took a long, deep breath. I had a sudden image of Harrold coming fast around the corner, spewing bullets of gravel up onto my car. I had a sudden image of myself and Caroline in the car, with Harrold hovering over us, trying to get in.

I wondered where he was now, what he was thinking, what he had done to find me.

There are stretches of my stay in St. Hilaire that are hazy to me now. The several days before Christmas, for instance. I remember clearly only Christmas Eve, the bonfire, but the days preceding it are now a blur.

On Christmas Eve day, Caroline cried a great deal; she was cutting two more teeth simultaneously and resisted my efforts to console her. Even the baby aspirin I had finally bought seemed ineffectual. As a last resort, I put her into the car and drove aimlessly up and down the coast road for at least an hour, so that she might sleep. The day was clear, transparent. To my left, as I drove south toward town, the gulf was strewn with jewels—glinting, restless, sparkling—in the high sunshine. I wore my dark glasses from necessity as

much as for camouflage. The green-and-white lobster boat had been gone when I bundled Caroline
into the car, and as I drove—first south, then
north, peering across the passenger seat out to
sea—I suppose I looked for a speck that might
have been a boat, emerging from the lee of an
island or idling amid a scatter of buoys.

During the day, men came and went on the
point. I would be aware of a motor, then perhaps
a voice calling to another. Short words, bursts of
words on the wind, with a hint of gruffness in
them, the greetings of men who do not stop
working when they talk to each other.

I think I imagined I would just have a look at
the bonfire, stay a minute or two, and then take
the baby home. I was curious about this event,
and I would have liked the sense of having somewhere to go, something to cap my day, but I was
worried about having Caroline out on such a cold
night.

I had not been on the coast road after dark,
except for that first confused drive to the motel,
but now that I knew the road better and had land-
marks to refer to, I could more easily pick out
houses that had grown familiar to me. The sky
that night seemed immense with stars, and there
was a moon, cream and low on the horizon, sending a rippled shaft of light across the sea and illu-
minating, from the east, the simple outlines of the
Capes and cottages and farmhouses.

Many of the houses had Christmas lights strung
up along the gutters, or electric candles in the

windows. Here and there, I could see a tree in a living room, and detached as I was that night, I was thinking about what an odd custom it was—to take a tree into your house and dress it with gaudy bits of glass and paper and put colored electric lights all over it. I was trying to imagine what I'd think of this custom if I had happened to visit Karachi or Cairo in the summer, and the people there, for a Muslim holiday, had brought a flowering tree into their house and decorated it in the same fashion. But I was not so detached that I did not sometimes have sharp memories when I looked into the windows on the coast road, memories of holidays with my own mother, memories of holidays she had made for me—stockings hanging from a bookcase; the fragile glass ornaments on the higher branches of our Christmas tree; our own electric candles in the windows; the pile of presents (handmade sweaters and gloves and hats; an array of toys).

You could see the glow of the bonfire from the edge of town. I parked in a small clearing behind the church, put Caroline into the sling, and wrapped my coat around her, so that only her head, in her woolen cap, peeked above the buttons of my coat. She had settled down some since late afternoon, and I thought she would probably sleep as I walked around.

I made my way toward the light of the fire, hanging back at an outer ring of celebrants. Already there were what looked to be a couple of hundred people in the common, most surrounding the fire. Closest to the fire were the young boys, their faces lit orange, darting recklessly toward the fire and back to the circle, throwing bits of twigs and debris onto the pyre, their faces upturned as a plume of sparks arced over the crowd. The fire was noisy, crackling, popping, and around it there was an equally loud commotion: boys squealing, adults admonishing, buzzing, greeting each other, slapping their hands together in the cold—although even in the outer ring, I could feel the fire's heat. Once or twice I saw an older teenager moving through the crowd, flashing a peace sign; another boy had a cardboard poster: "Stop the War." Where there were gaps in the ring, the light flickered outward, against the stone war memorial, against a green Volkswagen parked by the common's edge, against a tall straight tree I could not see the upper branches of.

To me the bonfire seemed dangerous, as if the sparks could easily ignite the old boards of the store or of Julia's house, or the trees overhead— but the townspeople seemed unconcerned about the danger. Perhaps they had had so many years without incident that they were complacent about hazard, or perhaps they had taken precautions I was unaware of. Possibly icy-cold branches do not easily ignite; I don't know.

There was comfort in the darkness of the outer ring, in being a voyeur, muffled in my coat and scarf, although I did occasionally get a knowing look. Probably most had heard already of a new

woman in town with a baby; perhaps some
thought me a relative who had come to spend
Christmas with a family in St. Hilaire. Most of the
men and women were wearing bulky car coats,
scarves wound around their necks, and knitted
caps. The night was frosty with puffs of conden-
sation, warm breath on cold air. Some of the men
took occasional nips from bottles concealed in
paper bags, and once or twice I passed through
the sweet drift of marijuana, but I did not actually
see anyone with a joint.

"It's made from wormy wood from the pots."

Startled, I turned to the voice at my shoulder.
Willis had a beer can down by his side, the other
hand in the pocket of his denim jacket. There
was frost on his mustache, and when the fire lit
his face, I could see that his eyes were badly
bloodshot.

"The fire," he said. "We make a pile of our
rotted pots and so on. Makes a blaze, don't it."

He was looking at me, appraising me, while he
said this. His leg was jiggling.

"Where's your family?" I asked quickly.

"Jeannine's taken the boys into the church for
cider and whatnot. I saw you from across."

He took a last swig of beer, dropped the can
onto the ground, and crushed it with his foot.

"So what do you think of our fire here? Wild,
huh?"

"It's really something," I said.

"We been doin' this fifty years, anyway. My

old man used to talk about it. You want me to get you a beer?"

"No," I said. "I'm fine."

"You want a toke, then? I could get us some joints."

I heard the *us*, didn't like it. I also did not like the picture that came to mind: Willis and myself smoking grass in the shadow of the church.

"I'd like to meet your boys," I said.

He swayed. He seemed confused.

"Yeah, sure. They'll be out soon," he said vaguely.

The singing began from nowhere, at no visible signal. There was a single man's voice for a bar or two, then half a dozen voices joining him, then a crowd, as people heard the carol, stopped chatting with their neighbors. By the end of "Silent Night," the town was in unison, the deep bass of the men offset here and there by the high trilling vibrato of the older women.

They began a heartier tune next—"Hark the Herald" or "God Rest Ye, Merry Gentlemen"— and I was watching the men and women singing. I had begun to sing myself; it forestalled conversation with Willis. He was moving beside me— swaying or jiggling, I couldn't tell. It was in the middle of that carol, or another, that I saw Jack, two or three people in front of me. He had his back to me but was slightly turned and bent toward a teenage girl beside him, so that I saw his face as he spoke to her. She had spilled her cider onto her gloves—that seemed to be the problem. I saw Jack take her gloves off and put them in his pockets, then remove his own gloves and give them to her. He held her cardboard cup of hot cider while she put his gloves on. I couldn't see her face—her back was to me—but I was struck by her hair spilling out from her hat: It was the color of her father's and was long and curly.

Possibly there was a subtle shift in the crowd, or a man in front of me moved and blocked my view, but I must have strained or craned my neck to watch the scene with Jack and his daughter, for I became aware suddenly that Willis was staring at me. He examined my face and then looked at the thing that had caught my attention. Then he turned back toward me. I met his glance; I looked away. I think I was embarrassed. I hadn't been able to read his expression—he'd been thinking—but his eyes had seemed clearer, sharper, than they had before.

"I'm getting some cider," I said quickly, and moved away from him.

The church was warm, brightly lit. People began shedding scarves and hats and gloves as soon as they entered, and those who wore glasses had to take them off and wipe the steam away. The cider was in the parish hall, I was told, a room adjacent to the sanctuary. I followed the others to a long table covered by a red tablecloth. On it were black ironware pots of hot cider, plates of cookies and cakes, and candles wreathed with holly. The tangy scent of the cider was delicious and filled the room. Garlands of silver tinsel had been strung from a green velvet curtain up on a stage, and there was a tall Christmas tree in a corner.

Caroline woke up and looked at me and rubbed her eyes. I thought fleetingly that I might have to nurse her soon and wondered if I should just drive straight home. I was hot in my scarf in the church. The cider smelled good, yet I was too uncomfortable to stay there any longer. I thought, also, that Caroline might begin to sweat, and I didn't relish having to unfasten her from the sling and undress her, just for a cup of cider.

Outside, the cold was almost a relief. I stood on the steps and watched the scene before me. A stiff wind had come up off the ocean, fanning the bonfire, causing it to intensify in brightness and sending even larger plumes of sparks out into the sky. A woman came out of the church, stood beside me on the steps as she put on her gloves, adjusted her hat. They were singing "Joy to the World" now, and I thought both the singing and the fire seemed to have reached a feverish pitch.

The woman beside me appeared to be thinking the same thing.

"I know we do this every year," she said, shaking her head, "but I said to Everett only this morning, one of these years he's goin' to have a fiasco on his hands."

She nodded briskly at me, tugged at her gloves, and marched down the steps and into the crowd.

I may have wanted to stay longer, but I didn't mind the prospect of returning to the cottage, nursing Caroline, and climbing into my high white bed. Caroline's teething was exhausting me, and I knew she would wake early. I made my way down the steps, feeling vaguely pregnant and ungainly again, with Caroline strapped to my belly, and was about to turn the corner to the clearing where I'd parked my car when I heard a shout, then a kind of gruff rumbling. The singing stopped, but the circle remained intact, still facing the bonfire. I edged toward the circle, wondering what the source of the sudden silence was. The wind blew hard across the common and stung my cheeks. I raised my scarf over my face, kept Caroline hunkered down inside my coat.

I reached the crowd, stood on my toes to see. There was fighting near the fire. A group of older boys were pitching back and forth, rolling toward and away from the flames. The "Stop the War" poster was on the ground. Men from the crowd moved forward to contain the fight or to stop it, and those who watched but were not involved had made a space, backing up into the crowd, compressing it. Those in the outer ring had moved forward, and it seemed that everyone was straining toward the center.

There were grunts and shouts, arms flailing, heads thrown back. I saw Everett in the fray. He held a boy by the zippered edge of his leather jacket, and then he was hit or slammed from behind, and the grocer's hat fell off. Willis was in the midst, wild and inarticulate with fury. I couldn't tell which side he was on, but I saw him kick a boy in the groin. Women closest to the scuffle were screaming and shouting, calling out names: *Billy! Brewer! John! John! Stop it! Stop it now!*

I backed away from the crowd, wound my arms around the baby. A jostle in the center might ripple outward, and I was afraid that Caroline might get hurt. The fire roared beside the fight, but no one was paying it much attention now.

The crowd parted, and Everett emerged. His face was flushed, his coat torn, and he had not retrieved his hat. He had a boy by the collar, and despite his age, Everett was racing the boy faster than the boy could walk. Other older men, in their forties, had boys in tow too, and the crowd turned to watch the procession. Everett took his charge into the church, and the others followed. Where else would they go? There was no police station.

The crowd then turned inward on itself. There was excited murmuring, the confusion of many witnesses. Someone said a group of kids had wanted to turn the bonfire into an antiwar demonstration. I heard a man near me tell his wife that the boys had been drunk, as if that were all the explanation anyone needed.

The fire burned unheeded; it couldn't compete now with the stories that were being passed from one puzzled or knowing face to the other. I looked over at the white houses lining the common, saw Julia standing on her porch. I thought that I would walk over to her, speak to her, wish her a happy Christmas. But I was reluctant to leave the crowd just at that minute, or to leave the fire. I was concerned about the fire, perhaps more so than I ought to have been. I had the idea that if I left, I would hear in the morning that a building or a tree had ignited, that something had burned down. Then I thought that I should mention my fear, but I didn't want to call attention to myself. I thought that I could say something to Julia Strout; she would know what to do.

I remember standing there, feeling somehow paralyzed with indecision, looking at the fire and the people. Images from the fight began to blur with images of the faces around me. I was sure I saw Willis again, striking a boy on the side of his head, his hand making an arc in the cold air. But the air was thin, leaving us. The fire was sucking the air from around us, and I was having trouble breathing. I looked around me to see if other people were having trouble breathing too. My heartbeat felt shallow, insubstantial. Then I looked up, and the trees began to spin.

Everett Shedd

After Christmas Eve, of course, everyone in the town got to know who she was, even if they hadn't heard any of the stories earlier. I don't know what caused it, exactly; the fight, I think it was. Maybe she saw things that brought back bad memories to her, don't you know. Or maybe she was just in a lot worse shape than any of us thought. I know Julia Strout blames herself, but she shouldn't. You can't be responsible for a person just because she rents a cottage from you.

Every year at Christmastime, we have a bonfire on the common there. It's a ritual; we been doin' it now, let me see, since probably 1910 or thereabouts. It started one year, the men made a fire outta their rotted gear on the green there, 'n' some folks got to singin' 'n' that, and each year it got a little more elaborate, until now we have a right fire from the traps that are useless—wormy, they are—and the townspeople, they gather 'round the fire and sing carols every Christmas Eve, 'n' the kids run around 'n' drink cider 'n' eat goodies, 'n' some of the older boys, they get a little wild and drunk, 'n' it's a way for folks to get together to celebrate 'n', to tell you the truth, to let off a little steam. My wife, she's a doomsayer; she's always tellin' me every year the bonfire is goin' to be a fiasco, but usually I think the bonfire is a good idea—keeps the boys pretty quiet for most of the rest of the winter, till they can go out on the water again—but this year things got a bit out of hand, 'n' we had ourselves a pretty good scuffle.

What happened is that a coupla the kids—Sean Kelly's boy and Hiram Tibbett's son—they had an idea to have a protest, don't you know, and there was this other group of kids—town boys—they got ahold of a couple of fifths of bourbon, 'n' I didn't realize it, they were drinkin' behind the church, 'n' then they come over to the fire, and the two groups, they got to exchanging words and then they got to fightin'—you know how boys are when they been drinkin'—'n' then somehow all hell let loose, 'n' the men were in it too, 'n' I had to go in and lay down the law. So all this is by way of explainin' to you that I was in the church when it happened, 'n' to tell you the truth, I'd been hit pretty bad, 'n' though I pride myself that I didn't let it show, I was feelin' a bit woozy, don't you know, so I didn't react as fast as I ought to have done.

The first I heard is Malcolm Jewett comes tearin' into the church where I got these boys under control 'n' we're sortin' out the damage to each other, 'n' he shouts that it's the woman with the baby, she's on the ground. Right away, I know who he's talkin' about, because I saw Mary earlier in the evenin'. Wanderin' around with the baby. He says she just fell, 'n' one of the women has got the baby off some contraption on the woman, 'n' the baby is OK but cryin'. So I leave the boys with Dick Gibb and hotfoot it out to the common, but already I can see Jack Strout has got her on her feet and is fixin' her scarf. Julia is there too; I think she seen Mary from her porch, where she always stays to watch the bonfire. She worries every year that sparks from the fire is goin' to blow over to her porch, so she stands there with a coupla buckets. I park the fire truck behind the store just in case we ever do lose control of the bonfire, but it never happened yet. We had years where we couldn't get much of a fire goin' because of a snow, but knock on wood, we never had an accident yet. Then Julia, she takes Mary 'n' the baby into her place. Jack, he didn't go inside, I'm pretty sure. But like I say, that's when anyone who didn't know who she was, they all knew by the time the night was done.

She just passed out, apparently. Fainted.

She was damn lucky, you want to know the truth. If she'd a fallen the wrong way, she could have really hurt the baby, don't you know. According to Elna Coffin, who was standin' beside her, she just went. Just like that. One minute she was standin' there, the next minute she was on the ground. At first Elna thought she'd been hit or bumped by the crowd, 'n' then the baby started cryin' 'n' then Jack was there, 'n' she came to. And that's about it, far as I can remember.

The next day people were askin' Julia 'n' me, whenever we saw anybody, and maybe they asked Jack too, I don't know, but he wouldn't have known anything anyway, how she was 'n' all, but Julia, she don't say much, 'n' she never had much to say about Mary Amesbury to people who was just curious or lookin' for a bit of gossip. And I think people, they kind of got the idea that Mary was in trouble.

So when that man come, you know, that fella from New York City—oh, let's see now, it was a coupla weeks later, don't you know, after New Year's—askin' questions about a woman with a baby, nobody would say much of anything. They took their cue from Julia; she carries a lot of weight in this town. If Julia had her reasons, people figured, those reasons would be good enough for them.

Though of course, I'm sorry to say, not everybody felt that way, did they? I mean to say, in the end, someone told that fella somethin'.

I have my ideas, 'n' I know Julia, she has her ideas, but I think that's about as far as I'm prepared to go right now.

Mary Amesbury sometimes came to my house with the baby for a cup of tea. And then I had her in the house on Christmas Eve. She fainted on the common on Christmas Eve.

I was on my porch, and I saw it happen. I had been thinking of walking over to Mary. I specifically wanted to make sure that Mary had somewhere to go on Christmas Day. I didn't like to think of her alone in the cottage, with nowhere to go on Christmas. I didn't want to leave my porch just then, however, as it seemed to me the bonfire was burning too intensely.

Everett has explained to you about the bonfire? I know we've never had an accident, but still I like to be prepared. I stay on my porch with a few buckets of water just in case of stray sparks. I do this, too, on the Fourth of July, when we have fireworks on the common for the children. Everett is in charge of the fireworks too. I know he says he's got his fire truck behind the store, but all it takes is one stray spark. These houses are very old and entirely built of wood, and if one were to go, there'd be no stopping it.

As I say, I saw her fall. I thought at first that she had been pushed, but when I got there, her face was white. I do mean white; you could see this even in the dark. This does happen to a person. I've seen it before. They say that my face turned white when they told me about my husband's drowning, but that's neither here nor there.

Jack Strout, my husband's cousin, was bent over her when I got there, shouting for people to give her air. Elna Coffin already had the baby out of the sling. The baby had been scared. That was all. You could see she was all right. And when I got the baby inside the house, I undressed her and checked her all over. Jack helped me get Mary to her feet. You couldn't leave a body on that cold ground. She would get pneumonia or worse. And as we got her up, she came to. I have salts in my house, and I think I might have told someone to go for them, but they weren't necessary. She came to right away. She was terribly embarrassed and kept asking me about the baby. She was badly shaken. There might have been an injury to the baby if she'd fallen the wrong way.

I took her into the house and tried to get some brandy into her and some hot tea, and I didn't want to let her leave until she'd had a meal, but she was in shock then and couldn't eat much. I thought she might have fainted because of malnutrition, that she wasn't taking care of herself, but she said no. She'd just gotten dizzy, she said, and I had an idea that the fighting had upset her.

Yes, if you want a reason, that's it. The fighting had upset her. Possibly it had triggered some unpleasant memories for her. That would be my guess. She didn't say much, and I didn't like to pry.

She'd taken it to heart, if you understand my meaning.

I offered to drive her home, but she said no, that she would be all right. She was quite insistent. She thanked me for the invitation to come to dinner the next day, but she said she didn't feel comfortable yet in front of other people, and she thought she would probably not come. But she did say that she had to make a phone call, and she asked if it would be all right if she came by the next day to use the phone, since the A&P would be closed on Christmas. I got the idea that she wouldn't want to be there when Jack and Rebecca and the children were there, so I told her to come by about noon. The others weren't due until three or so.

Yes, she did come to make the call.

*   *   *

She made the phone call in private, so I don't know who she called or what she said, and I'm not sure it's any of our business, anyway. But she did give me four dollars for the call. I wouldn't take the four dollars, so we settled on two.

I didn't see Mary for some time after that. I was very busy with whatnot, and after Christmas I always like to rest a bit, so it was nearly two weeks before I was able to get over to the cottage.

I mention this only because it took me somewhat longer than it might have to realize what was going on.

Mary Amesbury

I fainted on the common. I had never fainted before. It happened. It just happened.

I recognized a man's face over mine. His eyes were old, and his face was weathered. He was telling me that the baby was OK, and asking if I could stand. Then I saw Julia and remembered Caroline. Where was Caroline? I asked, looking frantically around. A woman next to me showed me Caroline but wouldn't give her to me. Caroline was fine, they kept saying.

I went inside with Julia and the baby. I felt the man's hands at my side, and then he was gone. I drank the brandy Julia gave me, but I had trouble eating the food. I couldn't tell her of what I had seen, of the images that had confused me. I was aware only that I had caused a scene and that people had been buzzing around me. I was aware, too, of how lucky I had been. When I thought of what might have happened to Caroline . . .

I don't remember Christmas Day at all. There is nothing about the day I remember. My mother says that I called her at midday and told her that Harrold and Caroline and I were just sitting down to Christmas dinner, but I don't remember any of it.

I did not sleep that night or the next.

I got your letter this morning. Yes, I understand about September and the timing of the article, and I will hurry with the next batch of notes.

I write all night now. I seldom sleep. My cellmate and I are a perfect pair. The more I am awake, the more she sleeps, as if to redress the deficit.

I sometimes wonder about your life. I have written you so much about myself, and yet I know almost nothing about you. I think about that imbalance, wonder what you will do with all these pages that I have sent you.

Several days after Christmas, a thaw, as predicted, warmed the coast. And with the thaw came the fog. One morning I awoke knowing something was amiss. I hadn't heard the motor on the lane. I went to the window but could not see out. I went downstairs and opened the bathroom window and watched the fog spill in over the windowsill.

I stood in the kitchen. I heard the foghorns then, one to the north, one to the south, slightly out of sync, one a low mournful note, the other slightly higher, speaking to each other across a vast expanse of wet gray air and water. In

between the foghorns you could hear a gentle lapping of the water.

We had six days of fog, off and on. On two or
three mornings during the thaw, I woke and there
wasn't any fog. And then, in the late morning,
while I was feeding the baby or washing the
dishes, the fog drifted in with stealth, blotting out
the colors, then the shapes, then the sun. First
there would be puffs of fog blowing across the
bar, and soon the island would be gone. That was
it—gone just like that. It didn't exist.

The green-and-white lobster boat did not go out
on the first day of the thaw, or the second, but I
heard the truck on the third morning. It was a
day on which the fog had not come in yet, and
I, not understanding the pattern of the fog, felt
buoyant at the sight of the islands becoming visible in the distance at daybreak. When I saw how
my own spirits had lifted with the return of the
sun—and we had only had two days of continu-
ous fog—I began to understand better the depression Willis had described, the depression that
sometimes settled upon the women of the town.
I wondered why it was that Willis had mentioned
only the women becoming depressed in the winter. Did the men not mind the days of grayness
too? Or was it easier for them because they were
able to meet the grayness as a challenge when
they went out on the water?

Caroline seemed to catch my mood and was
unusually contented and cheerful that morning.
She had been practicing balancing on all fours for

a couple of weeks now and had learned how to pitch herself forward. Crawling, I could see, as I watched her from the kitchen table, was imminent. But I had no impatience for anything. With Christmas behind me and no need to go anywhere or to do anything, I was becoming more and more content to allow the days to dictate themselves to me.

I was reading, and Caroline was napping upstairs, when the fog came back. First there were wisps, ethereal and transitory, and then the fog became a shroud, blanketing everything. The light dimmed so that it seemed like dusk when it was only midday. I had to turn on a light to read. With the fog, the room turned chill as well, or perhaps it only seemed that way, with the sun gone. I went to the window. I could not even see the fish house now, although I could make out the barest hint of the back of a red pickup truck. The end of the point had disappeared entirely.

There was a knock on the door.

Willis came in like a figure emerging from the sea. The fog seemed to cling to him in the form of billions of droplets of moisture—on his denim jacket, on his mustache, on his hair. He carried a mug of coffee.

"Brought my own this time," he said, shutting the door behind him.

I was glad I had gotten dressed early.

"Socked in," he said.

"I thought the fog was over," I said.

There was a recording of a string quartet playing on the radio. The elegiac music seemed to underscore the view outside my window.

He made a disparaging sound, the sort of sound you make when the other person has just said something incredibly naive.

"No way. We'll have fog for days yet. Hey, Red, better get used to it. Bother you?"

"No," I said, lying. "Not at all."

"Well, that's good." He took a seat at the kitchen table. He looked at my face.

"Jack's out," he said.

"Oh," I said.

"Probably thought he could beat the fog back."

"Oh."

"Wouldn't catch me out on a day like this."

"No."

"So what you goin' to do all day?"

"Same thing I do every day," I said. "Take care of the baby."

"You don't miss it?"

"Miss what?"

"Your old life. Where you come from."

"No," I said.

"Musta been pretty bad," he said. "Your old man."

I said nothing.

"Syracuse, huh?"

I nodded.

"Nice place, Syracuse?"

I shrugged. "I like it better here," I said.

"You're lookin' better," he said.

"Thank you."

He sighed.

"So OK, Red, I'll be off now. Goin' home for lunch. I'm supposed to start drivin' for a haulage company next week. I hate doin' it, but we got to have the money. You need anything?"

He asked me this every day.

"No," I said.

Caroline began to cry. I was glad.

"Hope I didn't wake her," he said.

I shook my head. He got up to leave. He walked to the door, opened it, and hesitated. The fog blew in around him.

"Keep your eyes peeled for Jack," he said, and smiled.

The green-and-white lobster boat did not come back at two o'clock, as was its custom. I thought that probably the fog would delay it some, so I wasn't exactly worried. It was merely that I was alert to the fact that it had not returned. As I have said, it was a kind of punctuation to my day to see the boat emerging from behind the island, and without it the day felt incomplete, like a sentence with no ending.

I was knitting a second sweater for Caroline, and I was halfway through the back piece. Caroline was in bed for her afternoon nap. I picked up the knitting, with the radio on in the background.

It's odd, now that I think of it, that I didn't write. Or perhaps not odd at all. To write would have required remembering.

The boat did not come back by three o'clock

or by four. I had become attuned to all sounds emanating from the water or the point, and I went to the window frequently to peer out into the grayness. By four, it had grown dark, and all of the trucks but one were gone. Indeed, when it was foggy, night fell early on the point. I carried Caroline, or I nursed her. I made myself a cup of tea. I listened to the news on the radio. Eventually I made myself some supper. At six, the darkness outside was impenetrable. I began to wonder if I oughtn't to walk up to the blue Cape and alert someone that the green-and-white lobster boat wasn't back yet. Was this my responsibility? I wondered. Who else would know that he hadn't returned? His wife and his daughter? Would they resent my alarm, my interference? Was this natural, not to come back from time to time? And what if he had decided to moor his boat at the town wharf? He had mentioned that when the weather was bad, he took his boat into town. Perhaps he had done that earlier, knowing of the fog to come, and I had waited all day for the boat's return for nothing. If I raised an alarm then, I would simply look foolish, as naive as Willis had indicated, and I would only draw even more attention to myself.

At six-thirty, I bundled Caroline into her snow-suit and into the sling and took us both for a walk. I could no longer bear it in the cottage. I didn't care that I wouldn't be able to see much of anything. I had to have some fresh air.

I made my way gingerly along the spit. I felt I knew the way well enough to walk without any danger to myself or the baby. I would feel the gravel underfoot, or the grasses, or the sand, and would be able to navigate with my feet.

The air was drenching. You felt it soak you through almost at once. I kept Caroline close to me. I could feel the pebbled beach under my sneakers. I hadn't walked fifty feet when I turned to look back at where I had come from. Already the cottage was gone. The lights burning in the living room were extinguished. I could see only about two or three feet ahead of my feet along the ground. That was it. The sensation was eerie and otherworldly. I don't think I was frightened, exactly, but it was a feeling I shall never forget. The world had disappeared entirely. There was only my baby and myself. I could hear, from time to time, sounds from the world I had come from— the foghorns, an occasional car along the road at the end of the lane, and a strange squealing overhead, like that of bats—but in that darkness you could not really believe in the world. Perhaps I *was* frightened, but I was also exhilarated. The anonymity, the privacy, the safety—it was perfect. No one, no one, could ever get to us now: not Harrold, not Willis, not even Julia or my mother, well-meaning though they might be. It was as I had imagined it in my dreams: my baby and myself, protected and enshrouded.

I heard the motor then. I knew its idiosyncrasies by heart. It grew louder; louder still; then it stopped. I wondered how he had found the mooring. I heard the slap of the dinghy, the sounds of the return ritual. Perhaps I walked in the direction of those sounds. Perhaps my feet knew the way better than I had imagined.

I wonder now, and I have often wondered this: whether things would have developed as they did if we had not come upon each other in the fog, if we had not had that perfect sense of isolation, of the world around us vanished.

He appeared out of the dark mist, as if emerging in a dream, and I must have too. It occurred to me that he'd be more startled to come upon me than I him, and so I spoke at once.

"You're back," I said.

I thought my voice sounded casual, cheerful.

He *was* startled. He'd been walking from the dinghy to the truck, but he stopped. He had two buckets, one in each hand. I could hear the lobsters inside those buckets more than I could see them.

He put the buckets down.

"Are you all right?" he asked.

"Yes," I said. "I'm fine."

"What are you doing out here?"

"I was just taking a walk. I'd been feeling cooped up."

He looked at my face, then at the baby in the sling.

"You shouldn't be out here," he said. "This fog is nasty today. You could lose your way."

"I don't see how," I said, but my voice lacked conviction.

"I've lived here all my life. I know the coastline and the water as well as I know my own kids. But in the fog, I'm a stranger. You don't trust anything in the fog. Nothing."

"Why did you go out, then?" I asked.

He looked out toward the water. "I don't know. I thought I'd beat it back. But I got caught the other side of Swale's. Took me all day to creep back in. Foolish. It was a foolish thing to do."

His voice was low, and he spoke matter-of-factly, without much emotion, but I understood that he sometimes took risks too. That he had been foolish was merely a statement of fact, not cause for much remorse. Beyond his voice, you could hear the foghorns.

"Your wife will be worried," I said.

"I've been on to her on the CB. She knows I'm in."

He looked at me as if he was thinking.

"You come with me to the truck, let me put these in, and then I'll walk you to the cottage."

"I'll be—" I started to say.

"I couldn't leave you out here without seeing you were safely back," he said, and picked up the two buckets as if there were nothing more to discuss.

I walked a little ways behind him. He had long sloping shoulders beneath the yellow slicker. His hair was covered with mist, and his slicker was wet. He wore tall waders that came up high over his knees, over his jeans. He had large hands with long fingers. I was looking at his hands gripping the handles of the buckets.

At the truck, he slid the buckets onto the bed.

"Well, then," he said.

He turned, and we walked in the direction of the house. He seemed to know better where to walk than I, and so I followed his lead, again a few steps behind him. He'd been right; I realized it at once. The fog was disorienting. I'd have gone in a different direction, south along the coast. I'd have missed the house at first, but I did think I would probably have found it after a few tries.

The cottage loomed out of the mist. First there was the glow of light from the living room, then the outline of the house itself. The light inside the rooms looked warm, inviting.

He walked me up the slope to the door. I had my hand on the latch. I felt like a schoolgirl who'd been seen home by a teacher who was too shy for conversation.

"Thank you," I said.

He looked at me. "I wouldn't say no to a cup of tea," he said.

His voice was so low I wasn't sure I had heard him right. "Would you like a cup of tea?" I asked.

"Thank you," he said. "I've got a chill on from the damp."

"Will your family . . . ?"

"They know I'm in. They won't be worried now."

I opened the door, and we both walked into

the cottage. I went directly to the stove and got the kettle, filled it, and lit the burner.

"Keep your eye on the kettle," I said. "I have to go upstairs and put Caroline to bed."

In the living room, I wriggled out of my coat and removed Caroline from the sling. I carried her upstairs, put her into her pajamas, and nursed her on the bed. After a time, I could hear the kettle whistling, then the sounds of cups and saucers being fetched from the cupboard. I heard him at the sink, washing his hands. The refrigerator was opened and closed. I heard him rummaging through the silverware drawer.

When I came downstairs, he was sitting at the table. The slicker was on a hook on the back of the door and was dripping water onto the linoleum. He had removed his waders and was in his stocking feet. I could smell the sea in the room, from the slicker or the waders. I watched him for a minute from behind, and if he knew I was standing there, he gave no indication. His back was very long, so long that his sweater rode up over the waist of his jeans. But his back was broad, and he was not as slope-shouldered as he'd appeared in the slicker. He sipped his tea and did not turn around. At the place at right angles to his own there was a cup of tea for me. He'd let it steep, taken out the tea bag. He'd put milk and sugar on the table.

I sat down. I looked up at him. I had never seen his face in bright light. He was still, and his eyes moved slowly. I was again struck by the deep grooves at the sides of his mouth. His face had color, was permanently weathered. He looked at me, but we didn't speak.

"It's some warmth," he said finally.

"Did you get many lobsters today?" I asked.

"I was having some luck before the fog," he said. "But all told, it wasn't much. Doesn't matter, though."

"Why?"

"Whatever you get this time of year you're grateful for."

"Why do you do it? Go out when no one else does?"

He made a self-deprecating sound. "Because no one else does, I suppose. No, I like it out there. I get restless. . . ."

"It seems dangerous to me," I said. "It seems I'm always hearing about men drowning."

"Well, you could. . . ."

"If you're not careful?"

"Well, even if you're careful. There's things you can't control. Not like today. I should have been smarter today. But you can't always control a sudden blow, or engine failure. . . ."

"What do you do then?"

"You try to get back the best way you can. You try not to make any mistakes." He leaned his weight on one elbow, turned slightly toward me.

"You've been all right, then," he said. "Since Christmas Eve, I mean."

"Oh. Yes. Thank you. It was awful, fainting

like that. I've never fainted. I don't know what came over me."

"Just a bunch of kids protesting the war," he said. "My son probably would have been in it too, except he was home with . . . my wife. You looked shocky. Like you were in shock."

"Oh," I said, looking down. "Did I?"

"What happened to you?" he asked quietly. "Why are you here?"

The question was so sudden, I felt I had been stung. Perhaps it was the quiet of his voice, or the way I had come upon him in the fog, or the way the simplicity of his question required a truthful answer. I put a hand up to my mouth. My lips were pressed together. To my horror, my eyes filled, as if I had indeed been stung. I couldn't speak. I was afraid to blink. I was afraid to move. In all of the days since I had left the apartment in New York City, I had not cried. Not once. I had been too numb to cry, or too careful.

He reached up and took the hand away from my mouth and put it on the table. He held my hand on the oilcloth. He didn't say a word. His eyes were gray. He didn't look away from me.

"I was married to a man who beat me," I said after a time. I let out a long breath of air after I had said it.

It sounded appalling, unreal, in the cottage.

"You left him," he said.

I nodded.

"Recently. You've run away."

"Yes."

"Does he know where you are?"

I shook my head. "I don't think so," I said. "If he did, he'd come and get me; I'm sure of that."

"You're afraid of him."

"Yes."

"He did that to you?"

He made a movement with his head to indicate my face. I knew the bruises were healing, were yellowish or light brown rather than purple or blue, but they were still visible.

I nodded.

"What do you think the chances are that he'll find you?" he asked.

I thought for a minute.

"Fairly good," I said. "It's what he does, in a way. Investigates things. He knows how to find out things."

"And what do you think will happen to you when he finds you?"

I looked at the place where he was holding my hand. His hand hadn't moved; it was firm on mine.

"I think he'll kill me," I said simply. "I think he'll kill me because he won't be able to control himself."

"Have you gone to the police?" he asked.

"I don't think I can go to the police," I said.

"Why not?"

"Because I've stolen his child."

"But you had to do that, to save yourself."

"That's not how it will appear. He's very clever."

He, too, looked down at where he was holding my hand. He began then to stroke my arm from the wrist to the elbow. I had a sweater on, and the sleeves were pushed up over my elbows, so he was stroking my skin, slowly and softly.

"You have a wife," I said.

He nodded. "My wife isn't—" He stopped.

I waited.

"She's sick," he said finally. "She has a chronic illness. We're together, but we don't have what you would call . . ."

"A marriage."

"No."

He was stroking my arm. I might have pulled it away, but I couldn't. I couldn't move. It had been so long since anyone had touched me this gently, this kindly, that I was nearly paralyzed with gratitude.

"We haven't . . . been together," he said, "for years."

"You haven't even told me your name," I said, "although I know it."

"It's Jack," he said.

"My real name is Maureen," I said. "Maureen English. But I've become Mary. I've taken it on. I'll stay Mary."

"Your daughter's name is Caroline," he said.

"Yes."

"That's her real name?"

"Yes," I said. "I couldn't call her something she wasn't."

He smiled. He nodded.

"I can't do this," I said. "I'm no good at this anymore."

But even though I said this, I did not pull my arm away. The stroking of his fingers was soothing and rhythmical, like a warm wave washing over me, and all I knew was that I didn't want it to stop.

"I'm afraid," I said.

"I know."

"You're old enough to be my father," I said. It was something I'd been thinking—just that minute or for days?—and I thought it ought to be said, soon, to get it over with.

"Not really," he said. "Well, technically maybe. I'm forty-three."

"I'm twenty-six."

He nodded, as if he'd already guessed my age, give or take a year or two.

Outside, the foghorns were relentless—insistent and scolding.

He took his hand away and stood up with his teacup. He took his teacup to the sink.

"I'm going to go now," he said. He walked to the door, where his slicker was hanging. "I've been gone long enough. I can't leave my wife alone too long."

I stood up. I didn't say anything.

"But I'll be back," he said. "I can't say when. . . ."

I nodded.

"You shouldn't be afraid of this," he said.

*　　*　　*

I woke when I heard the motor on the lane. There was just a smear of gray outside the windows, but I could see the tops of the trees. The fog had not come yet. I heard the motor stop, but it was not at the end of the point; it was below my cottage.

I threw back the covers and ran down the stairs to the kitchen. Harrold *can't* have found me yet, I was praying. My heart was drumming in my chest.

Then, through the window on the door, I could see just a glimmer of a yellow slicker.

I unlocked the door.

Jack came in and put his arms around me.

For a minute, I couldn't speak.

Then I said: "You smell like the sea."

"I think it's permanent," he said.

Later, before the sun had fully risen, we left my bed and returned to the kitchen. He had carried his clothes with him, and dressed standing on the linoleum floor. He showed no self-consciousness when he dressed, even though he knew I was watching him.

I had put on my nightgown and my sweater in the bedroom. I made us a breakfast of coffee and cold cereal. We did not speak while he dressed, and he lit a cigarette and smoked at the table while I made the coffee. I brought the bowls of cereal to the table.

"I usually make a breakfast before I leave the house, but I couldn't eat this morning," he said, putting out his cigarette on an ashtray I'd given him.

I smiled.

"Couldn't sleep, either," he said, and smiled back at me.

I wanted to climb upstairs to the bed and curl up against his chest and go to sleep with him, the blankets pulled up high over our heads.

"When did you decide to come?" I asked.

"Sometime in the middle of the night. As soon as I decided it, I wanted to get up right then and there and come, but I couldn't. . . ."

I nodded. I knew he meant his wife.

"Do you mind having to get up so early for your work?" I asked.

"It's all right," he said. "You get used to it. It suits me."

"Willis said you went to college and had to come back."

He snorted. "Willis," he said.

I watched him as he ate his cereal.

"I did," he said finally. "I was in my junior year; my father broke his arms on his boat. I had to come back to take it over."

He didn't elaborate further.

"Were you disappointed?" I asked. "Disappointed you couldn't finish school?"

At first he didn't answer.

"I might have been, for a time," he said slowly, not looking at me. "But then you settle in, have your house, your work, your kids. It's hard to regret the things you've done that have led to having your kids."

I looked at him. I knew what he meant. Even

though my own marriage had become unspeakable, I could not now imagine a life without Caroline.

Just then the sun broke over the horizon line, flooding the room with a bright salmon light. Jack's face, in the sudden fire, was aglow. I thought his face was beautiful then, the most beautiful face I had ever seen, even though I hated the sun, for I knew it meant he would have to leave. I could see it in his gestures, in the sudden tensing of his muscles, in the way he pulled back from the table.

He stood up, walked to the back door to get his slicker. He put the oilskin under one arm, came to stand behind my chair. With his free hand, he lifted the hair from the back of my neck and kissed me there.

"I can't give you much," he said.

I could feel his breath on my skin.

He left before the other trucks had come to the point. He drove his own truck down to his dinghy. He went out that day in the green-and-white lobster boat but came back before the fog had settled in. As it happened, when he returned, I was walking on the point with Caroline, and though he waved to us from the truck—a wave that would be construed by the men who were in the fish house as merely a friendly gesture—we did not speak. Later he took to parking his truck at his dinghy and walking back to the cottage, staying until the sun had risen. There was an understanding between us, though unspoken, that no one should know about his visits. There were his wife and children to think of.

He came every morning at daybreak. There would be the motor on the lane and then his footsteps on the stairs. I kept the kitchen door unlocked. I'd be sleeping when he came, and it sometimes seemed to me that he would enter into my dreams. It would be dark in the room, with just a tease of light, and I would see the shape of him standing at the foot of the bed, or sitting on its edge as he bent to remove his shoes. And when I rolled toward him, in the bed that I had warmed all night, it was as if our coming together were already one of the rhythms of the point, as natural and as necessary as the gulls who woke and called and foraged for food, or as the light that would be lavender or pink on the water when he left me.

After the first morning, I had moved Caroline to the downstairs bedroom. It was hard for me to separate us in that way, but I knew that the time had come for me to do this. The walls were thin in the cottage, and I could hear her easily from my bed when she cried.

Do you want the details? There are moments I will never give away for any purpose—memories, words, and visions that I hoard and savor. But I can tell you this much. He never asked from me more than I could give, and he was careful, as though I hurt all over. Sometimes he would hold me; that would be enough. At other times, I offered what I had.

On the third day, or the fourth, I waited until the sun had almost risen, so that there was light in the room. I got out of the bed and stood in front of him. I let him look at me. I made him look at me. I knew that I was damaged in some places, ugly in others, but I didn't mind his eyes. I felt no shame in myself, nor any sense of judgment from him. I didn't want him to say that I was beautiful; that wasn't what I hoped for. I think I wanted only to have it behind me, to have it done. But then he did a funny thing. He got out of his side of the bed. There was a line across his abdomen from a ruptured appendix, which he pointed out. He stood on one foot and showed me a dent from a rope burn on his shin. His hands had many nicks, he said, displaying them, and I saw a mark, like something made with jagged scissors, on his upper arm. He'd been a boy, he said, pegging lobsters for his father, and he'd gotten stung by a bee, lost control of the lobster, and it had clawed him. I began to laugh.

"All right," I said, and crawled back into bed.

"They're battle scars, that's all," he said, touching this one and then that one and then that one on my body.

We were intimate but not possessive. Oddly, we never said we loved each other, although I was certain that this was a form of love, one I had never thought to have. I think it was simply that although we trusted each other, we no longer trusted the word. I imagined that he, like myself, had once told his wife that he loved her—and had been perplexed and dismayed when certainty had become uncertain, then had turned to disappointment.

There was so much about each other that we didn't know, could never know. His life on the water had shaped him, formed him, as had my life in the city and with my mother. He would never know about deadlines and the pressure of putting words and sentences together in offices, just as I would never know what it was to be lost on the water in the fog and to have to rely on wits and instinct to make it back to shore alive. I did not know much about his marriage, either. By tacit agreement, he did not talk about his wife, and I asked few, if any, questions. It was an area of old sadness for him, around which I trod carefully, just as he was reticent to probe too deeply into the madness that had been my marriage. Although once he did speak up. I had said to him that I thought I had brought the abuse upon myself because I had been a catalyst for my husband's anger. Jack held me by the wrist and made me look at him. I was not responsible for the beatings, he said clearly. Only the man who hit me was responsible. Did I understand that?

One morning when we were in the bed together, I thought I heard a cry. I stiffened, to listen, and I felt Jack pull away from me, listening too.

It was Caroline, who seemed to be crying in

pain. I thought to myself: I must go to her—but I was strangely paralyzed, thrust backward in time to another bed, another set of cries. For a minute, I almost couldn't breathe, and there must have been on my face an expression of alarm, for Jack said, pulling even farther back and looking quickly at my face, "What's wrong? Are you OK?"

"It's Caroline," I whispered.

"I know," he said. "Go to her. Or do you want me to?"

The question snapped me back to the present moment. I flung back the covers and threw on my nightgown. I ran down the stairs to her bedroom. She was on her back, in her crib, her knees raised. She was indeed crying in pain. I picked her up and began to walk with her around the well-worn path through the kitchen, the living room, and her bedroom, but even the walking this time could not quiet her. Jack came down the stairs in his shorts. His hair was mussed, and he was barefoot—the floorboards were freezing.

"Give her to me a minute," he said on my second pass.

I handed her to him, and she looked at him curiously before she started again to cry. He walked with her to the sofa under the window and placed her, stomach down, on his knees, which were slightly apart. Then he began to make an up-and-down motion with his knees—in effect massaging her under her stomach. Almost immediately, she stopped crying.

"I don't know why it works," he said, looking pleased with himself, "but it does. I had to do this with my daughter all the time when she was a baby. It moves the gas bubbles up, I guess, or down. I can't remember now who taught it to me."

I stood across the room watching him with Caroline. They were a funny sight—Jack in his shorts, his eyes puffy, his hair flattened, Caroline stretched out on the tops of his long legs, looking up at me as if to say, *Now what.* It was so cold in the room, I'd begun to shiver. I went to him and picked up Caroline. She burrowed into my shoulder as if she wanted to go back to sleep.

"You're good with children," I said. "I saw you with your daughter at the bonfire."

"Good with children, lousy with wives," he said, getting up from the couch.

"You've had more than one?"

"One's enough." He crossed his arms over his chest and rubbed them to warm them.

"Is your marriage really so bad?" I asked, swaying lightly from side to side with Caroline.

He shrugged. "You make a mistake, you lie with it," he said.

It was an interesting choice of words.

"Why don't you leave?" I asked.

"I can't leave," he said. "It's not a possibility."

There was an air of finality to this pronouncement, and as if to underscore that finality he turned to look out the window, out to the horizon, where he saw the same thing I did—a crimson sliver of sun breaking over the water.

I was afraid that he had misunderstood me, and so I said, "I don't want you to leave; that's not what I meant."

He turned back to me.

"I know," he said.

We stood there looking at each other, and it seems to me now, remembering that moment, we spoke volumes to each other.

"I'd better go now," he said finally.

I went over to him and touched him lightly on the side of his arm, stroking his arm, as he had once stroked mine. It was all I could think of to do.

I did not know much about his life on the water, although one day near the end, on a Sunday, when the men did not come to the point, he took me out on his boat. When he first suggested the trip, I immediately thought of Caroline, but he said we would take her with us, in the sling if I liked. He used to take his own babies out onto the water, he said. Babies almost always fell asleep at once, from the rocking of the boat or from the vibrations of the motor. Indeed, when the men's wives had babies that were colicky, he said, the women would often beg to come aboard the boats with their babies for a day's fishing, just to get some rest.

I woke Caroline early, and we were ready for him when he came. The air was cold but still, and I could see all the way out to the lighthouse. The water's surface was unruffled, but I knew that by midmorning, the breezes would make it rougher. He untied the dinghy from the ring, slid it down to the water's edge.

"Get in the punt," he said, "at the bow."

The dinghy was pretty beat; even I could see that. He said that he'd been meaning to replace it all year, but somehow he hadn't gotten to it yet.

"We'll go slowly," he said.

I sat in the bow with the baby, as he had told me to do. He knelt in the stern rather than stand, so that he would not inadvertently tip us. When he got in, our combined weight seemed almost too much for the dinghy, and when I looked over the side, I could see we were riding pretty low to the water. I didn't move as he sculled us out to the channel and the boat, a distance of perhaps a hundred and fifty feet. Despite the short distance, the journey made me anxious. I wished I had a life vest, although I was remembering how Julia had said her husband went from the cold before he went from the drowning. I was, in fact, so frightened at one point that I surreptitiously dipped my hand into the icy water and made the sign of the cross on Caroline's forehead—a gesture that astonishes me now, when I think of it. I had not had Caroline baptized, and I could not bear the thought of being separated from her for all eternity—even though, if you were to ask me now, in this room, I would have to tell you that I don't believe in eternity.

As Jack sculled, I had a clear view of the point,

seen from the eastern end, and of my cottage. From the water, the cottage had even more of a sense of isolation than it did when you were on land. Surrounding it, in both directions for as far as the eye could see, there was only low-lying brush and coastline.

Jack managed somehow to get us all into the larger boat, though I was ungainly with the baby strapped to my middle and in the end had to be hoisted over. He told me to sit on a box in the cockpit while he got us under way. I watched him open the pilothouse, lift the lid off an engine box, and start the engine. He foraged forward and handed a life vest back to me. It was a regulation Coast Guard type, but I could see that it hadn't been used much. I put it on, over my coat, and when he looked back at me, he shook his head, raised his eyebrows, and smiled. Then we were off.

The port side of the boat was enclosed, with the foul-weather gear hanging from a hook. The starboard side was open. The wheel was there and a kind of hydraulic setup for pulling the pots. Above the wheel was a CB radio, but he didn't use it that day. There were other bits of equipment near and around the wheel—a depth sounder, he explained, and fuel gauges. In the cockpit beside me there was a bait barrel. He stood at the wheel and saw us around the island. Then he gestured for me to come up beside him.

I hung on to a center pole and watched the land recede behind the boat. It was hard to hear each other over the engine, so we didn't talk much. He shouted that he would take her straight out to the grounds, pick up twenty traps he'd set a few days before. At the end of the week, he said, he'd have the boat hauled. After he'd picked up his pots, he added, he'd take us over to Swale's Island. It was beautiful, he said. It had the prettiest beach in eastern Maine.

As soon as the engine started, Caroline fell asleep, and she did not wake up until we stopped the boat in the natural harbor of Swale's. The air was frigid, but if I stood close to Jack, inside the well of the pilothouse, I did not feel the wind. I thought that Caroline was probably warm enough, though I did not like to think of all the possible things that could go wrong and how quickly a person could die out there.

Jack was relaxed and loose and amused, smiling at me in a way he seldom did at the cottage. Perhaps he was enjoying the incongruity of myself and the baby on his boat, or perhaps he was just continually tickled by the way I looked with the baby at my front and the life vest tied around me. There were few boats on the water. Indeed, once we had put the coastline behind us, and there were only islands, I had a sense of being very far away. At first, I had been able to see the village of St. Hilaire from the water, but now that was gone, even the white steeple of the church. The sun was up, but the shore was just a hazy blue.

After about forty-five minutes, we reached a point where he cut the engine, idled the boat. He took the foul-weather gear from its hook, put on only the pants. He already had on his yellow slicker over his sweater. He wore the bib of the pants over the jacket, like an apron. I asked him how he knew where he was. He pointed to a small cove in a nearby island, then to a rocky ledge. They seemed identical to all the small coves I'd seen, all the rocky ledges. He laughed. He said he had the depth sounder too. And then, of course, all around us were his buoys—red on the top and bottom, with a yellow band in between.

I watched as he hauled his pots. As each came up, he would remove the lobsters, band the claws with elastic, put the lobsters into one of the buckets that he had filled with water, throw back into the sea any detritus that had been in the lobster pot, and stack the pot on those he had already retrieved.

"Normally I'd rebait them, throw them back, but I'm hauling them for the winter," he said.

It was hard work, and it had a certain kind of ugliness to it too. I did not think it was romantic, the actual hauling of the pots, only cold and difficult. He wore long cotton gloves, but I thought his hands must be freezing. The water splashed up on his bib and around our feet.

When he was finished, the small cockpit was jammed with buckets and pots and buoys, and I had lost my seat on the box.

He turned the boat south then, toward Swale's Island, which he pointed out to me when it became visible. On the north side of the island, as we approached, I could see several large wooden houses and what looked like fields.

"It's privately owned," he said, "though we all use the beach on the other side in summer. It's where we take our families for a picnic or whatever."

At the mention of families, he looked away from me and busied himself at the wheel. He checked the depth sounder, looked westward toward shore. I knew that it had cost him to give me this time on a Sunday, and that there might not be any more Sundays. The boat we were on had his wife's name on it, and I was sometimes reminded of this, as when he would say—a common enough expression—"I'll just take her out to the grounds."

He took the boat in close to the western shore of the island, so that I could see the rocky ledges there or catch a glimpse of a seal. Then he negotiated the cut, and we were in the harbor—a crescent bordered by a nearly pure-white beach. It was a wild beach, undomesticated. The only way to get there was by boat. He cut the engine and threw an anchor overboard. The baby woke up.

"I've brought us a picnic," he said.

"I have to nurse the baby," I said. I had never nursed her in front of him. He cleared two seats facing each other in the cockpit. He helped me off with the life vest and extricated Caroline from the sling. As he held Caroline, he said to me to go forward and see if I could find an old beach towel he thought was there. It would make a kind of tent, he said, to shield Caroline from the breezes while she nursed.

I went forward into the small cabin. I supposed there was an order to it that Jack understood, but to me it looked chaotic. There was hardware and ropes, a canvas tarp and rags. I opened a door to a cabinet. It was the books that first caught my eye. There were half a dozen paperbacks. I remember a book of poetry by Yeats, Malamud's *The Fixer*. The books were worn, dog-eared, and some had water stains. Also inside were old charts, folded and refolded a hundred times. A flashlight, some flares, a flare gun. A bottle, a third full, of whiskey. I saw the towel, picked it up. Under it was another gun, a pistol. I picked the pistol up, held it in my hand, put it back. I returned to the cockpit with the towel.

"I found the towel," I called to him, emerging, stopping a second to watch him holding Caroline, "but I also found a gun."

"Oh," he said. He seemed unconcerned, as if I'd found a watch he'd misplaced and not a gun. "We all have them," he added. "We all keep a gun for poachers, to warn them off. I'll fire it from time to time to keep it from getting rusty, but that's all."

"It's loaded?" I asked.

"Wouldn't be much point in having it if I didn't keep it loaded. Anyway, no one's ever on board except me."

"I also found some books," I said. "Paperbacks. Do you read when you're out here?"

He looked startled for a moment, embarrassed.

"If I get the chance," he said. He laughed. "Well, sometimes I make the chance. It's peaceful out here."

I took the baby from him and sat down. I opened my coat and raised my sweater. I immediately felt the cold air on my bare skin. He shook out the towel and placed it over my shoulder to shield Caroline's face from the cold. He went forward into the cabin and returned with the bottle of whiskey. Then he sat down and began to unpack the picnic. Occasionally, such as at that moment, I would shut my eyes, for just a second, and let the smallest picture come into my mind of what my life might have been like if I had met Jack years ago and not Harrold, but I immediately shook these pictures away. It was treacherous ground—shifting shoals.

He had made bacon sandwiches and a thermos of coffee. It was all he had made, but he'd made lots, and I was ravenous. My God, you cannot imagine how good bacon sandwiches are when you are hungry. He had toasted the bread, and even though the sandwiches were cold, they were indescribably delicious. He poured a generous amount of whiskey into the coffee. It seemed to be the custom here—to lace your coffee or tea with spirits. He gave me my coffee in the cap of the thermos; he himself drank from the canister. Around us the sun was brilliant and doing its best to try to warm us. It reflected off the white beach and the water. He sat across from me; our knees were touching. I ate with one hand, held the baby with the other. The boat was rocking gently. I looked at his weathered face, the wrinkles, his gray eyes. He had the collar of a flannel shirt up high under the sweater. It was just the two of us and all that water and all that sand and all that sky.

"This is . . . ," I started to say, but I couldn't finish.

He looked at me.

He adjusted the towel on my shoulder.

He nodded and looked away.

Perhaps we talked while we sat there eating the sandwiches. We must have, because I have bits of information I might not otherwise have now. We tended not to talk much in the mornings, and he was reticent by nature, not used to sharing thoughts and feelings—or possibly he was just long out of practice. I thought that in this way we were alike, for I had learned to be guarded, too, in conversation. If you cannot talk about the thing that is at the center of your life—cannot let bits slip out for fear of revealing the entire story—you develop what might pass for a natural reticence, a habit of listening rather than of telling stories yourself. But that day, I think he did speak of his family: not of his wife and children, but of his father and his grandfather. They'd been lobstermen too, or at least his father had, he said. His grandfather had fished for cod, then had switched to lobster when the demand for it had begun to increase after World War II. His grandfather was dead now, and although his father was still alive, living just south of town with his wife, he could no longer fish. I don't remember exactly what words Jack used to describe his father's accident, but I understood it and the early retirement it necessitated to be a calamity of serious proportions.

Though I never met Jack's father, I did sometimes have an image of an older, smaller version of Jack, a man with withered arms, sitting in an armchair in the living room of a Maine Cape, looking out across the gulf.

When we had eaten all the sandwiches, Jack said that we ought to be heading in. He would drop me off at the point, then take the boat over to the wharf to wash her down and set his pots on the dock. Easier to pick them up there, he explained, than to ferry them in the dinghy.

We didn't speak on the voyage home—again the engine was too loud—but the ride was comfortable and strangely warm. We were going with the wind.

We rounded a pine-thick island, and I could just make out the point and my cottage.

"Damn!" he said.

I tried to see what had caught his attention, but his eyes on the water were sharper than my own. I squinted in the direction of the cottage. And then when we had drawn a little closer, I saw it. A red pickup truck at the shack.

"There's a truck at the fish house," I said.

"You know whose it is?"

"Yes."

"We can't turn around. . . ."

"No, we can't," I agreed.

"All right, then," he said. "Jesus Christ, what's he doing here on a Sunday?"

I knew, but I didn't say.

He brought the boat to the mooring, lowered me into the dinghy, and sculled us to the shore. By the time he had pulled the dinghy far enough up onto the sand so that I could step out, Willis had traversed the length of the beach.

"Jack."

"Willis."

The two men greeted each other, but Jack did not look up in Willis's direction. Willis was smoking a cigarette.

"Red."

I nodded, bent my head to the baby.

"You out for a spin or what?" he said to Jack.

"Hauling some pots."

"On a Sunday. Good for you. I always said you were a hard worker, Jack."

Jack pushed the dinghy back into the water, prepared to get in.

"And you took Red here along for the ride."

Jack looked up from the dinghy at me. "Yes," he said.

No excuses. No explanations.

"So what'd you think, Red? You like it or what?"

Willis had sunglasses on, as I did. I couldn't see his eyes, but I looked straight at the sunglasses.

"It was instructive," I said. "Very instructive."

Jack pushed himself away from the shore with the oar. I thought he was smiling.

"So long, then," he said.

"Thanks for the trip," I answered as casually as I could.

I was thinking: In a few hours, I will see him again.

Perhaps he was thinking that too.

Willis walked me back toward the cottage. He said, "I saw your car was here. I tried the door a coupla times, no answer. I got worried, thought maybe you'd had an accident or something, or fallen into a honeypot. Another half hour and I'd a gone for Everett."

"That would have been silly," I said.

"It's dangerous you goin' out on a boat in the winter with a baby. You got to think of the baby, you know."

"I think of the baby all the time," I said. "And don't worry about me. I can take care of myself."

We were at his truck by then. I was not going to invite him in, even if he asked, and I suppose he sensed that, because he did not ask.

"Is that a fact," he said, touching the baby on the cheek.

Willis Beale

Well, I suppose someone's goin' to have to tell you the whole story about Jack and Mary. I don't mean to say that this has any bearin' on the crime itself, I wouldn't want you to think that. I'm not sayin' she did it because of this, that's not what I'm sayin' 'tall, although maybe you got to think of that a little bit, but the truth is she didn't waste much time before she hooked up with Jack Strout.

Has anybody told you the whole story yet?

Not too much of this came out at the trial, because nobody who testified would give too many details. That is to say, it was mentioned, and Mary, she had to say, didn't she, but the prosecutor, he didn't really get into the details. But I think if you're goin' to do this article of yours, you ought to have all the facts, even though I don't want you sayin' it was me or anything that told you. This is—what do you call it—undercover information.

Well, OK, background information.

So long as you don't put my name with this. But the truth is, it didn't take her too long, if you

understand my meaning. I can't tell you for sure
when it began, but I can tell you this. By Christmas Eve, I had kind of an idea about the two of
them. Just call it an instinct. I got a nose for people, you know what I mean? I didn't actually see
them together until, oh, at least a week or more
later, but I just began to get this idea from
watchin' 'em. Now you think about that. She got
here on December 3. Christmas Eve was only
three weeks later. Is that a fast worker or what?

So you think about that for a while, and you
start to get a little bit of a different picture of Mary
Amesbury. You know, maybe she wasn't quite
the injured party she made herself out to be.
Maybe she went after the fellas in New York City
a little too often, and her husband had what you
would call a real case against her, you follow me.
I don't know, I'm thinkin' if I had a wife played
around a lot—hey, you know, what if the baby
wasn't even his?—well, that could turn a fella's
head around, and he might get a bit hot under
the collar.

All I'm sayin' is, it bears some thinkin' about,
that's all.

Now, Jack, he was your basic family man.
Never a hint of any funny business from either
him or Rebecca. And to tell you the truth, this
whole thing is a really sad story. When I think
about what happened . . .

So what I'm tryin' to tell you is, I don't think
Jack made the first move, you understand me? I
know Jack. He's as straight as a die. Loyal to his

wife, even with all his troubles. Never even looked at another woman, far as I know, and I'd probably know. So you tell me what happened. I mean, Mary Amesbury, she was a pretty good-lookin' woman, even with all what happened to her, and I suppose even Jack, I mean if a woman really goes after you, sometimes, well, we're all human, right, and maybe she was just too much for him. What I mean to say is, I just can't see Jack makin' the first move. He's not the type.

Yeah, I saw 'em together. Caught 'em red-handed, so to speak, although they weren't actually . . . you know. It was a Sunday afternoon, and I was over to the point to get some gear from the fish house, and I thought I'd just stop by, see if she was OK. You know I felt responsible for her a little bit, seein' as how I was practically the first person she met in town, and I noticed that her car was there, but she was nowhere to be seen. I started to get worried after a while, that she'd had an accident or something, and then I saw 'em comin' in. He took her out on the boat. On a Sunday, no less. So right then you knew it wasn't on the up and up. 'Cause how come he takes her out when he knows no one will be on the point? Right? So I go down to say hello, be friendly, and they're both lookin' guiltier than shit. All over their faces. And there she is with the baby, no less. I'd like to know what they did with the baby when they . . . you know. Anyway, that's none of my business, is it?

Fact is, he used to go there in the mornings,

afore he went out on his boat. It got to be kind of general knowledge around town, though whether it got to be general knowledge afore or after is hard to say now. I can't really remember. I knew, but of course I wouldn't a told anyone. Except possibly Jeannine. I might of told Jeannine. I was pretty disappointed in Mary Amesbury after that. I thought she was what she was, but she wasn't, if you follow me.

So, like I said, probably this is neither here nor there. I just thought you ought to have all the facts, that's all.

Mary Amesbury

That night I woke up to the sound of Caroline crying. The cries were high-pitched and insistent, and when I reached her room, she was on all fours in the crib, trying to pull herself up the bars. Her face was scrunched and reddened with pain. I reached for her, and I could feel at once that she was feverish. I put my hand on her forehead. She twisted away from me. I'd never felt such hot skin before.

Immediately, I went into the kitchen and crushed a tablet of baby aspirin. It dissolved imperfectly in the apple juice, and when I tried to give the juice to Caroline, she flung her head back and screamed, refusing the bottle. Not knowing what else to do, I walked with her around the familiar path, but the walking was useless. I tried to hold her close to my chest to comfort her. When I did so, however, she kept twisting her head away and then flopping her face from side to side against me. I wanted to stay calm, to think clearly, but this flopping alarmed me.

Jack came just before daybreak, as was his custom. I had Caroline on the orange mat in the bathroom. I had stripped her of her pajamas and diaper and was trying to give her a sponge bath with cool washcloths to bring the fever down. The touch of the washcloths must have been searing on her skin, however, for she shrieked even louder when I did this.

Jack stood at the door. He had his slicker on and his high boots.

"What's wrong?" he asked.

"She's hot, feverish. I can't make out what's wrong."

He crouched down to touch her face.

"Jesus," he said. "She's burning up."

I had been trying to convince myself that her fever wasn't all that serious, but when he said *Jesus*, I knew it was. "I was going to wait for the clinic in Machias to open," I said in a rush. "But I don't know. What do you think?"

He looked at his watch. "It's five-thirty now," he said. "There won't be anyone there till nine."

He stood up, unfolding his long body. His boots and slicker crinkled.

"I'll go up to LeBlanc's," he said. "Call the doctor on duty."

"You can't do that," I said, looking up at him. I was thinking that his going up to the blue Cape on my behalf would give him away, be too risky for him.

"I'll say I was on my way out to the boat when you came to the door and called to me and asked for help."

"They won't believe you," I said.

"I don't know," he said, "but I don't think you can afford to worry about that right now."

When he returned I was in the bathtub with Caroline. The water was dreary and cold and felt miserable even to me, but I couldn't think of anything else to do. Bringing the fever down was all that seemed to matter.

"Let's go," he said from the doorway. "The doctor's going to meet us there."

I looked at him questioningly. His eyes, his gray eyes, were focused and alert.

"Should you . . . ?" I started to ask.

He shook his head, as if to toss away my question. "I'm taking you. Get dressed."

I stood up and handed Caroline to him. He wrapped her in an orange towel. He held her while I went upstairs and dressed myself. Then I came downstairs and dressed the baby. Through all of this, she continued to scream, twisting her head from side to side, alarming even Jack, who I had thought was unflappable. Once, when I had her on her back and was trying to get her foot into the leg of her sleeping suit, she began to bat at the side of her face. I looked at him, but he wouldn't return my gaze. I abandoned the thought of dressing her then, simply wrapped her in a woolen blanket.

Jack held her as I climbed up into the cab of his truck. The sky was violet, and on the western horizon I could still see stars. There was no traffic on the road to speak of, but in the houses there were lights on in the bedrooms. The town of Machias was still and silent when we drove though it, as if it had been abandoned.

The doctor was at the clinic. He had turned on the light by the door. He came around a corner as we entered the waiting room, and I was surprised to see how young he was. He couldn't have been more than thirty, and he didn't look like a doctor. He wore blue jeans and a wrinkled blue work shirt, as if he had stepped into the clothes that had been lying on the floor by his bed. He ushered us into an examining room and asked me to unwrap the baby. As I did so, I told him of how she'd been shrieking and twisting her head, of how she'd batted at the side of her face.

He didn't take her temperature. He seemed not to need to do that. He examined her throat, then looked into each of her ears.

He stood up. He felt her forehead then. "Ear infections," he pronounced matter-of-factly. "Thought it might be that. She's got a couple of lulus."

He reached into a cabinet for a small bottle and put a drop of liquid into each ear. "This'll stop the pain for a bit," he said. "But we'll have to put her on antibiotic straightaway. Actually I'd like to give her an injection right now, if that's all right with you, and then you can get a prescription when the pharmacy opens up. Quite frankly, I don't really like this fever, and I think we probably want to get that down as soon as possible." He felt her forehead. "I'll take her temp, but my

guess is the fever's close to a hundred and five."
His voice was calm, but I understood that the
fever worried him.

The room went hollow then, airless, like the
inside of a bell jar. The floor sank perceptibly. I
put my hand out for the edge of the leather gurney. I tried to think, to remember. But what I
needed to remember was just beyond my grasp,
like a mystifying calculus problem that will not
yield up its secrets.

"Oh, no," I said quietly, almost inaudibly.

The doctor heard me, but he misunderstood
me. Jack looked puzzled too. Ear infections were
good news, weren't they? Compared to what it
might have been?

"She'll be all right," the doctor said quickly to
reassure me. And perhaps there was a note of
false heartiness in his voice. He removed a rectal
thermometer from a glass jar filled with liquid and
held Caroline's legs while he inserted it. She
twisted and wriggled in protest, but his grasp was
firm. "I wish I had a nickel for all the ear infections I see in a season, believe me," he said. "If
I give her an injection now, the fever will probably break before the day is out. By tomorrow,
she'll be her old self, though you'll have to continue the antibiotic for ten days."

I shook my head.

"What's wrong?" It was Jack. He was looking
at me oddly. In the harsh light of the examining
room, his roughened skin and the two deep
grooves at the sides of his mouth were pro-

nounced. I thought that my bruises, though nearly healed, must be prominent too. I wondered if Jack had been here before, if he had stood as he was standing now, with his wife where I was, with his own child on the gurney.

"She's allergic to one of the antibiotics," I said as calmly as I could, "and I don't know which one."

"Well, there's no difficulty there," the doctor said, extricating the thermometer. "Yup," he said. "One-oh-five on the nose. Don't want to fool around with this. I'll give her something for the fever too. Who treated her? I'll make a call. It must be on her chart."

Jack understood then. He shifted his weight, looked at me again.

"She was three months old," I said, more to myself than to the doctor or to Jack. "She had a fever, but her pediatrician couldn't figure out what was causing it. He gave her something, and I don't know what it was, but it made her break out in hives and swell up. So they gave her something else, but I don't know what that was, either. I'd say it was penicillin, but I'm not positive. They also gave her a sulfa drug, I think, and I just can't remember which was which."

There was a silence in the room.

"I'm sorry I can't remember," I said. "I wasn't very—"

"Well," the doctor said, interrupting me. He sounded impatient with my inability to grasp the ease of the solution. "It *is* important. An allergic reaction like that can be fatal the second time around. But it's not a problem we can't solve. As I said, if you can give me the name of where she was treated, I can call up her chart."

Jack's face was impassive. "Is there any drug you can give the baby that wouldn't be either of the ones Mary mentioned and that might be safe?" he asked.

The doctor looked at Jack, then at me. You could see on his face that he was beginning to understand.

"I'll make the call," I said quickly.

The doctor shook his head. "No," he said. "I think I have to. They probably wouldn't give you the information, and you might not understand it, anyway. And I don't think we want to lose any time."

I started to speak, then hesitated.

"There's a problem here, isn't there?" the doctor asked.

Caroline, whose pain was temporarily gone but who was wrung out from her fever, looked up at me from the gurney.

"No," I said quickly, and perhaps too loudly for such a small examining room. "No, there's no problem here."

I gave the name and address of Caroline's pediatrician in New York City. I even knew the phone number.

We left the clinic and walked to the black pickup truck parked out front. Jack carried Caroline. He said to me that it was a long shot, that my husband wouldn't have thought of the pediatrician, that the odds were a million to one against it. I, in turn, to reassure him, said that I agreed with him, the odds were a million to one.

But I didn't agree with him. I didn't at all.

Jack drove me back to the cottage with the baby. Dawn was breaking as we bumped and jostled down the lane, and already the ocean was turning a bluish mauve. The air was clean and crisp, as though washed through, and cold. It had been clear and frigid for three days, and I sensed that the thaw was over, that we would not have any more fog or moderate temperatures for some time now. Jack had said the day before that he would soon be hauling his boat.

He left me off at the cottage and drove back into Machias to wait for the drugstore to open so that he could fill the prescription for me. This would mean that he would be delayed going out onto the water and that he might be seen by the men in the fish house coming to my cottage with the medicine. I had said to him that I would go into town to get the prescription, but he wouldn't hear of it. I should be inside with Caroline, he said. He would go.

As it happened, the red pickup truck was at the fish house when Jack returned. He came to the door and gave me the package. He asked me how Caroline was. I told him that she seemed better, was sleeping now. I willed him to come in, and I sensed that he, too, wanted to step over the threshold, to close the door to the point behind him, for he held the door open with his shoulder and hunched forward as though poised on the brink of a decision.

"Come in," I said, knowing even as I said it that he would have to refuse. It was full daylight now, and I sensed that Willis was peering at us from the salted windows of the fish house. I expected him to emerge at any minute from the door.

"I can't," Jack said.

I reached my hand forward and tucked it inside the collar of his flannel shirt and his sweater. It was a gesture that could not be seen from the fish house. His skin was warm there. I was trembling from the cold and from pure longing. I saw on his face the same need I had. Beyond us the gulls twirled and looped in an early-morning feeding frenzy.

Time had become compressed—perhaps even more so since the events of the morning. I knew that Jack felt now as I did, that minutes together could not be wasted. When he hauled his boat in a few days, he would not be able to come to me any longer in the early mornings—not until the season began again in the spring. He couldn't come to me while he was working on his gear at the fish house; the others would see. And he couldn't leave his bed at four in the morning. He would have no boat to go to, which his wife would know. Did we have three mornings left or four?

"I have to go now," he said.

I withdrew my hand.

"You'll come tomorrow?" I asked.

"Yes," he said, and turned abruptly to jog down the small hill to the end of the point.

I nursed Caroline through the day and the night, dozing when she slept, just holding her when she was awake. The antibiotic had knocked her out, but she didn't seem to be in much pain, for which I was grateful, and her fever was abating as well. Toward evening, she recovered a bit more of her spirits, and we played together on the braided rug. I lay down on it and she crawled over me, then I'd capture her and whisk her through the air or lay her down beside me and tickle her. She giggled and laughed—deep belly laughs that made me want to squeeze her all the more.

Jack came just before daybreak. I was awake and waiting for him. His footsteps seemed urgent on the stairs. He was already shedding his yellow slicker as he opened the door to my bedroom. I rose in the bed to meet him, and he embraced me before he even had all his clothes off. His need was high-pitched and keen that morning, and we roiled in the bed like a churned-up sea. I felt in him something new—a frustration, the wanting of more than we could reasonably have. Afterwards, he rolled onto his back.

"I want to leave her," he said. "I want to come here and be with you."

I started to speak, but he stopped me.

"I can't leave her," he said. "Yesterday morning, when you gave the doctor the name and the number in that way you did, I thought for a just a minute that if you could risk so much, so could I. And all day I was trying to work it out, trying to figure a way I could leave her without harming her and come to you, but I couldn't. There just isn't any way to do it. Because it isn't a question of my risking anything for myself. I'd be risking her things—her family, her home, what little stability she has. And I can't do that to her. I don't have that right. She's too fragile, and this would just—"

I rolled over onto him and pulled the covers up to our shoulders. I put my hand over his mouth, laid my head on his chest. "Don't think about any of that," I said. "Let's just have this."

He wrapped his arms around me, held me close to his body.

"I'm sorry," he said.

There was a silence in the room.

"You know," he said after a time, "I don't want you to go, but maybe you should think about that, just to be on the safe side." His arms had stiffened against me. "Just to another town or something, somewhere a little further north maybe."

I had had this thought too, almost immediately, at the clinic in Machias, but I had rejected it even before it was fully formed. I couldn't leave the cottage now. I couldn't leave Jack. I didn't have the strength. I knew that.

"When does the season start up again?" I asked.

"April," he said. "But I could push it a little. Get her in mid-March."

"Do that," I said.

Later, when he was sitting at the kitchen table and I was making tea, I asked him what it was that he had studied in college, what he had thought he might do with himself after he graduated. It was still dark outside, and I could see our reflection in the windows: myself in my flannel nightgown and my cardigan sweater, my hair too long and loose over my shoulders; Jack in his flannel shirt and sweater, his body half turned toward me so that he could watch me at the stove. We looked, in the windows, like a fisherman and his wife, who had risen early to prepare her husband's breakfast. I thought that we did not look anything like a love affair—rather something homelier, more familiar. This vision in the windows held me for a moment; we appeared to be something we were not, could not ever be.

"What's wrong?" he asked.

I shook my head. I brought the tea and some toast to the table.

"You'll laugh," he said, "but I suppose I thought I'd be a college teacher one day. I went to school on a track scholarship, and I thought I'd be a track coach myself. I loved running—there's nothing like it, not even lobstering—and then I had a great professor for English lit, and somehow I sort of thought I'd do both: teach and coach."

"Do you ever think of going back to it—school, teaching?" I asked. I was thinking of the books I had found on his boat.

"No," he said quickly and dismissively. "Not since I left."

"Do you mind?"

"No." He said it with finality, as if it were something he had put behind him years ago.

We ate the small breakfast. He said that he would haul his boat on Friday if the weather was decent, and that he would then begin to mend his gear. He always took his wife and daughter on a small trip in February, he added, a kind of vacation. He wasn't sure where exactly they would go this year; he himself wanted to go down to Boston to see his son, who was at school there, but his daughter was vigorously lobbying for somewhere warmer. There was an edge to his voice; he talked more rapidly than he usually did, and I responded the same way, as if we sensed that whatever it was that we had wanted to tell each other, or might want to tell each other during the winter months, we had better say it now. I was wondering if I would continue to wake early, before daybreak, after he was gone.

The sun broke the horizon line. I could see there a sliver of molten red. I thought how odd it was to hate the coming of the day, as if we were night creatures who disintegrated with the light. I stood up and went to the door, waiting for him. I always hated the moment when he left the cottage. I watched him rise from the table, put on his waders and his yellow slicker.

"Maybe I won't let you through the door," I said playfully, snaking my arms around him between the slicker and his sweater. "Maybe I'll just keep you here all day."

He buried his face in my hair. He put his arms around my nightgown, lifted the nightgown so he could feel my skin.

"I wish you would," he said.

The next morning—it was the Wednesday—Jack didn't come. I woke, as usual, just before daybreak and waited, but I didn't hear his footsteps on the stairs. I lay in bed, straining for the sound of his motor on the lane, but I heard nothing except the first cries of the gulls, the lapping of the waves against the shingle. I watched as daybreak came, then the dawn itself. When the sun broke above the horizon line, I knew that he would not come at all. It was the first time since the fog that he had failed to visit me, and I felt empty, as though the day itself had lost its color.

Caroline woke shortly after sunrise. She seemed, as the doctor had predicted, perfectly fine, but I continued the antibiotic as I had been told to do. I put her on the braided rug after I had fed her, and looked out my windows to the end of the point. The green-and-white lobster boat bobbed in the water as though mocking me. Eventually trucks came and parked by the fish house, and men got out, but Jack was not among them. I tried to think of all the reasons why he had not come. There had been a crisis at home. Perhaps Rebecca had caused a scene of some kind. Possibly Jack had told her after all. Or Jack had decided to make a clean break with me—that would be like him. Yes, that was it. When he'd said goodbye yesterday, he'd known it was for good, and that's why he'd held me in that way. He'd said goodbye, only I hadn't known it.

I tried to come to terms with this possibility, tried to believe it and accept it. But I couldn't. I walked around the rooms, empty-handed, while Caroline played on the floor. I couldn't sit still. Was he telling me I should go now? Leave this town and find another?

But I couldn't leave. I had no will to leave. And I couldn't go without first speaking to Jack. I had to know if he meant never to come again.

I dressed myself and then the baby. I wanted to drive into town and find his house and ask him why he hadn't come, but I knew I couldn't do that. Down by the fish house, I could hear men talking. I wanted to go down there, ask of Jack— the hell with Willis—but I knew that was an absurd idea too. Instead I bundled Caroline into the sling and took her out for a walk. I didn't think a walk would harm her, not if she was dressed warmly enough.

The air was dry and light and stinging, like chilled champagne. It hadn't been the weather that had prevented Jack from going out on his boat, I knew that. I walked fast down to the edge of the point and back again. If someone had seen me walking, he would have said that I looked angry. I glanced up at the cottage, but I didn't want to go inside it yet. I veered south, walked along the shore toward town. Because I was walking fast, I went farther than I ever had been before. The tide was peeling back, leaving a firm patch of sand. The low-tide smell drifted in on a breeze from time to time and then wafted away on the fine, dry air. I walked until my legs ached and my back was sore from the weight of Caroline in the sling. But it was what I had wanted, I realized—to tire myself out.

I walked back more slowly than I'd set out. I'd been gone almost two hours when Caroline began to cry. It was past the time when I should have fed her again, and I knew I had to get back to the cottage soon to do that. I picked up my pace.

I rounded a bend and saw the cottage on its promontory. Outside the cottage, on the gravel drive, there was a car I hadn't seen before, an old black Buick sedan. Julia Strout was standing on the steps to the cottage, looking out over the point.

She saw me then and waved. I waved back. I made my way up the slope.

"Thought you might have gone for a walk," she said. "The baby's OK?"

"She's hungry," I said. "I've got to nurse her. How are you?"

Julia said, Fine, thank you, and held the door for me; we both entered the cottage. I took Caroline out of the sling and shook off my coat. I sat on the couch in the living room and gestured for Julia to sit down too. She did so but did not take off her coat.

"I got a call from Jack Strout this morning," she said, looking at me carefully as she said this. I tried to keep my face composed, but almost immediately I could feel a sharp squeeze inside my chest. I took a deep breath of air. I wanted to open a window.

"He said that the baby had been quite sick," she said. "And that you'd asked him for help morning before last and he'd taken you into Machias, to the clinic."

I nodded.

"Baby's all right now?" she asked.

"Better," I said. "A lot better." I realized that I was sitting stiffly in my chair, that I was breathing shallowly. I also became aware of the fact that the milk was no longer flowing. Caroline had stopped nursing and was looking up at me. I tried to breathe evenly and deeply to relax, to let the milk flow again. Take it easy, I said to myself.

"Anyway," she said, "he wanted me to tell you that he had meant to come by today to see if the baby was OK and if you needed anything, but his wife, Rebecca, got sick in the night herself—a bad stomach virus, he said—and he couldn't leave her. And he thought, if I was coming out this way, I could look in on you myself."

"That was . . . that was nice of him," I said feebly. "And of you," I added quickly. "You can tell him that Caroline is fine now. I'm fine. We're all fine."

Julia looked at me oddly. My voice sounded high and tight in the small room. I was trying to figure out how to get a message back to Jack through Julia, but I couldn't think clearly.

"Actually," she said, sitting back in her chair and unbuttoning her coat—it was warm in the cottage—"I was on my way out here, anyway. This may be nothing, and I don't want to alarm you, but I thought you ought to know. I saw Everett at the store early this morning—I go over every morning to get the milk and the paper—and he said there was a fellow from New York into the store last evening asking questions about a woman named Maureen English."

I may have blanched then, or perhaps the shock registered some other way on my face, for Julia said quickly, "Are you all right?"

"I'm having some trouble," I said, making a gesture that indicated the nursing.

"You're sure?"

"Yes," I said. "This man . . . ?"

"Everett thought the fellow was some kind of private detective, although the man didn't say exactly," she continued. "Everett said he knew of no one named Maureen English, and then the fellow described the woman he was looking for and said she was traveling with a baby, and Everett said he didn't know of anyone like that, either."

I shut my eyes.

"The man left and hasn't come back," Julia said. "Everett thinks he's gone on to another town. He told him to try Machias, but the man said he'd already been there that afternoon. He said he was trying all the towns along this part of the coast. He'd had a tip the woman he was looking for was in the area."

I opened my eyes. I tried to breathe normally. There was no hope of any more milk now, and Caroline had begun to fuss.

"I have to make her a bottle," I said, and got up.

Julia followed me into the kitchen.

"I think you'll be OK," she said. "Everett thinks the man believed him. He thinks he's moved on."

I nodded. I wanted to believe her.

"Does Everett know if this man spoke to anyone else in town?" I asked.

Julia shook her head. "He doesn't know, but he doesn't think so. It's only logical that someone would try the store first. It's the only place that looks half alive in town."

Normally, I'd have smiled at that.

"Let me hold her while you fix the bottle," she said.

I gave Caroline to Julia. I warmed some milk on the stove. My shirt was sticking to my back, and I realized I'd been sweating.

"You should go to the police," Julia said. "I don't mean Everett. I mean the real police, in Machias. If you're that afraid."

I shook my head. "I can't do that," I said. "I'm better off if he doesn't know where I am at all. If I went to the police, they might have to notify my husband and tell him where I am. I don't know how this sort of thing works, but I can't take any chances."

I took the bottle from the stove and retrieved Caroline. We went back into the living room. Caroline resisted the bottle at first, but then settled down to it. Julia sat across from me, as before. She still had her coat on.

"Would you like a cup of tea?" I asked.

"No," she said. "I can't stay."

She said that, but she did not get up to leave. She watched me giving the bottle to Caroline. I thought that she might be lingering to make sure that I was all right before she left.

"Jack's been around?" she asked.

I kept my face focused on Caroline. The meaning in Julia's question was unmistakable. She hadn't said, "So my cousin was helpful, was he?" or, "So you've met Jack, then." She'd said, *Jack's been around?*

I didn't know how to answer. Perhaps she was only fishing.

"Well, he helped me that one time."

She nodded slowly.

There was a long silence in the room.

"I'd be glad if Jack had some happiness," she said finally after a time.

It was, if she really didn't know anything, an extraordinary thing to say. But even as she said it, I could feel the ground begin to shift. I sensed that somehow we had entered new territory now. Where it was better not to lie. It was tempting territory. Or perhaps I only interpreted it as such, because *I* wanted not to lie, to tell someone the truth.

"I think he's had some happiness," I said cautiously, looking away from her and out the window.

She changed the subject then. "Your face looks better," she said. "A lot better."

I nodded and tried to smile. "Well, that's good at least," I said.

She stood up then.

"Now I've got to go," she said, all business. "I'm on my way into Machias. Can I get you anything in town? Anything for the baby?"

I shook my head. "No," I said. "We're fine." I stood up too. "Thanks for coming by. I mean it."

She put on her hat and gloves and walked toward the door, and I thought she would leave then, as briskly as she'd come in. Instead she paused, looked out at the cars parked by the fish house. I sensed that she was on the verge of saying one thing more, of saying the one thing she'd really come to say, but that her reserve, her code, inhibited her.

"I'll be by to check on you again in a day or two," she said. "Or Jack will."

"I love him," I said recklessly.

She turned. She looked stunned at first, but I knew that this was because I'd spoken, not because she didn't suspect the truth. Then she nodded slowly, as if confirming her own imaginings.

"I thought that might be it," she said.

She studied me then as if I were a daughter who had grown too fast for safekeeping, who was now beyond a mother's reach.

"You be careful," she said.

Jack did not come the next morning, either. It was the Thursday, and I thought that he would be hauling his boat on Friday. At best we had only one more morning left. I waited in the bed until the sun rose. Then I got out of bed and walked downstairs to the windows in the living room. I looked out at his boat. The white paint had taken on a salmon hue.

In the afternoon, I went into town, to the store. I did this almost every day, from habit even more than from necessity.

That afternoon, when I parked my car across the street, I saw, in front of the Mobil pump, a black pickup truck with a cap. I knew this truck well, knew its dents and rust marks even better than those of my own car. In the front seat, on the passenger side, there was a woman. I turned off the ignition and looked at her. Her hair was gray, pulled back severely off her face. She wore a silk-like kerchief in a navy-blue print. She had high cheekbones in a face you sensed had once been beautiful but now was painfully thin and white. Her lips were narrow, pressed together tightly. She had on a navy-blue wool coat, and it seemed that her hands were folded in her lap, although I couldn't see them. She must have sensed that someone was looking at her, in that way that one does, for she turned slowly to look in my direction.

I saw then her eyes, and looking at them I felt what it was that Jack had had to live with. Her eyes were pale, a milky blue, or perhaps I have that impression of their color because they seemed cloudy, clouded over. And yet they had a hunted look, a haunted look. They were pinched at the sides. Looking at them, you could not describe what it was these eyes were seeing, but you sensed that it was something terrible. I had the immediate impression that this was a woman who had lost her children to illness or to an accident, but I knew that wasn't true.

I looked away—as much because I didn't want to see those eyes as because I didn't want her to know I'd been examining her. When I glanced up again, she was facing straight ahead, waiting.

I thought then that I ought to start the car up, go home. But I knew he was inside the store. I couldn't pass up this chance to see him, even if I couldn't talk to him.

I got out of the car and removed Caroline from the baby basket. I walked with her around the back of the black pickup and up the steps into the store. The bell tinkled overhead, announcing me.

He was standing with his daughter at the counter. She wasn't wearing a hat, and her hair fell in curls down her back. She had on a red

woolen jacket and a white scarf. She turned to
see who had entered the store, and when she did
this, he turned too. Everett nodded, said hello. I
was looking at Jack. I didn't know if he would
speak, if he would dare to acknowledge me. He
looked at his daughter and then said, in as casual
a voice as he could, "How's the baby?"

"She's better," I said.

Everett was looking at both of us.

Jack said to his daughter, "I don't think you've
met Mary Amesbury, have you? She's living in
Julia's cottage over to the point."

And to me, "This is my daughter, Emily."

I said hello to Emily, and she said hi in a shy
way, as fifteen-year-olds do.

I saw Jack glance briefly through the window
at the truck. I knew he was wondering if I'd seen
Rebecca.

"Mary's baby had a fever the other day," he
said to his daughter. He turned to me. "But she's
better now?" he asked.

I nodded.

Around me, the canned goods and the fluores-
cent lights began to spin. It was a reprise of that
first evening in the store, only now there was
Jack. In the spinning, I had locked onto his face,
and I became aware that I was standing there
longer than would have been natural. With an
effort of will that seemed monumental, I made
myself walk forward, made myself say lightly, "I
need some milk and things. . . ."

I waited at the rear of the store until I heard

the bell over the door. When I walked back to the counter, Everett said, "Julia told me the baby was sick. Looks OK now, though."

He rang up my purchases. I had no idea what I had bought. Outside, I heard the truck start up, the familiar motor.

"Rebecca's poorly," Everett said, nodding to the sound. "Jack's had to do for her."

That night I was lying in the bed. I heard a motor on the lane. The room seemed darker than it ought to be, and I was thinking that he'd come earlier than usual. This would be our last morning together, and like myself he'd been impatient. Perhaps he'd told his wife that he'd be leaving early, that he had a lot to do before he could haul the boat.

I heard his footsteps on the linoleum floor in the kitchen. He didn't come straight up the stairs as I had thought he would, but instead seemed to be getting a glass of water from the sink. Then I heard him open the door into Caroline's room. Yes, I thought, he's checking on the baby. He's been worried about her.

Finally, I heard his footsteps on the stairs. I rose in the bed to greet him. He opened the door.

"Jack," I said with relief in the darkness.

A figure loomed into the room, hovered over the bed.

It wasn't Jack.

January 15, 1971

———————

Everett Shedd

You're askin' me now did I know about Mary 'n' Jack afore that terrible business over to the point. Well, that's a hard one to answer. I know Julia 'n' me, we talked about it at length, but whether it was afore the killing or after it, I'm not sure I can say now. Memory is a funny thing. 'Specially so in this case, because I do know this, that when Julia did say somethin' to me about Mary 'n' Jack, I remember thinkin' to myself that I already had an idea about that.

She came into the store just afore the end. And Jack was here with Emily, 'n' the two of 'em, Mary 'n' Jack, they had a little bit of conversation between 'em, 'n' I think even at that point I might of been sayin' to myself, Those two know each other. Course I did know that he'd helped her with the baby the morning the baby got the fever. Do you know about the fever? It's important, because that's how she got found.

As I understand it, the baby got the fever on the Monday morning, 'n' Jack come by—well, who's to say; maybe he was there already—'n' he drove her into Machias to the clinic there, 'n' Dr. Posner, he's this young fella from Massachusetts come to take over the clinic when Doc Chavenage retired, he saw the baby, 'n' somehow because of the baby bein' allergic to some kind of medication, he had to call down to New York for the baby's records, 'n' I guess he had to give his name 'n' all, 'n' the husband, he'd already alerted a nurse in the office there to Mary's disappearance, 'n' so forth. So it wasn't too long after that morning that the private detective come by askin' questions.

He didn't waste much time, I'll tell you that, 'cause it was Tuesday evenin', 'n' I was gettin' ready to close down the store for my supper, when this fellow walked in. Actually he kinda caught my attention afore he walked in, due to the fact that he was wearin' these shiny black shoes 'n' he slipped on the steps 'n' caught himself, 'n' I heard him cuss on the steps. So he came in, 'n' he was blowin' on his hands; he didn't have any gloves—I tell you, some people don't have the sense God gave 'em—'n' he asked me if I'd seen a woman named Maureen English around. I didn't know the name, of course, but I had an idea, right off the bat, what was up, so I asked this fella to show me some identification, 'n' he did, 'n' then I told him I was the town's only officer of the law, 'n' this seemed to please him. I suppose he thought he'd come to the right place for help. And then I asked him what the woman was wanted for, and he said it was a private matter, she'd run away from home, 'n' so forth. And then he showed me a picture, 'n' if I'd a had any doubt, I wouldn't have then, but of course, I didn't have any doubt in the first place, so I told the fella I'd never seen anyone like this, 'n' if anyone in town would know, I would know. Then I wished him well and told him he ought to try Machias.

That's when he told me he'd already tried Machias. He'd got a tip that she'd been to the clinic there, as I told you. Dr. Posner, I got to hand it to him, he didn't let on much more'n he had to. I don't know whether she didn't give the doctor her address, or she gave it 'n' he wouldn't give it to this fella, but the fella told me the doctor told him he'd treated the baby but had no idea where she was; in fact, he'd had the idea she was just passin' through, on her way north.

Course, none of this matters much now, does it? I mean to say, someone got on to this fella, didn't he? My guess is the fella was on his way out to his car 'n' saw some trucks down by the co-op, and thought, just for the hell of it, don't you know, he'd go down there, snoop around, ask a few questions. And someone down there must of said they'd seen her and where they'd seen her, and that was that.

I got the call 'round five-fifteen in the mornin'. I picked up the phone, 'n' this voice said, *Everett.* I said, *What?* And the voice said, *It's Jack.* And I said, *Jack.* And he said, *You better get out here.* And I said, *Rebecca?*

And then there was a long silence, 'n' I thought he'd gone off the phone.

And then he said, *No, Everett. It's not Rebecca.*

Mary Amesbury

I think you aren't like me. I think you wouldn't have let this happen to you. I see you in your khaki dress, your summer suit, your eyes clear and unwavering, like your sentences, and I think you couldn't have loved Harrold. You'd have left him after the first night.

Do you have a lover? Do you go to bars after work at night? Do you stay at your lover's place, or does he come to you—when *you* want, when *you* say?

I imagine you reading this. I imagine you thinking to yourself: Why did she let this go so far?

I write all night and all day too. I have learned to write through the light and the noise and the numbing routine. I sleep badly and infrequently, napping under the lights, amid the din.

When I dream, I dream of Harrold.

Harrold stood at the foot of the bed. I was kneeling on the mattress with the covers pulled up to my neck. He reached for the switch and flipped it on, lighting the lamp on the table.

The bright glare momentarily blinded us both, and when I looked at him, he was squinting. He had on a heavy crimson sweater and a pair of jeans, with his navy cashmere topcoat over them. The skin of his face was mottled and drawn, and I could see that he hadn't had a haircut since I'd left. He rubbed his eyes. There were dark circles under them, and the whites were bloodshot.

"Why are you naked?" he asked.

I said nothing, didn't move.

"Put something on," he said. "And come downstairs. I need some coffee." His voice was flat, as if drained.

He turned and left the room. I heard his footsteps on the stairs. I was nearly as stunned by his sudden departure as I'd been by his entrance.

My blocking the light behind me cast a long shadow on the opposite wall. I was still frozen on my knees, with the bedcovers drawn up to my chin. Below me I could hear a chair scrape on the linoleum floor. He was sitting at the table. I had a vision of myself slipping out the dormer window, shimmying down a drainpipe, crawling in the window of Caroline's bedroom, snatching her, getting into the car, driving off. But I didn't even know if there was a drainpipe; I had locked Caroline's window to keep out drafts; my coat was on the hook at the back of the kitchen door; my keys were on the kitchen table.

I looked down at my own nakedness. What time was it? Two-thirty? Three?

I dressed as quickly as I could. I put on layers:

A long-sleeved T-shirt, a shirt, a sweater, my cardigan over that. The layers felt protective. I put jeans on, and my boots.

When I came down the stairs, he was slouched in a chair by the table, his head thrown back, resting on the top rung. He had his eyes closed, and I thought for a moment that he was dozing. When he heard my footsteps, he sat up and looked at me.

"I drove straight through," he said. His voice was low, husky with lack of sleep. But it was also without inflection, as if he were on automatic pilot, or as if he were trying hard to modulate his emotions. "I haven't slept in a couple of days," he added. "I need some coffee."

I walked to the stove.

I took the percolator from the burner, filled it with water and with coffee from a canister. I knew that he was watching me as I performed this task, but I didn't return his gaze. He'd been drinking—I'd guessed that when I'd seen his eyes, and I'd smelled it when I passed him—and I was afraid to look at him, to say or do anything that might be a trigger.

"I'm not going to hurt you," he said, as if reading my thoughts. "I've just come to talk."

"To talk?"

I put the percolator on the stove, turned on the gas underneath the pot. I stood in front of the stove with my arms crossed, staring at the flame. Just beyond me, to the left, was the door to Caroline's bedroom. I imagined I could hear her turning in her sleep, crinkling the plastic that covered her mattress under the crib sheet.

"How's she been?" he asked. "How's the fever and the ear infections?"

How had it worked? I wondered. The pediatrician had called Harrold? Harrold had called the private detective he'd used on his stories, and the man had driven north, talked to the doctor in Machias? The doctor had known Jack, given the detective Jack's address?

No, Jack wouldn't have said anything, I knew. And Everett wouldn't, either. Someone else had. But who?

"How did you know?" I asked.

"Your mother called, did you know that?" he said, slightly off the subject. "When you talked to her on Christmas Day, apparently you sounded so out of it that she called back to talk to you again, and I had to tell her, of course, that you weren't there, you'd left."

I shut my eyes. I thought of my mother, of how she must have worried. I realized, too, with some surprise, that I hadn't spoken to her since Christmas.

"But it was Caroline's doctor's office put me onto you. I'd told a nurse in the office to give me a call if she heard from you, and she did. She called Monday morning. So I got in touch with Colin—you remember Colin—and he drove up here that night, and found you the next day, apparently. Didn't take him more than a day. I knew it wouldn't. Some guy in town—Williams,

Willard: something like that—told him there was someone new in town staying at this house, so Colin put two and two together." He leaned forward in his chair. "Listen, I don't want a scene here. I didn't come for that. I just came to get you, and take you and Caroline home where you belong."

I watched the coffee begin to perk.

"Your mother was relieved when I called her," he said. "I told her yesterday I was bringing you home, and she was relieved."

I watched the bursts of coffee in the glass bubble at the top of the pot.

"Caroline's fine," I said. "The fever's gone now."

He shook his head.

"She wouldn't have had any fever if you hadn't had the *idiocy* to come up here," he said suddenly. I froze. "The nurse told me it was high, *life-threatening,* for God's sake."

I didn't move.

He must have seen that he'd frightened me. He opened his hands. "But we won't talk about that now," he said in a more conciliatory tone. "That's behind us. All that nonsense is behind us."

I wondered if by nonsense he meant my coming up here or the way that he had been just before I'd left.

"Look, I'll go into therapy if you want," he said, answering my question. "It won't ever happen again. OK, I was in the wrong. You had to leave. But now all that's behind us. We can be a family again. Caroline needs a father."

I turned off the gas under the pot. I brought the pot to the counter and poured coffee into a mug. I took the mug to the table. I put the mug in front of Harrold. When I did, he looked up at my face, took my hand in his.

I may have flinched. I wanted to withdraw my hand, but he held it tight. He began to knead my hand with his fingers.

"You look good," he said softly.

There were faint traces of the bruises still on my face, but I knew that he would not allow himself to see those.

"Sit down," he said.

I sat in the chair at right angles to his own. He let go of my hand.

"How long will it take you to pack?" he asked. I could see that he hadn't shaved in a couple of days. "I think it's best if we get out of this place as soon as possible. We can drive for an hour or so, stay at a motel. I don't think I can make it all the way home unless I get some sleep."

"How's the magazine?" I asked carefully.

He rubbed his eyes. He looked away from me. "Oh, you know. The same," he said. "I'm taking a few days off now."

He moved his hand in front of his face. I could smell stale liquor on his breath. He took a sip of coffee, winced as he burned his tongue. He blew over the rim of the coffee cup, met my eyes.

"So let's go," he said. "You want me to help you pack?"

I put my hands in the pockets of the cardigan, drew the pockets around to my lap. I crossed my legs, looked down at my knee. Around us there was silence, though not silence at all. There was the wind against the windowpanes, in the dormant beach roses; a drip in the sink. The refrigerator hummed behind me.

"I'm not going," I said quietly.

He put the cup down slowly.

"You're not going?"

I shook my head. "I'm not going," I repeated. I sat very still. I was waiting for the reaction. Instinctively, I had tensed. To ward off his raised voice, perhaps even a blow.

"Is there anything to eat?" he asked.

"What?" I thought I couldn't have heard him right.

"Eat," he repeated. "I'm hungry. Have you got anything to eat?"

I felt dazed, thrown off guard. "Eat," I said slowly. I thought. "Yes," I answered finally. "There's food in the refrigerator."

He got up from the table and went to the refrigerator. He stood there with the door open for a moment, looking at the contents, the light spilling out around him, and then he withdrew a bowl. He still had on his navy overcoat. Was this a tactical maneuver, or was he simply hungry? Was it possible that Harrold had changed while I'd been away?

"What's this?" he asked.

I tried to remember. "It's sort of a macaroni and cheese," I said.

"All right; I'll eat this, then."

He took the plastic wrap off the bowl and set it on the counter. He moved slowly, deliberately, as if he had to think about his movements in advance. He seemed whipped. He opened a cupboard over the sink and removed a small plate. He pulled out a drawer, looking for silverware, but the drawer contained pot holders.

"Where's the silverware?" he asked.

I gestured toward a drawer at the end of the counter, near where I sat at the table. He walked toward the drawer, bent down over it, one hand on the counter, one hand on the drawer. He was bent like that, rummaging through the drawer, when I stood up.

"So that's all right with you," I said.

"What's all right?"

"That I'm not going with you. That I'm not leaving here."

He stayed bent over the drawer. I could hear the rattle of cheap metal as he searched for a fork. I was thinking—what was I thinking?—that now was the time to say what had to be said, to say it all.

I was, in that moment, not afraid of him. Perhaps it was the curve of his back, or the domesticity of looking for a fork. I took a step forward. He looked tired, punished. I was thinking: I used to love him. We made a child together. We made Caroline, and she is as much his as she is mine.

I had a sudden brief vision of the bed in the apartment in New York City, the kitchen table there.

I put my hand out toward his back, withdrew it. I was thinking that we would simply get a divorce like other people, and he'd have visitation rights, and that would be all right, he would see that.

"I think you and I can work this out," I said, tilting my head a bit to speak to him.

The movement was swift and stunning. I did not actually see the arc of his hand, merely felt the rush of air, like an electric charge, then the shock of something sharp on my face. He'd straightened up in a flash, swung his arm around. There was a silver object in his hand. It was a fork. I put my hand up, looked at my hand. There was blood on my fingers. The tines had scraped my cheek just below my eye. He could have blinded me.

I whirled around to get away from him. He grabbed my hair. He snapped my head back, so that I lost my balance, staggered, but he was holding me up by my hair. He pulled me to my feet. He wrenched my hair tightly with his fist; his forehead was against the side of my head. He pressed the tines of the fork into the hollow below my neck. I thought: It's only a fork. What can he do with a fork?

But I knew that he could kill me with the fork. He could kill me without the fork.

"Did you really think you'd get away with this?" It seemed he hissed the last word. "Did you think you could humiliate me, take Caroline, get away with this?"

"Harrold, listen . . . ," I said.

From the back of my head, he shoved me into the living room. I fell against the couch, regained my balance, sat down. I pulled the cardigan tightly across my chest. He held the fork in his fist, as a child would. He took his coat off, slipped the fork through the sleeve.

"Take your clothes off," he said.

"Harrold . . . ,"

"Take your clothes off," he repeated. His voice had risen a notch.

"Harrold, don't do this," I said. "Think of Caroline."

"Fuck Caroline," he said.

The air around me billowed out, then in, like a sail that had filled suddenly with wind and then emptied. Nothing—nothing—Harrold had ever done or said up to that point was as palpable as those two words. They were words I'd have said a human being couldn't pronounce together, as if, in combination, they were unintelligible. But Harrold had said them.

I knew then that he was beyond reaching, that in the days I'd been away from him he'd crossed a line.

"Take off your clothes," he yelled.

I began to undress slowly, stalling for time so that I could think. There was a knife in the same drawer in which he'd found the fork. Could I get to it? And if I did, would that help me? What in God's name could I accomplish with a knife?

I pulled the sleeves of the cardigan from my arms. He stood across from me, watching. He looked impatient, annoyed with my slowness. I laid the cardigan on the couch, actually thought of folding it, crossed my arms to slip my other sweater over my head. I had the sweater up over my face when he grabbed my arm, pulled me toward him and onto the floor.

"You fucking bitch," he said.

He unsnapped my jeans, yanked the zipper down in thrusts with his free hand. I did not resist. This was not important to me, being raped by him; I had survived this before, though it hurt: His body was abrasive against mine, he tore at me, and he kept the fork pressed hard against my neck. It was only near the end, when in his frenzy he had the fork pressed too tightly against my skin and I thought that he would puncture me, that I tried to lift my shoulders, shake him off. He rose up over me then and slammed his free hand into the side of my head.

I was unconscious only seconds, I think, though when I came to, I lay still, did not open my eyes. I let him think that I was out cold. I did not have a plan then, but I sensed that if he thought I was out, he might loosen his grip.

How long did I lie there? A minute, five

minutes, ten? At first I felt the full weight of him, and then he seemed to slip to the side, to roll over onto his back.

I didn't move; I was completely limp. This, at least, I did well.

I listened for sounds of Caroline awakening, but I heard nothing. In the distance a dog barked.

After a time, I felt Harrold get up from the floor, heard him pull up his jeans. He walked away from me, but I didn't open my eyes. There was the clink of something metallic on the table. Then it seemed that he had opened the door, and he was gone.

I lay still and listened. I thought. He hadn't taken his coat. That meant he would return. There was no point in leaping up, grabbing Caroline, and making a run for it. I wouldn't get past the door.

I was careful not to alter my position on the floor, though I was exposed—my jeans were down below my knees—and that exposure was painful, as though a spotlight were aimed at me.

The door opened, and he came in again. I felt his eyes on me. I heard him walk to the couch, sit down. I heard the slosh of liquid in a bottle, heard him take a swallow.

Was he concerned that I hadn't come to yet? If he was, he didn't show it. He didn't bend down over my body, or pull my jeans up, or speak to me, or slap my face. He just drank, almost rhyth- mically, with a minute or two between the swal- lows. I knew it was whiskey. I could smell it, and

I knew he'd never drink gin straight as he might whiskey.

How long did I lie there then? Twenty minutes, forty-five? Sometimes I imagined that he was waiting for me to twitch, to make the slightest move, so that he could pounce. But that was just my imagination, wasn't it? What he was doing was drinking himself into a stupor.

Eventually I heard the sound that I'd been waiting for. It was faint at first, then heavier, deeper. He was snoring.

I moved just a foot, then a hand. Then I pressed my teeth together for courage and rolled over, away from him. The snoring didn't stop.

I sat up, turned my head, dared to look at him. His mouth was open, his head was leaning at an angle against the back of the couch, the bottle was in his lap. A bit of the whiskey had spilled out onto his thigh.

I pulled my jeans on and zipped them up. I stood up. How much time did I have? A minute? An hour?

I thought: If I get Caroline and run to the car with her and drive away, he will find us again.

I thought: If I run up to the blue Cape and call the police, they will arrive and see that a husband has come to reclaim his wife and his child.

I thought: If I tell them that he has raped me, they will look away. A husband cannot rape a wife, they'll be thinking.

I walked to the silverware drawer, opened it as quietly as I could. I removed a long kitchen knife with a black wooden handle. I held the knife in my hand, tested its weight. I put the knife behind my back and walked toward Harrold. He was lying on the couch, still snoring. I brought the knife from behind my back, held it in front of me, not two feet from his chest. I said to myself, *Do it, just do it,* but my hand didn't move. Instead I found myself wondering if the knife would go through the sweater and the shirt. And if, when I got to the skin, I'd have the strength to push it through.

I looked down at the knife. It seemed preposterous in my hand.

In the end, it wasn't so much a question of strength as it was of physical courage. I didn't have the courage to thrust the knife forward. Perhaps if he'd awakened and lunged toward me, and I'd held my ground, I might have gotten the knife into him, but short of that, I knew, I couldn't do it. I lowered the knife. I eased back into the kitchen, put the knife silently back in the drawer.

I put my head into my hands. *What,* then?

I lifted my head up.

I had it.

Because I had my boots on, my progress was slow and clumsy on the smooth round stones of the pebbled beach, and several times I had to catch my balance to prevent a fall. I had put my coat on, but I felt the cold air, like the sting of dry ice, on my hands and face and through the cotton of my jeans. I was not cold inside, beneath the coat, however; I was trying to run, and that kept me warm.

I abandoned the south side of the point for the sand beach. Because I was running, the heels of my boots sank and caught occasionally in the sand. It was low tide, I could smell it, though it was so dark I couldn't see the tideline. A layer of cloud had pasted itself over the moon. I moved more by instinct than by sight. I was bent over a bit, my knees in a slight crouch, my arms extended in front of me, in case I should suddenly hit a dinghy or a rock or a large piece of driftwood.

The sand grew softer, muckier, wetter, sucking in my boots, making a squelching sound when I pulled them free. I guessed that I had veered too close to the low-tide mark, that the harder sand was to my right. My progress seemed absurdly slow; I felt that I was trying to run through molasses, the sticky medium of childhood nightmares. I thought of Caroline and pulled a boot free with a smack from the muck. What if she woke up and began to cry? Wouldn't that wake Harrold? And if she woke Harrold, mightn't he just take her with him, leave with her in his car? I plunged on more frantically.

I turned to my right, in the direction of the harder ground of the spit, expecting the ground to begin sloping upward to the dunes. But the ground seemed flat all around me. I stood still, disoriented. I took a deep breath, tried to think clearly. I could see nothing, not even a shape I thought might be the fish house. Above me, the paste was moving slowly over the moon. If there were a break in the clouds, I thought, the moon might provide enough light for me to see my way.

I took a step forward, then another. It seemed to me that I had badly miscalculated somehow; the ground was growing soupier, not firmer. I backtracked, tried another direction. This was slightly better, but my inner compass was spinning in confusion: This certainly was the wrong direction. I retraced my steps, went back to what I thought was the position I'd been at before I began to maneuver. The moon broke free just at that moment for only a second or two, but I could clearly see the end of the point, the dinghy, the boat. Confidently, I took a step forward.

The ground gave way like a trapdoor in a stage. My leg vanished up to my knee. I fell to the sand, as if someone had yanked my foot from under me. When I put out my hands to stop my fall, my arms plunged into a vat of glue.

It felt like that in the darkness—a vat of gritty glue; it had that consistency. I couldn't pull my arms out. I couldn't pull because I didn't have any leverage. The vat of glue seemed to have no bottom. My foot was sinking and my arms could not find firm ground.

I thought, in rapid succession: *Honeypot. Willis. Caroline. This can't be happening to me. Caroline. Jesus God, Caroline.*

Lie flat, I told myself. Had I read this in a child-hood story about someone caught in quicksand?

I tried to spread myself out and lie as still as I could. Nothing happened. I didn't sink. If I didn't pull and twist, I realized, I'd be better off. I felt hard spots under my shoulder and the knee that was free. I used these for leverage, and as slowly as I could, I began to roll over, away from the muck. I could feel the muck in my hair, in my ear, inside my collar. Close to me, I could hear the crawling of a wave up the sand. A crab or something small scurried over my face. I made a sound and tried to blow it off me. Gently I rolled and began to pull. One arm slipped free, then another.

Inch by inch, I slithered back onto the harder ground. Pulling my leg out was more difficult than freeing my arms had been: My knee was bent, and heavy with the muck. If I called out for help, the only person who could conceivably hear me would be Harrold.

I began to shiver then. The soupy ground was cold and wet with icy salt water. The water had already seeped through my woolen coat, my sweater. I was thinking: If I lie here any longer, I will die from exposure, and dying is not a possibility, because I can't leave Caroline.

I gritted my teeth and groaned audibly with the effort.

Then I said out loud, *Goddamn fuck*, and I didn't care if Harrold heard me.

I pulled my leg free.

I rolled over and over, away from the honeypot.

I was crying, mixing tears with the muck that covered my face.

The paste slipped past the moon. I could see my way. I rose to my feet, stumbled forward. I began to run then to the dinghy.

The rest was nothing by comparison. I pushed the dinghy into the water, got inside. I lay forward in the bow, paddled with my cupped palms over the edge. The water stung, felt colder than ice.

I tied the dinghy to the mooring, slipped along the bow of the lobster boat, and fell into the cockpit. I opened the door to the cabin. Only then did it occur to me that it might have been locked. This thought took my breath away. I so easily might have gone through all of that horror with the honeypot only to find the bulkhead door locked tight. But it wasn't.

I found this fact momentarily encouraging, as if the ease of opening the cabin door were a sign that I was doing the right thing.

I felt for the cabinet with my hands, fished around in the darkness for the small object I had come for.

When I got back to the cottage, Harrold was in the same position as when I'd left. What I should have done, what I ought to have done, is to have walked straight up to him and fired.

Instead I sat at the kitchen table with the gun in my hand. My hands were shaking so badly that I was afraid I might shoot myself. I put the gun on the table. I could not stop the shaking. I felt a sudden wave of nausea, got up quickly, and vomited into the sink, trying to stifle the sound of my retching. I wiped my mouth, saw my reflection in the window over the sink. My face and coat and hair were black with muck. It was as if I had on a mask, were not really myself at all. I smelled like low tide.

I went back to the table, sat down. I thought it astonishing that Harrold had not come to when I had vomited.

I tried to breathe deeply so that I could stop the shaking. I felt another wave of nausea, fought it back. I was waiting for the shaking to stop. I was thinking: I have no life as long as he exists.

I put the gun in my hand, felt its weight. This weight, or the cold metal of the object, calmed my hand. I stood up, walked to where Harrold was sprawled against the couch. I heard only a high ringing in my ears. I raised my arm and aimed. I was thinking: Is it better to aim at the heart or at the head?

Behind me, I heard a hoarse, whispered shout and a gasp, or perhaps it was the other way around. I turned to see. It was Jack, in his yellow slicker and his boots. He had come at the accustomed time. Our last morning together. I stood with the gun in my hand. He looked at me, then at Harrold, then at me again. I must have seemed to him a sea monster, a mucky creature from the deep with an incomprehensible object in her hand.

But he comprehended soon enough. He started to cross the room.

"What the . . . ?" he said.

On the couch, Harrold stirred.

I thought: If he exists, I have no life.

I was aiming at Harrold's heart. Jack's hand was only inches from my arm. I fired. Harrold bounced forward from the couch, clutching his shoulder.

Jack shouted and turned toward Harrold. Harrold opened his eyes, looked, understood, didn't understand.

"Maureen . . . !" he said.

I shook my head.

"My name isn't Maureen," I said.

I fired again.

Or perhaps I fired first, then said my name wasn't Maureen.

I lowered my hand.

I stood as if paralyzed, rooted to the floor.

Above me and around me then I could hear a strange sound. It was a sound that began slowly at first, then gathered pitch. I looked at Caroline's door, but the sound wasn't coming from there.

I looked at the couch, but the sound wasn't coming from there, either. Harrold had fallen forward onto his knees, and I was certain that he was dead.

I looked at Jack, as if he might tell me about the sound, but he didn't seem to be able to. I could see that he was not its source. He was looking at me, saying my name. He was wearing his yellow slicker. His face was weathered, he had deep grooves at the sides of his mouth, and he was saying my name. I remember that he had his hands out, palms upward, as if he had an object in them he wanted me to see.

The sound became a keening.

I looked out the window to the end of the point. I could see the green-and-white lobster boat bobbing in the water. There was a mist of daybreak just above the horizon.

I thought then of the woman in the hospital, of the woman behind the wall in the labor-and-delivery room.

The sound became a howling.

I think it was then that Caroline began to cry.

January 15—Summer 1971

———————

Everett Shedd

When I got there, good Lord, there was a sorry sight. I hope I don't ever see anything that sad again, 'n' that's the truth.

Mary was on the floor, holdin' this man in her arms. Jack was cradlin' the baby, walkin' with her in the living room. There was blood everywhere— on the couch, the floor, on the wall behind the couch. All over Mary Amesbury.

Well, Mary, you wouldn't of believed Mary. She had her coat 'n' her boots on, 'n' she was covered with mud—from the low tide, don't you know. On her face 'n' hair 'n' everything. And that mixed with the blood . . . well.

Mary, she just kept her eyes shut. She was holdin' this man—course I know now it was her husband, Harrold English, but I didn't then, not right away—'n' makin' this sound 'n' rockin' back 'n' forth, 'n' it was the sorrow you felt in that room, not the horror of it all at first, but more like somethin' very deep 'n' sad had kind of settled itself in there.

I went out to the car 'n' called over to Machias

to ask for a car 'n' an ambulance, even though I knew that was a dead body in that cottage. And then I went back inside.

Jack, he was as white as a milk sky, he was. But he hung on to the baby 'n' tried to get her to stop cryin', 'n' he kept lookin' at Mary, 'n' then I said to him, *Jack, what happened here?*

Jack, I think he'd been waitin' for me to ask this. He cleared his throat and stood over by the sink. He's got a deep voice, don't you know, husky, and he spoke slow that mornin', like he was thinkin' as he spoke. He said he'd come around four forty-five. He didn't say *why* he had come, 'n' I pretended to make out as how he was just goin' down to his boat, but I think he knew I knew that wasn't strictly the case. Anyway, he said he saw the car, 'n' then the lights on in the cottage, when normally there wouldn't be any, 'n' then he thought he saw this man get up from the couch 'n' hit Mary at the side of her face. So Jack, he started up the slope to see what was goin' on, 'n' by the time he made it to the back stoop this man had Mary up against the table 'n' was beatin' her. He said the man looked as if he would kill Mary, 'n' Jack opened the door, 'n' then there was the shot.

A shot? I said.

Just the one, Jack said, 'n' I think he regretted that straight off, because even I could see there'd been two shots.

Whose gun was it? I said.

Jack was holdin' the baby, mind you, 'n' I think

this question might of stopped him a second, but then he said, straight up, it was his, he'd given it to Mary Amesbury a week or so earlier, for protection, one night when she was scared 'n' thought she'd heard a prowler.

Then Mary said, from the floor where she was holdin' the man—her husband, that is—*Jack, don't.*

Jack, he looked at her 'n' then at me, 'n' then he just turned away from me.

And then Mary got up 'n' came over 'n' sat down at the table. And as I say, she looked pretty dreadful, 'n' I was wonderin' what had happened to her she got all that muck all over her, 'n' she began to talk.

This is what she said that mornin', 'n' she never wavered from it, neither.

She said her husband had come around two-thirty or three in the mornin', 'n' he'd been drinkin'. He raped her, she said, 'n' hit her once while he was rapin' her, 'n' knocked her out. And he'd attacked her with a fork once afore that.

A fork? I said.

And she said, *A fork.*

After he'd raped her, he'd fallen asleep or passed out, 'n' she had gone out to Jack's boat, 'n' got the gun in the cabin there, 'n' come back 'n' shot her husband while he was asleep. Once in the shoulder 'n' once in the chest. And then she said that Jack had come in the door after he heard the shots, but that Harrold was already dead by then.

And then Jack started to say, *That's not—*

And then Mary interrupted him and said to me, *That's what happened*, 'n' she got up 'n' went to Jack. They stood there for a minute just lookin' at each other, 'n' I'll tell you, I was embarrassed to be in the same room with 'em, to have to look at 'em, at somethin' that *raw* between 'em, 'n' then she kissed Jack on the mouth, with the baby between 'em, 'n' then she took the baby from him 'n' sat back down again at the table.

And I thought to myself: If she tells this story to the police from Machias when they get here, they aren't ever goin' to see each other again.

The trouble was, Mary was her own worst enemy. It wasn't that she was proud of what she'd done, or that she was glad of it in any way. That wasn't it 'tall. It was more that this was the most *important* thing she'd ever done, 'n' she wasn't goin' to lie about it.

So there we were, the three of us—well, the five of us, if you want to get technical—'n' the sun come up, 'n' I said to Mary, *Why?*

And she thought a bit, 'n' then she said, *Because I had to.*

And that was it.

They were goin' to put her in the county lockup, don't you know, but they couldn't really keep her there, 'cause it wasn't a fit place for a woman prisoner of any duration, so they made arrangements with the state, 'n' Mary, she's at the Maine Correctional Center now in South Windham, which is where the women go.

Now, since that mornin' I've had lots of time

to think about all this 'n' mull it all over, 'n' this is what I think now. I think Jack was in the house with her when she shot Harrold English, but he couldn't say that, could he? Not because he wouldn't want to implicate himself. Oh, no—that's not our Jack. But because he saw right away her only hope was in self-defense, 'n' she's got no self-defense case if he's standin' right there beside her. I don't know exactly how it went—maybe he tried to get the gun away from her. And Mary, she wouldn't say he was there because she didn't want to get him involved. Sort of like that great old story "Gift of the Magi." You ever read that one? By O. Henry, it was. My kind of story, don't you know. Well, it weren't exactly like that, but the feelin's were the same, you follow me?

Anyway, at the trial, all this was confusin' to the jury, weren't it? The defense lawyer, Sam Cotton, local boy from Beals Island, his argument was this: Mary shot her husband while he was asleep—they allowed as that's what happened, even though actually, Mary said, he'd woken up when she pointed the gun—but she did it in self-defense because she believed that *eventually*, that day or that night, he would kill her.

Tricky.

It was the "eventually" that was the problem, wasn't it?

The prosecutin' attorney—Pickering—he argued that Mary had had time to call the police—me, if it came to that—'n' have Harrold English arrested for assault. But the problem was that Mary didn't go *up* the hill to the LeBlanc place, where there was a phone; she went *down* the point to Jack's boat, where she got the gun 'n' come back 'n' shot her husband in cold blood.

Now, Mary, she kept talkin' about the rape 'n' the blow that had knocked her out, but the problem is, in Maine, a husband can't legally rape his wife, and maybe everywhere else as far as I know, so the prosecutin' attorney, he made short shrift of that one—settin' aside the blow almost as easy as he set aside the rape.

And then there was the fork.

Unfortunate, that, the fork. Well, I mean to say, a *fork.* How much damage can you do with a fork? Pickering, he made mincemeat out of the fork. Even got a laugh out of the jury, if I remember correctly.

So you see, Mary Amesbury, she just didn't help her case 'tall, did she? And even with me 'n' Julia 'n' Muriel testifyin' as to how beat-up she looked the first day she come to us, it wasn't enough, was it? Particularly so when you had Willis Beale testifyin' that Mary herself had told him the bruises were from a car accident, 'n' Julia, she got recalled 'n' had to say Mary had told her the same thing too—very damagin', that was—and in light of the fact that Sam Cotton couldn't produce a single witness from New York City to say they'd ever suspected anythin' amiss between Harrold English and his wife, or who had ever seen any bruises on Mary.

Well, that was it, wasn't it? And I guess it was too much for the jury—got ourselves a hung jury, didn't we? Pretty much split down the middle, far as I can make out.

After the trial, don't you know, the judge thanked the jury for their services and dismissed them, and straight off, Sam Cotton, he asked for a dismissal, but Pickering stood right up and said there was goin' to be another trial, and he asked for a date.

And then about ten days ago, Sam, he must have heard who the judge assigned was, 'n' it was Joe Geary, who everybody in Machias knows has a soft spot for women. He gives 'em light sentences, don't you know. So Sam, he decided to waive Mary's right to a jury trial—I think he figured she'd make out better with Geary—'n' so the whole thing gets thrown to Joe Geary in September, when they have the next trial. It was in the papers.

So there you are.

It's in his hands now, in't it?

The muck? That was from a honeypot. Those are nasty patches in the flats. Can suck you in, give you a fright, I'll tell you. Like quicksand. Mary Amesbury had a run-in with one, tryin' to get to Jack's boat.

The baby? Julia Strout asked to take her. Has her still.

Willis Beale

Well, I'll tell you right off the bat what I think happened that night. This guy, this Harrold English, he done what any guy woulda done; he drove up to get his wife and kid and bring 'em back home, and he surprised Mary and Jack in bed, in flagro delecti, if you catch my meaning, didn't he? And there was some kind of a scene between the three of them, and there was Jack with his gun, and one or the other of them shot the poor son of a bitch, and that's what I think.

There's your motive, if you're lookin' for one.

Mary's coverin' up somethin' for Jack. Even Everett, he thinks so. He didn't say so to me, but I heard this around.

I think, near the end, they didn't care who knew what was goin' on. You ask LeBlanc. He'll tell you Jack was there five-thirty in the morning the day the baby got sick. It was Jack went up LeBlanc's place for the phone. And I myself saw Jack comin' and goin' all that day to Mary's cottage, like they was real old friends. I saw him from the fish house. He didn't kiss her in public, but they weren't foolin' anybody.

Maybe they had a plan. Who's to say? I mean, what were they goin' to do when Jack hauled his boat? How was he goin' to see her every day? You ever think of that?

At the trial I had to say, didn't I, that she said the bruises were from a car accident. I was under oath. I know some people from town, they don't understand that, but bein' under oath is serious business to me.

I don't know how she got found. I do recall this fella up from New York City, he come down the co-op askin' questions. I mighta said, if he asked was there someone new in town, that there was this girl with a baby, but I wouldn'ta let on where she lived or anythin' like that. If Mary didn't want to get found, that was her business, wasn't it?

I'm real curious now about Judge Geary's verdict in September. She'll probably get off, 'cause he's partial to women.

Julia Strout

Yes, I had to testify at the trial. I testified as to the condition Mary Amesbury was in when she first arrived in St. Hilaire. Then I had to say that she'd told me that the bruises were from a car accident. But I was quick to say, before the lawyer interrupted me, that I hadn't believed her.

I could not have done what Mary Amesbury did. I don't believe so. I don't think I could have shot a man, but who is to say what a person might be driven to? I know that they say she killed this man, her husband, in cold blood. She could have asked Jack or Everett for help. She could have done any number of things, I suppose. But then who is to say that an act of passion, of hot blood if you will, has a finite limit of only a minute or two? Who's to say an act of passion couldn't last all the way through going out to the boat to get the gun and returning with it and shooting the man who was hurting you? Who you were sure would hurt you again. Who might eventually kill you. Who's to say an act of passion couldn't last for weeks or months if it came to that?

* * *

So I can't tell you what will happen to Mary in September. They say she might get off, and I hope that's true.

But when I think about this terrible business over to the point, what I feel most is . . . distressed. I feel distressed for Mary and for Jack, and distressed about Rebecca, and most of all now, worried for Emily and this little baby I'm taking care of now. It's Emily and the baby I feel for.

Listen. Do you hear that? That's the baby now. It always takes me by surprise. It's a strange sound in this house after all these years. But a welcome one. My husband and I, we didn't have any children ourselves, and I was always sorry about that.

I just have the baby until Mary gets out.

Would you like to see her? I saw his picture. . . . She looks like her father.

The Article

———————

The Killing
Over to the Point

by Helen Scofield

Sam Cotton seemed preoccupied. He looked uncomfortably hot in his best blue suit and in his shiny black wing tips, which were getting ruined in the sand. It was unseasonably warm on Flat Point Bar this September afternoon, and the talk in this small coastal town of St. Hilaire, Maine, 65 miles north of Bar Harbor, was that the temperature would hit 85 before the day was out.

Cotton put a finger between his collar and his neck, then wiped his bald pate with a handkerchief. He was headed for the end of the bar, also known as "the point," so that he could get a better look at a green-and-white lobster boat that was bobbing in the channel. When he finished examining the boat, he made his way back to the other end of this small peninsula that juts into the Atlantic. There he stood next to his car below a modest white cottage that overlooks the point and the water. Apart from the odd wave to a fisherman heading for shore in his dinghy, Cotton said nothing and spoke to no one. The entire round trip, including the time he spent gazing at and thinking about the boat and the cottage, took about twenty minutes. He does this every day.

Defense attorney Sam Cotton, 57, has been practicing criminal law in eastern Maine for almost 30 years. But his current case, at the Superior Court in Machias, may be the most complicated defense he's undertaken. It is certainly the most celebrated. The case is known around here as "that awful business up to Julia's cottage," or "that terrible story about the Amesbury woman," or "the killing over to the point." Sam Cotton must prove his client, a 26-year-old woman, innocent of murdering her husband last January in the small white cottage Cotton has spent so much time studying. And there isn't much time. Next week, at the conclusion of the second trial of a woman known both as Maureen English and as Mary Amesbury, Judge Joseph Geary is expected to deliver his verdict.

As Cotton has told it, the bare facts of the case are these:

Following two years of domestic violence at the hands of her troubled and alcoholic husband—including repeated rapes and physical assault, even while she was pregnant—Maureen English left her home in New York City last December 3 with her infant daughter, Caroline, and drove 500 miles to the small fishing village of St. Hilaire to seek refuge. There, under the alias Mary Amesbury, she rented the white cottage on Flat Point Bar and settled in to a life of quiet tasks, centered around caring for her six-month-old daughter and nursing herself back to both physical and emotional health.

In the early morning of January 15, after six weeks in hiding, Mary Amesbury was surprised and frightened by her husband's sudden appearance in her bedroom. Harrold English, 31, a successful journalist with this magazine, had driven to Maine to confront his wife. He'd been tipped off to her whereabouts by a physician at a local health clinic Mary Amesbury had visited.

Sometime during these early-morning hours, English assaulted his wife with a sharp instrument, raped her, and hit her so violently in the head she was knocked unconscious.

Believing her life was in danger, Mary Amesbury waited until her husband had passed out from excessive drinking and then made her way to the end of the point. There she crossed a short expanse of water and located a gun she knew was kept on a green-and-white lobster boat moored in the channel. She returned to the cottage, and fearful that her husband would kill her when he came to, shot him twice—once in the shoulder and once in the chest.

Cotton claims she acted in self-defense. So does Mary Amesbury. "I had to do it," she says. "I had no choice."

Last June, a jury was unable to reach a verdict in Mary Amesbury's case, and the trial ended in a hung jury. There were seven votes for acquittal; five for a guilty verdict. Cotton immediately moved for dismissal, but D. W. Pickering, the prosecuting attorney, asked for a new trial date in September. In a surprise move in early July, Cotton announced that his client would waive her right to a trial by jury. Cotton has not commented on his strategy, but sources close to the defense attorney suggest that Judge Geary's reputation for leniency toward women may be the explanation.

At both trials, Cotton likened his client to a modern-day Hester Prynne, the heroine of Nathaniel Hawthorne's classic *The Scarlet Letter*. Both, said Cotton, were wronged women, romantic figures, living out quiet exiles in cottages by the sea and both fiercely protective of young daughters. Both women were outcast and doomed by love to carry the scarlet "A" on their breasts. In the case of Mary Amesbury, the "A" stood not for adultery, but for abuse.

When Mary Amesbury tells her own story, however, she comes across as somewhat more complex than just a "wronged woman." And her story sometimes raises more questions than it satisfactorily answers.

To prevent her husband from finding her, Maureen English assumed the name Mary Amesbury when she arrived in St. Hilaire on December 3. She refused at both trials to answer questions when addressed as Maureen English. The prosecuting attorney solved the problem, addressing her as "Mrs. English/Mary Amesbury." Cotton deftly avoided using either name when he addressed his client on the stand.

For seven weeks this summer, I conducted a series of exclusive interviews with Mrs. English while she was awaiting her second trial. Despite the tension and fear she was obviously feeling, Mrs. English was often eloquent. She was also sometimes sad and occasionally angry, but she was always forthcoming, even at times appearing to contradict testimony she had given in court. One of these interviews was conducted in person. The rest were carried on through the mail.

Because there were no adequate facilities in Machias for long-term female prisoners, Mrs. English has been remanded to the custody of the Maine Correc-

tional Center at South Windham. As she sat in the
visitors' room, she looked older than her 26 years.
Her skin was pale and lined about the eyes and on
her forehead. Her red hair, one of her most striking
features, had been cut short, and there was a thin
streak of gray over her left eye. Her posture was
tense and angular beneath the gray sweatshirt and
pants of her prison garb. When she spoke, she had
a nervous habit of twirling a strand of hair between
her fingers. Those who knew Maureen English less
than a year ago find the changes in her appearance
startling.

I had met Mrs. English only once prior to our
prison interview—at a party at this magazine's office
in Manhattan. Although she had once worked there,
she had left before I joined the staff. At the party
she wore a black velvet dress and looked radiant as
she showed off her infant daughter, Caroline, to her
former colleagues. She struck me that evening as a
happy woman, well-off and well-married, and content to take a few years off to start a family. Harrold,
her husband, was almost constantly at his wife's
side and kept what appeared to be a loving and
protective arm around her shoulder. The idea that
he might be beating his wife in the privacy of their
home was inconceivable.

During the course of telling her story, Mrs. English
spoke at length about her childhood and her upbring-
ing. The illegitimate daughter of a soldier and a secretary whose immigrant Irish family hailed from
Chicago's south side, she spent most of her youth in
child care, while her mother worked to support them.
Mother and daughter lived in a small white cottage in

the suburban town of New Athens, 20 miles south of Chicago. Mrs. English appeared to have been close to her hardworking mother and to have respected her values: "My mother would often tell me that things happened to a person and that you should learn to accept those things," Mrs. English said, "but I also understood from an early age that neither my mother nor I would be happy unless I did what I was supposed to do. Unless I seized for myself a life she had been denied—a life with a husband and a stable family."

A talented student, Mrs. English was accepted at the University of Chicago in 1962. She studied literature and eventually became an editor on the university paper. A svelte, redheaded beauty with pale skin and large hazel eyes, Mrs. English eventually made her way to New York City. In June 1967, she was hired as a reporter with this magazine. She met Harrold English on her first day of work.

Colleagues recall Maureen English as a diligent worker who learned her trade quickly. Although she was well liked, she was something of a loner. With the exception of Harrold English, she made no serious lasting friendships at the magazine. Still, she was promoted in near record time to the National desk.

"She was fast," says a former editor who worked closely with her. "Give Maureen English an assignment, and she'd have a solid story back to you before the day was out."

Despite the disparity in their backgrounds, Maureen and Harrold appear to have been attracted to each other at once. Harrold came from a wealthy Rhode Island textile family and was educated at Yale. A tall, well-built, dark-eyed young man whose good looks and journalistic successes made him attractive to his female colleagues, he had been a reporter for the *The Boston Globe* before moving to New York City. He distinguished himself as both a national and foreign reporter and was a 1966 Page One Award winner for his series on the race riots in Watts. "He did some great pieces for us," says Jeffrey Kaplan, editor in chief during most of English's tenure. "He was an excellent reporter and was very aggressive in the field. His writing style was clean and straightforward. He was an extremely intelligent man."

The pair began dating almost at once, and were seen as a "perfect" couple, both up-and-coming journalists, both very much in love. According to Maureen, Harrold gave her presents, tutored her in her reporting, and significantly aided her career.

"I loved him," she said. "Even on the day I left him, I loved him."

Co-workers maintain that there was never the slightest hint of friction between the couple, who almost immediately began living together in Harrold's Upper West Side apartment. "These reports of friction between Maureen and Harrold are unbelievable," says Kaplan. "I have trouble believing it even now. You hear about stories like this once in a while, but it's always some poor woman with six kids, married to an alcoholic. Never, I mean never, do you hear about this kind of thing with people like Maureen and Harrold."

Yet alcohol and abuse are exactly what Mrs. English asserts formed the fabric of her marriage. The violence began even before the couple were married, she said. It started one night when she refused to have sexual relations with Harrold and he became angry. He'd been drinking a lot, she said. Eventually that became a pattern: Excessive drinking would often trigger violent mood swings in her husband. He assaulted her in their kitchen that night, she said, and "raped" her.

Later, Mrs. English said, Harrold repeatedly had sex with her against her will and then physically assaulted her—striking her in places where the bruises wouldn't show.

"I think he believed if you couldn't see the bruises, it hadn't ever happened," said Mrs. English.

She also said that her husband raped her and hit her even when she was pregnant. "I don't know what it was about the pregnancy that angered him so," she said. "Perhaps it was the fact that I was doing something that was beyond his control. He seemed to be happiest only when he was controlling me."

Curiously, however, Mrs. English described herself as sometimes "complicitous," and hinted at S&M sex games between herself and her husband that may have turned rougher than she anticipated. "I was part of it," she said, referring to "silk handcuffs" tied to a bed on their very first date. Sometime after a particularly brutal evening of sex that she subsequently began to think of as "rape," Mrs. English found herself wondering, "Was what had happened that night so very different from all that had gone before?"

At other points in her account, she suggested that she was "a passive player" in the ongoing, furtively violent drama that was her marriage.

In her interviews, Mrs. English came across as a passionate woman. Beneath the cool, contented, and hardworking exterior she presented to colleagues at work is a woman who uses words such as "ravenous," "lost," and "burning" to describe herself in relationship to her husband. "I was a toy top someone had spun and walked away from," she said, of their first date. She also described herself as being under the influence of "erotic fevers," as being "ensnared," and as having struck a "secret bargain" with her husband. For example, she described in detail a night of unconventional lovemaking but gave no hint that she thought the episode distasteful. To the contrary, she suggested she found it pleasurable. The implication in these revelations is that something in her own passionate nature may have contributed to the couple's unusual relationship.

This ambiguity about the nature of the violence in the English household is crucial to any moral or legal judgment about the murder.

One witness at the trial, Willis Beale, a lobster fisherman and something of an old salt, even at the tender age of 27, addresses this issue of the relativity of domestic violence from another angle. "I'm not saying she was lying, or anything like that, but we only ever had her say-so, didn't we?" says Beale, who seems to have made a point of befriending Mrs. English while she was in St. Hilaire—walking daily over to her cottage from the fish house where he mended his lobster pots on Flat Point Bar, to see if she was all right. "Most couples get into a little pushing and shoving at some point in their marriages. Nothing heavy. Just a little something. It takes two to tango, right? I'm just saying, how are we ever going to know?"

*   *   *

The relative severity of the domestic feud between
Harrold and Maureen English raises troubling ethical
questions—particularly insofar as it casts a shadow
of a doubt on her self-professed motive for the
shooting—but there is an even more serious legal
difficulty with Mrs. English's assertions of abuse
and alcoholism in her marriage: No one has been
able to produce a single shred of evidence to support them.

Despite Mrs. English's testimony at her two trials,
and her interviews with me, there has been no cor-
roboration of scenes of violence between husband
and wife. Although Mrs. English now says that her
husband beat her up on at least three occasions and
hit her repeatedly throughout their marriage, there
is no evidence that she told anyone about this violence while it was happening.

At the office party they attended together, none
of those present had any hint of discord. While it is
certainly possible that the scars of domestic violence
might have been hidden, there were no visible
marks on Mrs. English. She left the party early, telling former colleagues that she had to put her baby
to bed. Now she asserts that her husband made her
leave because he had seen her talking to another
man and that when he arrived home from the party,
he beat her severely. It was this beating, she said,
that prompted her flight. "I prayed for my husband's death," she said.

But if her situation was as bad as Mrs. English
now asserts, why didn't she go to the police? Prosecuting attorney Pickering raised a similar issue at
both trials: "If these allegations of violence are true,

why didn't Maureen English leave her husband sooner, when the abuse began?"

Upon arriving in St. Hilaire, Mrs. English told townspeople that her bruises were caused by a car accident. She also falsely claimed to be from Syracuse, facts that several St. Hilaire residents had to testify to at both trials. She declined to go to the police even after she ultimately told about the beatings.

Mrs. English's charges that her husband was drinking heavily during their marriage have also been called into question. Editor Kaplan dismisses the claim: "Harrold was no alcoholic," says Kaplan. "He drank like the rest of us drank. A martini at lunch, maybe two if the occasion called for it. But that was it."

Whatever actually happened between Harrold English and his wife, there *is* evidence that friction began to develop not long after the wedding. According to Mrs. English, the traveling demanded by her job incited Harrold's jealousy. Like most national reporters, Mrs. English often had to travel around the country with male reporters and photographers. While she always had her own room, she acknowledged that there was usually an easy camaraderie among the crew and that her colleagues would often visit her in her hotel room. Her husband, she said, found this familiarity intolerable and once beat her badly upon her return from a business trip. She was then forced to lie to her editors, telling them that she suffered from motion sickness and could no longer travel in airplanes or automobiles. Her editors released her from reporting duties and relegated her instead to rewriting other people's stories, a move that effectively derailed a promising career.

Mrs. English said that she was driven to seek the help of a psychiatrist, and that at one point she considered suicide. It's also possible that her pregnancy aggravated her despair. She quit her job at the magazine unusually early in the pregnancy and seldom left her apartment after that. On one occasion, she ran away to her mother's.

Alcohol, too, may have exacerbated her downward spiral. Both she and her husband, she said, were drinking excessively during this period. "We drank like we were drowning," Mrs. English explained. They drank in bars and then drank at home. Curiously, Mrs. English continued to drink in Maine. By her own admission, there was always beer in her refrigerator at the cottage on Flat Point Bar, and she often offered Willis Beale a drink when he came to visit.

Even after she reached St. Hilaire, Mrs. English's emotional health appears to have been unstable. At one point, she said, she began to have hallucinations, to hear her husband in the cottage long before he actually found her. She also apparently passed out from fright at a community event—a festive holiday bonfire on the town common on Christmas Eve.

Undoubtedly Mrs. English was under great stress during her stay in St. Hilaire. She had taken her baby from the apartment in New York City and driven 500 miles to a strange town. When she arrived, the temperature was 20 degrees below zero. Both her own and her baby's health were fragile. She was living on funds she'd taken from Harrold's wallet on the night she left him. She'd been unemployed for nearly a year and had no clear prospects for employment in Maine. She was lying about her name, lying about her background, and telling varying stories to those she met. She was trying to begin a new life—that of "Mary Amesbury."

Everett Shedd's general store has always been the hub of the small fishing village of St. Hilaire, but these days it is bustling. Each day, after "the doin's over to Machias," residents of the town gather in the small store filled with groceries, sundries, fishing gear, and cold beer to talk over the case. They speculate as to who came out on top that day in court, and comment about how "Mary Amesbury" looked on the stand.

On the surface, St. Hilaire is a classic New England coastal village—charming, picturesque, and sleepy. There's the typical white steeple, the common, the old colonial houses, the tidal rhythms of the harbor. But underneath, life in St. Hilaire is not always as simple as it seems. According to Shedd, who has one glass eye, a thick Down East accent and doubles as the town's only officer of the law, St. Hilaire has seen better days.

"The town was big in shipbuilding 150 years ago, but now it's economically depressed," he says. "Most of the houses are abandoned. The kids, when they get out of high school, they lose heart and leave town."

The fishing for lobster, clams, and mussels makes up the heart of the economy of this and other towns like it along the coast. Further inland, a few residents have been able to eke out meager livelihoods on scrubby blueberry farms, but an aura of hard times permeates the area. The houses, while charming, do not look prosperous; small pink and aqua mobile homes, many of them rusty with age, mar the landscape. It is a town, says Shedd, where women frequently become depressed during the winter months, where insularity has led, on occasion, to inbreeding (according to Shedd, one local woman has three breasts; others have what appears to be a ubiquitous familial trait—gapped front teeth), where men sometimes drown off their lobster boats, where unemployment and alcoholism are pervasive. It is a town of lapsed ventures and failed hopes.

"You read the tourist brochures," says Shedd. "The shortest paragraphs are about St. Hilaire. There's nothing here."

Into this bleak and frigid coastal town came Mrs. English on the night of December 3. She spent one night at the Gateway Motel just to the north of town and then rented a cottage on Flat Point Bar from Julia Strout, a prominent local widow. Mrs. English then, according to her own testimony, settled down to a tranquil, Hester Prynne–like existence. Like Hawthorne's heroine, she even took up needlework. "I loved the cottage and my life there," she said. "I read, I knit, I took care of the baby, I took walks. It was a simple life, a good life."

Indeed, this tranquil domesticity might have helped her more at her trials were it not for one critical detail that some observers have found at odds with her assertions of a simple life.

Barely a month after she arrived at St. Hilaire, Mrs. English took a lover—a local fisherman with a wife and two children of his own. He was Jack Strout, 43 (a cousin of Julia Strout's husband), and he was there on the morning Mrs. English shot Harrold English.

"By Christmas Eve, I could see there was already something between Jack Strout and Mary," says Beale. "And I can tell you this: It wasn't Jack who started it. He was always, before he met Mary, very loyal to his wife. I always liked Mary, but I have to say, in retrospect, she was a pretty fast worker."

Strout is a tall, lanky lobsterman with light-brown, curly hair. His daughter, Emily, 15, is still at home, and his son, John, 19, is a sophomore at Northeastern University. Strout attended the University of Maine and hoped to become a college professor. But after his sophomore year, his father broke both of his arms in a fishing accident, and young Jack returned home to take over his father's lobster boat. Strout refused to be interviewed for this article, but he appears to have been well-respected in St. Hilaire. For years he has kept his green-and-white lobster boat moored off Flat Point Bar.

According to Mrs. English, she met Strout on the point one night while taking a walk. The two became lovers shortly afterward. She has described the affair in some detail in her interviews. Strout came to her bed at daybreak and made love to her each morning before he went out on his boat. She said that their relationship was very "natural"—that they needed each other.

The two appear to have been discreet at first, but Beale, who was often on the point, mending his pots, recalls seeing them together.

"I saw them come back on Jack's boat on a Sunday," he says, "and I would see them at her door, acting in a very 'friendly' way."

The need for discretion was important because Strout's wife, Rebecca, was almost incapacitated by depression, which appears to have begun shortly after the birth of her first child. Strout was afraid of what his wife might do if the affair became public.

Even so, on the Monday before the shooting, Strout accompanied Mrs. English to a clinic in Machias when her infant daughter developed a 105-degree fever. After this visit the local doctor called the child's pediatrician, who subsequently alerted Harrold English to the whereabouts of his wife. It was on that Monday, too, that Beale saw Strout in broad daylight at Mrs. English's door, acting in a "friendly" way.

According to Mrs. English, she and Strout were anticipating an end to their daily predawn trysts because he would soon have to haul his boat, and then he would no longer have a reason for leaving his home before daybreak. The prospect was causing them both anxiety about the future. In her interviews, Mrs. English stated that she knew the last time Strout would be able to come to her cottage would be on Friday morning, January 15—the morning she shot her husband.

More than just calling Mrs. English's character into question, the love affair has crucial significance because prosecuting attorney Pickering contends that it was this, and not self-defense, that was the true motive for the murder of Harrold English.

In court, D. W. Pickering, a 32-year-old graduate of Columbia Law School who moved north from Portland to practice law in Washington County two years ago, has presented a formidable contrast to his older opponent, Sam Cotton. Pickering, whose height (6′5″), booming voice, and penchant for theatrics have given him at least a performer's edge in court, has seemed at home and unruffled, first before the jury and now before Judge Geary. Unlike Cotton, who sometimes sweats in the courtroom and who has a slight but noticeable stutter, Pickering seems positively to be enjoying himself. And perhaps never more so than with the business of the fork.

According to Mrs. English, her husband attacked her in the cottage in the early hours of Friday morning, January 15, with a sharp instrument. Upon cross-examination during the first trial, it was revealed that this object was a fork with which Harrold was about to eat a casserole he had found in the fridge.

"You mean to say you were worried that your husband would kill you with a fork?" Pickering asked her under oath. There was, in his tone, an unmistakable note of disbelief.

"Yes," Mrs. English replied, in her quiet, straightforward manner.

"The same fork he'd just eaten the macaroni and cheese with?" the prosecutor asked. The disbelief in his voice had risen a notch.

"He hadn't started it yet," she replied.

A wave of laughter washed over the courtroom.

Each side then called "expert" witnesses to the stand to attest to the fact that a fork could or could not kill a woman, but Pickering's amused incredulity tainted the testimony, giving it a frivolous backbeat and mitigating Harrold English's intent.

Pickering was no less incredulous when it came to the shooting itself. As he pointed out at both trials, if Mrs. English was truly concerned for her life, she certainly had time, after her husband fell asleep, to go up to a neighbor's house at the top of the lane, barely 200 yards away, and telephone either Everett Shedd or the police in Machias.

Instead she made an extremely difficult journey in the dark out to the end of the point, where she got into a dinghy and rowed out to Strout's lobster boat, on which she had once seen a gun. She had some difficulty en route with the wet sand of low tide, once falling into a treacherous quicksand-like pocket the locals refer to as a "honeypot."

When she returned to the cottage, she says her husband was still asleep. He woke up just before the bullet hit his shoulder. Then she fired again. Strout, she has said in court, entered the cottage after the two shots were fired.

According to Pickering, at his summation at the first trial: "Maureen English had obviously hurt Harrold English, if not disabled him entirely, with the first bullet. If all she were concerned about had been self-defense, she'd have achieved that then. But she fired again. She meant to kill her husband."

Instead of self-defense, Pickering maintains, the murder was premeditated. Because Mrs. English was now in love with Strout—and her husband, who had driven 500 miles to reclaim her, was unlikely to agree readily to a separation or divorce— she believed she had no alternative but to rid herself of her husband altogether. Hence the difficult trek to the lobster boat instead of to the neighbor's house. Hence the shooting in what Pickering has called "cold blood."

Both Mrs. English and Strout have testified under

oath in court that they were "friends," and Strout admitted he went to the cottage on the morning of January 15 with the intention of "visiting" Mrs. English. When Pickering asked the defendant if the "friendship" included a sexual relationship, she would say only that she and Strout had "a relationship."

Both have testified that Strout entered the cottage seconds after she shot her husband.

In her written interviews, Mrs. English has been somewhat more revealing. She states that Strout entered the cottage just seconds *before* she fired two bullets at her husband. Even allowing for the confusion of the moment, it seems apparent, if we are to believe Mrs. English's statements in her interviews, that Strout was physically present in the cottage when she shot her husband. "I raised my arm and aimed," she said. "I heard a noise. It was Jack. He started to cross the room. I aimed the gun at Harrold's heart. I fired."

Shedd, who arrived moments later, believes that the two have publicly denied Strout's being in the cottage at the moment of the shooting to protect each other: "If Jack were to say he was in the cottage when Mary shot her husband, there would be no case whatsoever for self-defense. And Mary has changed the moment of Jack's appearance because she doesn't want to involve him."

However, if Strout entered the cottage before Mrs. English fired, *why did she shoot her husband?* Wasn't Strout's presence in the room security enough? Or did she, as Pickering has argued, have an additional motive, above and beyond that of self-defense, for wanting her husband dead?

Mrs. English insists her motive was self-defense, and she will say only this: "If Harrold lived, I had no life of my own."

Although Pickering claimed in his opening remarks that the love affair was the motive for the shooting, he was noticeably gentler with Strout on the stand than observers had anticipated. At neither trial, for example, did he ask Strout if he had had a sexual relationship with Mrs. English. At Shedd's store, Pickering's treatment of Strout has been the subject of much speculation. Some have suggested that the prosecutor has been unwilling to harass Strout about the affair because Mrs. English's statement about "a relationship" said enough. Others have maintained that there may have been some local reluctance to trouble a man already racked by guilt and grief—and that badgering Strout might have sat poorly with both a jury and a judge.

For perhaps the saddest aspect of the story is the death of Strout's wife, Rebecca, less than twelve hours after the shooting.

Upon returning home on the morning of January 15, Strout appears to have told his wife of the shooting at Flat Point Bar. Whether he also told her of his affair with Mrs. English, he has never said. But later that day, while Everett Shedd was taking him to the police station in Machias to give a statement, Rebecca drove her husband's black Chevy pickup truck over to the point.

Mrs. Strout was a tall, thin woman of 43 who had once been a beauty queen in high school. In recent years, however, as a result of her chronic depression, she was seldom seen in public.

On the day she drove to Flat Point Bar, she wore a long navy-blue coat, a blue kerchief, and a pair of black rubber boots. She appears to have taken her husband's rowboat out to his lobster boat—a boat named after Rebecca herself—and climbed aboard. Then she stepped off the boat into the Atlantic Ocean.

Her pockets and boots were filled with stones from the beach. The autopsy indicates that she drowned at once.

Townspeople searched for her all night long and found her body the next morning. Mrs. Strout had washed up on the low-tide flats of Flat Point Bar— ironically, just below the little white cottage where her husband's lover had committed murder the day before.

"When I think about Rebecca, I just get so upset," says Julia Strout. Mrs. Strout has asked for and received temporary custody of the Englishes' baby daughter, Caroline.

"It's the children I feel for now," she adds. "Rebecca's children, John and Emily, and now this baby. . . . It's such a tragedy."

Throughout both trials, Cotton has retained his mild demeanor. Cotton's father was a fisherman off Beals Island—an island connected by a causeway to Jonesport, just south of St. Hilaire—where the lawyer still lives, with his wife and three children. A familiar presence in these parts, he has defended local fishermen who have taken well-aimed potshots at poachers. Rumor has it that he might be tapped for a seat on the bench this year—making this case particularly important for him.

Cotton has two advantages. The first is that while Mrs. English's initial trial ended in a hung jury, the final split was tipped in her favor. One juror, a Native American woman from Petit Manan, seemed to speak for those who had voted for acquittal when she said on June 23, "You couldn't *not* believe that woman." Although Mrs. English's presence on the stand has occasionally been a problem for her, she has, at times, struck a distinctly sympathetic chord.

Cotton's second advantage is the previously mentioned tendency of Judge Joseph Geary to be particularly lenient toward women. Although Geary has not shown Mrs. English any favoritism in court so far, the word over at Shedd's general store is that with Geary on the bench, "Mary Amesbury is in good hands."

Still, Cotton has been dogged by several key aspects of the case. The most serious is the core of the defense itself. Because Harrold English was asleep when Mrs. English shot him, she cannot claim that her life was immediately in danger. Instead she has stated that she believed that her husband would *eventually*, that day or that night, kill her. Trickier still is the fact that Mrs. English herself says that while her husband was physically abusive toward her, he did not actually verbally threaten to kill her that morning. She simply *believed* that he would seriously harm her, if not kill her outright, sometime that day.

The allegations of abuse themselves have also been a problem for Cotton. As previously mentioned, he has not been able to provide a single witness to testify that Harrold English beat his wife. He did, however, put several residents of St. Hilaire on the stand—Shedd, Julia Strout, and Muriel Noyes, the owner of the motel where the defendant spent her first night in Maine—to testify that when Mrs. English arrived in St. Hilaire on December 3, her face was covered with bruises and her lip was cut and swollen. This testimony was later somewhat weakened when both Beale and Mrs. Strout testified that Mrs. English herself had told them that the bruises were the result of a car accident.

Lastly, Cotton himself seems to be baffled by the love affair between his client and Strout. In court, he tried feebly to skirt the issue, but to no avail. Cotton will not comment on his strategy during the trials, but sources close to the defense attorney have suggested that he was loath to put Mrs. English on the stand because of the damage the revelation of the affair might do to her case. It was only when he was unable to locate any witnesses to the domestic violence that he was forced to let her tell her own story—thus leaving her prey to Pickering's skillful cross-examination. The tragedy of Rebecca Strout further complicated the case. It suggested that the affair not only provided a motive for Harrold English's murder, but also led directly to the death of Strout's wife.

Cotton knows, perhaps better than anyone, that the case is a complex one. During a brief telephone interview, he said only that "this is an extremely serious case" and that his client serves as an important test case for all women.

The defense attorney must wonder if he has taken too great a risk in advising Mrs. English to waive her right to a trial by jury, and if her presence on the stand has done her more harm than good. Whether or not Cotton's gambles succeed, in many's people's minds there are larger issues at stake; and even after Judge Geary reaches his verdict next week, many of them will linger:

• What really constitutes domestic abuse between husband and wife? In the privacy of the bedroom, where "normalcy" is an elusive concept, where is the line drawn between sex play and abusive behavior?

• What role did Mrs. English actually play in fostering the dark undercurrent of sado-masochism that she admits to condoning, however passively? Was she an innocent victim or an unwitting accomplice?

• If Mrs. English's motive was self-defense, as she has said, why did she fire *after* Strout entered the room?

• And finally, did she have a motive above and beyond that of self-defense? Was the shooting truly prompted by a will to survive? Was it the result of an unstable frame of mind? Or was it a love affair with another man?

Cotton reached his blue Pontiac. He put his hand on the door of his car, but before he got in, he raised his eyes to the cottage. It has been uninhabited since Mrs. English was taken from it on the morning of January 15. Surrounded now by wild beach roses, it sits spare and lonely on its small promontory. To one side is a weathered lobster boat on the sand, abandoned years ago. The water was unusually still, but gulls swirled about the roof and the dormer windows. Cotton took one last long look at the cottage, as if it would yield up its answers.

But the answers he was looking for are ones only Mrs. English, or "Mary Amesbury," can reveal now.

Perhaps Willis Beale put it best: "Before Mary Amesbury came here, this was a peaceful little town. Then she came, and it was like a hurricane had blown through. I'm not saying she tried to cause trouble. It's just that she did, didn't she?

"By the time she left us, we had one murder, one suicide, and three kids had lost their mothers.

"She's got something to answer for, doesn't she?"

Night had fallen by the time I returned to the dormitory. I had guessed at how long it would take Caroline to read the notes and transcripts. Now I would have to let her confront me.

The corridors were quieter than they'd been earlier. I didn't announce myself by calling up to her room. Instead I simply knocked on the door.

She said at once, "Come in."

She was standing by the only window, holding a small doll made of yarn and bits of cloth. She looked straight at me when I entered. Although I could see at once that she was shaken, she didn't avert her eyes from mine. The notes and transcripts were in a neat pile on her desk.

"You've finished it," I said.

She nodded her head.

"Are you all right?" I asked.

She nodded again.

"It wasn't so much the article that upset me," she said, setting the doll on the windowsill. "I had guessed about that. It was the pattern of my mother's words. That was how she spoke, did you know that?"

I hadn't known the mother well enough to be able to answer that question.

"Have you had dinner?" I asked, gesturing toward the door. "We could go to a café or something, have a late supper."

She shook her head quickly. "No," she said. "I'm not hungry."

I edged closer to the center of the room. I felt uncomfortable in my coat and scarf. Although I didn't want to stay long—indeed, I wanted this interview to be over as soon as possible—I thought it would be better to sit. So I did, again on the only chair in the room.

She herself did not move to sit down, but instead rested her weight on the sill.

"I'm not sure I understand why she wrote all of that to you," she said. "Why did she tell you all that? Why did she contradict what she'd said in court?"

I shifted in my chair, unwound my scarf from my neck. It was hot in the room—a fact I hadn't noticed earlier in the day.

"I've often asked myself that question," I said to her. "I'm not sure what your mother's motivation was in sending the material to me. I think that at first she was trying to comply with the interview process, but on terms she could manage. Later the process itself became a kind of catharsis for her and may have brought her some relief. So she wrote in great detail, almost as if she were writing a memoir. I think she wanted to tell her story once and for all, and it was for her-

self that she did this. And because it was for herself, she had to tell the truth."

"The truth? But you didn't accept it as the truth!
It's outrageous what you did!" she screamed. She
sat up quickly and wrenched her hair out of her
ponytail. "Outrageous! How could you have done
this to her?"

I turned my head away and looked at the wall.
Oh, yes, I wanted to tell the daughter, I had
known her mother's story was the truth. In spite
of what I'd done.

"I'm sorry," I said. "I know that's not much,
but I *am* sorry."

She shook her head violently, as if to toss away
my apology. Her hair fell all around her face.

"Why?" she asked, gesturing with her hands.
"Why did you do it?"

I took a deep breath. The answer was complicated.

"That's a complicated question," I said.

I paused, searching for the answer.

"The truest reason, I suppose, is ambition," I
said. "I know that's inexcusable, but that's the
truth. I was looking for a cover and a book contract. I knew that to get a book contract, I had
to leave the reader with unanswered questions—
make it seem like a real puzzle. I knew I also
had to suggest that I had more material from your
mother's notes—material I could reveal at a later
date."

She looked down at her feet. Her lips were
pressed tightly together.

"But there are other reasons you should know

too. Not to excuse myself. You should just know them."

She didn't speak, so I went on.

"It's true that my article was different from the story your mother told in her notes. But I don't think that when I wrote the article I deliberately set out to hurt her. It seemed to me, at the time, that the truth of the story lay in its complexities—in its different voices, different angles."

It was now extremely hot in the room, so I took my coat off.

"And there's something else," I said. "There's the process itself. It's hard to explain, but in the process of writing an article, a writer has to pick and choose. He has to edit a person's words, select some quotes and discard others, perhaps even change what a person said to make the meaning clearer. When you do this, it's almost impossible not to change the story in one way or another. . . ."

Outside, in the corridor, I could hear students talking.

"And another thing," I continued. "The article was a product of its times. It couldn't be written today. We didn't know a lot then about domestic violence. I mean, we didn't know *anything* about domestic violence. Wife-beating wasn't part of our thinking in 1971. To a lot of people it wasn't even considered all that terrible. . . ."

Truth was sometimes relative to the era in which it was spoken, I was tempted to add, but

I didn't think the girl in front of me would find that much consolation.

"She was in there twelve years!" Caroline shouted from across the room. "That was my childhood!"

I leaned my head back, looked at the ceiling.

"I know," I said.

My article had gotten more play than anyone had anticipated. It had been picked up by the wire services, had been quoted on TV. Judge Geary, in rendering his verdict, had said he had not been swayed by recent reports in the media. But I had wondered. Judges are not required to sequester themselves during trial, because it is thought they have the professionalism to remain immune to publicity. But I didn't think he had remained immune when he had found Maureen English guilty of first-degree murder and was then required to sentence her to life in prison, with a possibility of parole in twenty years. Basically, he'd thrown the book at her.

Today, I thought, she'd have gotten five years for manslaughter, if that.

I'd been afraid when the article had come out that Pickering would subpoena my notes. But he hadn't. After Geary had found Maureen English guilty of first-degree murder, what was the point?

Maureen English's sentence had been commuted by the governor of Maine after she'd served twelve years. I knew that Julia Strout, along with various feminist groups, had lobbied for the commutation. I had even thought of joining their efforts, but I didn't.

When I looked down at the girl across from me, I saw she'd been crying. She took a tissue from her pocket and blew her nose. She'd been crying earlier, too, I suddenly realized.

"She wasn't complicitous, was she?" Caroline asked in a small voice after a time.

"No," I answered as truthfully as I could. "But I didn't know that then. Your mother often describes herself in the notes as complicitous, but I didn't know in 1971, as I do now, that most victims of marital abuse feel as your mother did. I didn't know then, as I do now, that this sense of guilt and complicity is part of the destructive process that the victim suffers."

I paused.

"What did your mother die of?" I asked, changing the subject. "The obituary didn't say."

Caroline didn't answer me at first. Then she moved to the bed and sat on it.

"Pneumonia," she said finally. "She'd had it on and off when she was in prison, and was prone to it. Jack and I were always careful. . . ." She trailed off.

Her face seized, as if she might be going to cry again, but she gained control of her features.

"I'm sorry," I said.

There was a long silence in the room.

I cleared my throat. "I was glad to see from the obituary that she'd been survived by Jack and yourself," I said. "I mean I was glad to see that she had married Jack in the end, and that she had been able to eke out some happiness for herself."

Caroline nodded dully. "They were happy," she said.

"If you don't mind my asking, I'm just curious, but I was wondering what happened to some of the people."

She looked up at me, her eyes vaguely unfocused. "Who?" she asked.

"Well," I fumbled, "Julia, for one."

She answered me, but she seemed preoccupied.

"I lived with Julia until I was twelve," she said. "My grandmother asked for custody, but my mother wanted me near her in Maine. And then, when my mother got out, she and Jack and I moved into his house. This was . . . this was hard for me at first. I loved Julia. I thought of her as my mother for a long time. . . . Emily had left by then. She's an engineer in Portland."

"And you," I said. "Will you be a writer, like your parents?"

She shook her head slowly.

"No," she said. "No, I don't think so. I'm thinking about a program in architecture right now."

"Jack stayed a lobsterman?" I asked.

"Oh yes," she said, as if it were a silly question.

"Oh. And Willis?"

"I was taught to hate you," she said. There was a sudden anger in her dark eyes, almost threatening; but more than anger, there was confusion.

I'd been prepared for this, but the heat came

up into my face even so. I made a small gesture
with my hand. I couldn't remember how I had
planned to respond.

"Well, not taught to hate you," she said, "but
it was understood."

I nodded. It was all I could do.

"I've felt bad," I said. "I feel bad. It's why I'm
here."

She looked away from me.

"Why do you do it?" she asked.

I thought a minute. Hadn't I already answered
this?

She saw the incomprehension on my face.

"No, I mean," she said, "why do you write
about violence, about crimes?"

I looked down at my hands. I twirled a gold
bracelet on my wrist. It was a question I had, over
the years, often asked myself—sometimes with
alarm, sometimes with complacency. Why was I
so drawn to other people's stories of murder,
rape, and suicide? It seemed to me a question that
went to the very heart of my existence, my life's
work.

Could I possibly explain to this young girl the
draw of the unnatural act unfolding naturally? Or
tell her of my fascination with the violence and
passion just beneath the veneer of order and
restraint? Could I admit to this girl that it was
precisely that excess, that willingness to permit—
to commit—excess, that had so drawn me to her
mother's story? Could I reveal to this child the

trembling of my hands when the packages from her mother had arrived at my desk?

"I'm interested in the extremes to which people will go," I said.

It seemed to suffice.

"When I read of your mother's death in the *Times* last week," I said, "I spent an entire afternoon walking the streets. The memory of your mother triggered many powerful associations for me, many questions that I'd tried for years to brush aside. And when I got home, I went into my files and dug out this material and reread all of it. It's a very different thing reading something in the heat of ambition and then twenty years later. . . . When I had finished it, I felt you should have it."

She shook her head slowly back and forth.

"There was a book," I said.

She nodded. "I know. I've never read it."

"I have a copy here for you, if you want it," I said, bending and reaching into my briefcase. "Though it's just a longer version of the article, the same themes and so on."

But I saw when I looked up that she was shaking her head again.

"No," she said. "I don't want it."

I put the book back into the briefcase.

"The truth is," I said, "your mother's story made me rich."

I stopped. I looked down at my boots.

"She trusted you," she said. "Despite her reservations, despite what she knew of the process."

It was an indictment I could not protest. I gathered my coat into a heap on my lap.

"The title of your book . . . ," she said.

"Strange Fits of Passion."

"It's from Wordsworth," she said. "We read the poem last year. I'd heard the title years ago, from Jack or Julia, and was surprised when I came across it in class."

"He meant the phrase differently than in the modern sense. He meant it to describe grief," I began. But the mixture of gravity and grief in her own eyes stopped me.

"Look, this is difficult," I said, bending forward and reaching into my pocketbook. "But the truth is, I made a lot of money from your mother's story. My success with the book enabled me to write other books—have other successes. Over the years I've tried to share some of the income with her, but every time I sent her a check, the envelope came back unopened. I have a check here that will help you with your education. I hope you won't refuse it merely on principle. I believe that your mother should have shared in the money from the book."

I had no hope that she would take the check. I felt foolish as I held out my hand to her. I saw myself as she must have seen me—a middle-aged woman with a bribe. She stood at the desk a long time, longer than was necessary to humiliate me. So I was stunned when she took the check and put it into her pocket.

Stunned and then immensely relieved.

"I need the money," she said simply. "My father's legacy has run out. Jack hasn't much, and I don't like to ask."

She didn't thank me. I thought she understood and believed the money to be her mother's, and therefore hers.

"Well, I'll go now," I said, standing up and putting my arms into my coat.

Her taking the check, that was an unexpected bonus. There was absolution in that.

"There's just one more thing I have to ask you," she said.

"Sure," I said, perhaps a bit too flippantly.

I was thinking already of finding a place for a late supper and then returning to the motel room I had taken earlier in the day while she'd been reading. And then tomorrow I could return to my apartment and to my work.

"Do you think my mother told the truth?" she asked.

I stopped in mid-gesture, my coat half on and half off. Caroline had turned her back to me and was looking out the window. But there was dense blackness outside the window, and the only thing to be seen was the wavy reflection of both the young woman and myself.

"What do you mean?" I asked. I was confused. "Do you mean, did your mother tell the truth in her notes?"

"Yes," she said, turning to face me. "Mightn't she have edited her own story a bit, changed a quote here and there, exaggerated or altered something in order to help herself?"

The question lay between us like an abyss. An abyss in which the story and the storyteller were endlessly repeated and diminished like images in two reflecting mirrors.

Who could ever know where a story had begun? I wanted to say. Where the truth was in a story like Mary Amesbury's?

And then I wondered if she was thinking of her father. If she wanted to see him in a better light.

"I don't know," I said to the daughter.

Outside, a bell rang. From a campus church tower, I imagined. I counted eleven tolls.

She seemed to shrug, unsatisfied with my answer. I continued getting into my coat.

"I'll be at the Holiday Inn if you have any more questions," I said. "I won't be leaving until around nine tomorrow morning. And you can always reach me at home. My address and phone number are on the check."

"I won't have any more questions," she said.

"Well, take care, then," I said.

I turned to leave.

I had my hand on the door.

"Don't forget this," she said behind me.

When I pivoted, I saw that she was holding the stack of pages.

"No," I said, shaking my head. "It's for you. I brought it for you."

I was aware that I had backed away from her.

To my embarrassment, I had actually put my hands out in front of me, as if warding her off.

She took a step forward. "It doesn't belong to me," she said. "It belongs to you."

I shook my head again, but she put the neat stack of typewritten pages into my hands, a final gesture.

"Julia died," she said, "a year ago. And Everett still has the store."

I walked down the long corridor to the stairs. Behind some of the doors I heard voices and music. Outside, on the stone steps in front of the dormitory, I saw that it had begun to snow again, and so I tried, with my free hand, to pull my scarf over my head. In doing so, I dislodged the stack of papers in my arm. They cascaded in a fan down the wet steps.

Perhaps I thought then about how my father had once told me that the story was there before you ever heard about it and that the reporter's job was simply to find its shape, but when I put down my briefcase and began to gather up the already soggy pages, I saw that they had spilled in total confusion.

There was no hope, in the darkness, of remaking a neat bundle.

Save up to **$400** on *TWA* flights with
The Great Summer Getaway
⊘ from Signet and Onyx! ⊜

Look for these titles this summer!

JUNE

EVERLASTING
Nancy Thayer

EARLY GRAVES
Thomas H. Cook

THE
GREAT
SUMMER
GETAWAY

JULY

INTENSIVE CARE
Francis Roe

SILK AND SECRETS
Mary Jo Putney

AUGUST

AGAINST THE WIND
J.F. Freedman

CEREMONY OF INNOCENCE
Daranna Gidel

SEPTEMBER

LA TOYA
La Toya Jackson

DOUBLE DOWN
Tom Kakonis

SAVE the coupons in the back of these books.
REDEEM them for TWA certificates
(valued from $50 to $100 depending on airfare)
The more GREAT SUMMER GETAWAY coupons you collect,
the more you get. (up to a maximum of four)
IT'S THE BEST DEAL UNDER THE SUN!

• Send in two 2 coupons and receive: 1 discount certificate
for **$50, $75,** or **$100** savings on TWA flights
(amount of savings based on airfare used)

4 coupons: 2 certificates
6 coupons: 3 certificates
8 coupons: 4 certificates

B O N U S

And to get you started, here's a BONUS COUPON!

B O N U S

•This bonus coupon is valid only when sent in with three
or more coupons found in the books listed above.

Employees and family members of Penguin USA are not eligible to participate in THE GREAT SUMMER
GETAWAY Offer subject to change or withdrawal without notice Offer expires December 31, 1992